EMBER'S ASHES

L M LISSETTE

Copyright © 2026 L M Lissette
All rights reserved
The characters and events portrayed in this book are fictitious. Any similarity to real persons, living or dead, is coincidental and not intended by the author.
No part of this book may be reproduced, stored in a retrieval system, or transmitted in any form or by any means, electronic, mechanical, photocopying, recording, or otherwise, without the express written permission of the publisher.
ISBN-13: 979-8-9904134-5-0

Cover design by: Dreams In Ink
Printed in the United States of America

For my dog, Ruairi.
Don't judge.
He makes my world a better place.

Contents

Dedication   iii

Chapter 1	1
Chapter 2	10
Chapter 3	18
Chapter 4	27
Chapter 5	36
Chapter 6	47
Chapter 7	58
Chapter 8	67
Chapter 9	76
Chapter 10	86
Chapter 11	95
Chapter 12	106
Chapter 13	117
Chapter 14	127
Chapter 15	136
Chapter 16	145
Chapter 17	154

Chapter 18	163
Chapter 19	172
Chapter 20	180
Chapter 21	189
Chapter 22	198
Chapter 23	207
Chapter 24	216
Chapter 25	227
Pronunciations	237
About the Author	238

EMBER'S ASHES

Chapter 1

The crowd's hush sends a shock wave of electric tension through the air as we round the first bend. The opening upright looms ahead, daring Beau to rush at it, but a lifetime of training has prepared us for this. There isn't a course on Earth that could shatter our Olympic dreams. Beau stays in my hand, confidently cantering with his head high as I count the strides before takeoff.

I exhale as we safely land on the other side. 28 to go.

My breaths match Beau's cadence as his long strides eat away at the course, one jump at a time. The triple combination looked impossible from the ground when I walked the course earlier today, but my talented steed meets the challenge with exceptional skill and grace. Looking back would disrupt Beau's balance and cost me this medal. I just have to trust that he left them up.

We bank to the right, setting our sights on the water jump. At nearly six feet across, it's the widest spread we've faced and virtually unheard of in a three-day event challenge. Our team stands frozen by the fence just beyond it. I hate that they are braced with their hands out in front of them as if they could fathom holding the reins of a horse as powerful as Beau.

I earned my spot on this Olympic team with determination and talent. My subpar teammates probably paid their way. Although their horses are incredible, their lack of skill has forced me to carry this team to victory. Once we complete this round, they will hold their heads high with a medal around their neck because Beau and I have become an unbeatable force.

My horse tugs at his reins, asking for his head. After all these years competing together, I know when to let him take the lead. I remain poised over his back, ready to rise as he launches. Beau's powerful form soars over the water without hesitation, clearly demonstrating his undying devotion to our partnership. His hooves crash to the ground with a deafening thud on the far side.

Leaping to their feet, the crowd erupts with cheers, but I can't hear them over my raspy breaths. Each exhale matches the downbeat of my horse's stride while we collect ourselves for the final fence. The hedge was a late addition. Five feet tall wouldn't be so bad if it weren't an oxer with a four-foot spread.

After an exhausting course of 28 jumps, number 29 is a career killer. Every competitor today has failed its test. Many years of pain, sweat, and solitude have boiled down to this exact moment. One more cleared jump, and that gold medal is mine.

Counting the final strides, I push the distracting thoughts and hatred for my worthless team to the back of my mind. Three, two—Beau takes off a stride too early. I latch onto his mane and attempt to pull myself up to meet him, but get left behind, slamming into the back of the saddle.

A blinding flash of light accompanies the explosion of Beau's hooves colliding with the top rail. My fingers lose their grip on his mane, and I suddenly find myself alone, tumbling through a dark cloud of dust. My flailing arms can't connect with anything until my back slams into the ground, knocking the wind out of me.

Beau's scream in the distance sounds as though he's fighting for his life. Another blast discharges nearby, making my ears ring. I clutch my chest and gasp for air, but smoke fills my lungs instead. My eyes burn and begin tearing up when I open them, causing my vision to blur.

My bedroom door crashes open. "Wake up, Ember!" Alice's panicked voice pierces through the air. "Girl! Where are you?"

I rub my hands over the cool hardwood floor underneath me. My sheet is wrapped around my body, holding my legs in the air from when I'd fallen out of bed. I yank at it until I'm free and feel around for Alice.

"I'm down here," I sputter through the smoke. "What's going on? Is there a fire?"

I'm hauled off the floor and dragged across my room. Alice stops, but my momentum throws me into the wall.

"What are you doing?" I spout, trying to rub my shoulder despite her unrelenting grip on my arm.

Although I was too young to remember, I've heard the tale of how I came to be Alice's charge many times. My family's trusted ally placed me in her arms when I was just two months old and ordered her to keep me safe. She said it was my father's will. I suppose Alice could've just told me she was my mother. Instead, she has always just referred to herself as my guardian and corrected any attempt to call her anything else.

"Shush, child," Alice hisses urgently. "We need to hurry. They've found you. You're not safe here anymore." She pulls me down the hall to the stairs. "Come. Beau's waiting."

I hear my horse cry out again in the distance as if he knows we're talking about him. I ride Beau to Olympic victory in my dreams every night and firmly believe that one day we will earn a record number of gold medals. Our bond as horse and rider is unbreakable, but I'm unsure why he would be waiting for me in any situation.

"Alice, I don't understand," I forcefully whisper, hoping she'll answer me now that I'm not yelling. "Who has found me? And why were they looking for me?"

We stop at the bottom of the stairs. Brushing my hair from my face, my guardian cups my cheeks. "We have kept you safe since you were a baby," Alice says, sounding rushed. "I will hold them back. Just get on Beau. He will take you to your grandfather."

"My what?" I sputter just before a fiery ball crashes through our living room window behind Alice.

My guardian leans into me, creating a shield from the debris flying across the room. The splintering wood and shards of glass shower us for an impossibly long time. Alice leans back to inspect me in the blast's remaining cloud of destruction. While checking for injuries, she turns my face, and my gaze travels through the hole in the front of the house.

I gasp at the sight before me. Beyond the front field, high atop the tree line, two large golden eyes stare so intensely at me that they could peer into my soul. The cat-like appearance makes me wonder what animal could be large enough to look over those towering trees. Time stands still until the eyes blink, and loud crashes and splintering wood surround us again.

Alice shoves me toward the front door and yanks it open. Beau paws at the ground just beyond the porch steps. When I reach him, he turns to the side, and Alice leans over to give me a leg up onto his back. I try to protest amidst the steady barrage of fireballs crashing around us, but the two seem to work together, and I'm suddenly astride my bay stallion.

"Go, Beau," Alice shouts. "Guard her with your life!"

The horse's muscles roll under me when he turns to face my guardian. She presses her forehead to his before stepping back to nod at me. I grab Beau's mane as he spins away from her and darts toward the woods beside our farmhouse. His thundering hooves are nearly silent among the deafening blasts and crashes of a war raging behind us.

Images of the events and Alice's words race through my mind for the rest of the evening. As the roaring fire bombs fade into the distance, Beau's steady hoofbeats take over, giving me something less terrifying to focus on. The trees whip past in the darkness. I lay against Beau's neck to escape the branches he isn't avoiding.

I close my eyes and squeeze back the tears that want to leak in my panic. Alice is the only caretaker I've ever known. I'd asked about my parents, but she only told me they had done their best to keep me safe by placing me in her care. Although I'd tried to learn more about them, she always responded, "It was in the past, young one. We learn to move forward because looking back is dangerous."

I understand why they would hide me from a gigantic creature that can devastate lives in a hail of firebombs.

Beau was my other constant. He's been present since my earliest childhood memory. Alice told me that Beau would always take care of me, and he has. We spent countless days riding through the mountains around our Montana ranch. I never knew a moment of danger until today.

My fingers are stiff when Beau finally slows to walk into a stream. I open my eyes at the familiar splash of his hooves. My grip on his mane yanks me over his shoulder when he drops his head for a drink. Without being able to release his hair, I roll before landing on my already sore rear end in the water, ripping handfuls of mane from the crest of his neck.

"Great," I huff, shaking the loose tufts from my fingers. "Hope you didn't want that back."

Beau shoves me with his nose before returning it to the rippling water. I look around in the meager light of dawn. We've been to this creek many times over the years. It marks the southern border of Alice's ranch.

I join the horse, leaning to touch my lips to the water and pulling large gulps between breaths. It's a cool mountain spring that has served as a boundary since I discovered it ten years ago, when I was seven. I'd fought with Alice about wanting to go to school with other children. Beau galloped dangerously at full speed upon my urging, but slammed on the brakes once reaching this creek.

Although I have tried to cross the water and see what is on the other side many times, Beau has consistently refused to go further. I considered going alone a few times, but the thought of leaving my handsome equine behind hurt my heart. I poke at the small fish swimming in the calm waters and quickly recall all the strange occurrences I've grown accustomed to over the past 17 years.

"You're not a normal horse, are you?" I accuse Beau, sitting back on my heels. "What was that back there?"

Beau lifts his head and drops a mouthful of water back into the creek. He stares at me for a moment before bopping a fly on his chest. The horse sinks his muzzle into the creek to splash water at me. I narrow my eyes, watching him cross the creek and stand proudly, his ears pricked toward the forbidden forest.

"Someone blows up our house, and suddenly it's okay to cross the creek?"

The horse snorts and slings his head toward the unpleasantly dark forest.

Climbing to my feet, I quickly bounce through the shallow water. The chill of the mountain spring reaches my bones since there hadn't been time for shoes during the fireball bombardment.

"Where to now, mighty protector?" I spout as I step beside him.

Beau turns west and steps toward the thickest section of trees.

"I just ran away from a hailstorm of fireballs, found out I apparently have a grandfather, and now my horse is leading me into the darkest pit of a mountain forest," I grumble, rolling my eyes. "I'm sure nothing horrible is waiting in there. What else could happen?"

Beau shoves me with his nose and paws at my heels until I have no choice but to push past the thick brush. The oppressive woods hit instantly with their concentrated darkness. The temperature around us drops at least ten degrees, and the air becomes so still that it creates a heaviness, exhausting my limbs.

Hoping to avoid a display of fear, I latch onto Beau's mane and carefully pick my way through the dark woods. My grip on him is the only thing keeping me on my feet through my violent shivers. None of the warmth from the rising sun seems to touch this part of the forest. A heavy gloom fills the air, only sharpening the temperature's bite.

"I think we should turn back," I suggest after hours of unrelenting darkness. "Nothing about these woods seems to be welcoming, Beau. We shouldn't be here. Alice was right to warn me about them."

But Beau doesn't stop. He continues to trudge deeper into the woods until it's clear that the day is ending. Although it's not much of a change, it's obvious when the sun sets, as the small amount of light that made it through the canopy of leaves disappears.

At a slower pace, Beau remains on course to wherever he's dragging me. I've had to rely on his eyes when we stayed out too late on cloudy nights. I'm stiffer than any of those occurrences, but I still easily recognize his cues as he moves me from side to side to avoid obstacles. My exhaustion is determined to get the best of me, though.

"Beau," I whisper through chattering teeth, "I need to stop." I stumble a bit before crashing to my knees. "Can't we rest for the night?" The bay stallion tries to urge me forward, causing me to crawl until I collapse against a cold, damp boulder. "It's too dark for anyone to find me here, Beau. Just a short break."

I can barely make out his silhouette, but Beau's muzzle is unmistakable when he rests it on my shoulder. His warm breath penetrates deeper than my skin and sends a sense of comfort through my muscles. My horse's actions defy all reason, but this warmth is appreciated even as one of the most bizarre feelings I've ever experienced.

When my shivering ceases, I scratch his cheek. "What are you?" I half expect him to answer my question, but he just shoves my shoulder until I climb to my feet and push him away. "All right, we won't stop in the forest of doom, but I was serious. I need to rest. How do we get out of here?"

Beau lies down and nudges me toward his back. This is how I used to get on him when I was little. Alice said she taught him to do it, but now it seems he figured this out on his own. I grew up on Beau's back and trusted him with my life. However, my faith has led me into a dark pit of despair, and I'm not so sure I'll survive the stifling hell he's determined to stay within.

Beau shoves me again, and I glare at him from the corner of my eye. "If I die, I will haunt you until the end of time," I hiss.

I swing my leg over Beau's back and hang onto his mane as he lurches off the ground. He gives me a minute to situate myself on his back before resuming our journey through the darkness. The steadiness of Beau's cadence soon allows my body to relax, and his warmth causes my eyelids to droop. I lie over his neck and lace my fingers into his mane for support.

As my eyes close, I notice Beau's hooves aren't making any sound as he continues forward. His shoes had been clinking on stones all night, but now they are silent. He's moving steadily forward without turning or sidestepping to avoid any debris on the forest floor. Only the sound of our matched breathing reaches my ears before I drift off to sleep.

Chapter 2

I can't remember the last time I slept without dreaming. I've always enjoyed my dreams, having never had a nightmare. Beau is in most of them, so I pretend I'm still asleep when I wake to his muscles rhythmically moving under me. I could stay in a dream where we left the fiery bombs and splintering wood behind. There is no place within my reality for those large eyes that loomed over the tops of trees.

Beau's breathing is the only sound that continues to echo through the silence. It's labored but slow as it filters over the blood pulsing in my ears. When Beau stops, I push against his neck to sit upright. Looking around, I squint through the trees as if I could ever get my bearings.

Although the stifling darkness of the thick forest still surrounds us, the air seems lighter. Beau lowers his head and splashes some water with his nose before drinking. I slide from his back and feel along his neck until my hands reach the refreshing pool he'd found. I bring the chilly water to my lips with cupped hands, pulling large gulps to quench my thirst.

"Do you know where we're going?" I ask, sliding my hand over Beau's cheek.

My horse leaves his mouth in the water and ignores me. I sit back on my heels and replay the sights and sounds of the attack. All I saw was smoke until we reached the bottom of the stairs. Alice was holding my jaw, and I was facing the large bay window that looked out over the front of the ranch before the fireball erased its existence.

Beyond it, to the west, is a line of trees that curves with the driveway, which remained untouched by the flames. Focusing above the trees across that front field, I watch the large golden eyes again. Until they blink, they nearly resemble a painting or photograph. I can't recall any reaction or movement, even when the next ball of fire was hurled in our direction. There is no emotion in them at all.

"Someone was there," I growl, standing. "Alice said they found me. Who is after me?" I stare at Beau, unsure if he would have any way to answer me. "Whatever was out there was large enough to see over the trees. Nothing's that big. A dinosaur, maybe."

Instead of acknowledging my confusion, Beau shoves me with his nose until I stand up. He pushes me with his shoulder, and I find myself absentmindedly walking beside him, my eyes narrowed in thought.

"I saw a cat with gold eyes once," I murmur.

The eyes remain before me as if part of the foliage slapping at us as we make our way through the humid forest. They are calm, almost curious. Time remains still, allowing them to study me uninterrupted. My chest hurts from the amount of air I pull as I allow my imagination to run wild. The different creatures I picture beyond the trees that may own the eyes become incredibly strange.

"Do you think it saw me?"

Beau stops beside me and turns his head to block my path. When I allow my eyes to focus on our surroundings, it's clear that the sun has begun to rise. The forest isn't any more inviting, but the treetops allow some light to filter through. Although I may not feel the same impending doom, there is still a sense that caution must be taken, almost as if we are being watched.

I reach for my horse's head, but he moves away, revealing that he'd stopped before a large wall of vines. "Where are we?" I whisper.

Beau nudges his nose toward the vines, so I move forward and reach for the leaves. I snatch my hand back as they move away from me. They fall quietly into place upon my retreat as if they'd never been disturbed.

"What the hell?" I mumble, my eyes widening.

I rub my thumb over my fingertips while twisting my other fingers into Beau's mane before reaching for the plants again. The vines move away, and the closer I get to them, the wider the opening becomes. I move my hand from side to side and watch the vines swing erratically, attempting not to touch me.

"Beau, what is this?" I ask, smiling at the dancing plants.

My horse snorts and shoves me into the vines. They part in a flourish to reveal a grand archway. Beau continues to push me forward into the tunnel until its darkness engulfs us. The air is cool and smells of damp earth. Beau propels me through the abyss, filling the stillness with heavy breaths and the soft thuds of his hooves on loose soil. My arms stay stretched out before me until bright lights suddenly blind us.

I try to stop, but Beau presses his head to my back and forces me forward while I shield my eyes. My feet slide along the ground, feeling only damp grass and soft dirt. I drop my hands from my face and reach out to my side when Beau stops pushing me. My fingers tangle into his mane, giving me the confidence to continue forward blindly.

With his guidance, I slowly open my eyes, allowing them to become accustomed to the brightness. Blinking repeatedly, I use my hand to block out most of the light until my vision clears. We're in a bright green meadow with stone walls separating crops from grazing fields. In the distance, several trees and a small pond are visible, with large white birds floating peacefully through the reeds.

I release Beau's mane and cup a long, dew-covered leaf of a fern bush with tiny red berries, captivated by the peaceful scene. Beyond it, sitting high atop a hill, is a small cottage with a thatched roof. The smoke streaming from its chimney swirls as if dancing to a merry tune. The tiny moving specks beside it could be goats or sheep, and a cow bell is ringing from somewhere in their direction.

"Where are we?" I whisper, my curiosity piqued as I step around the berry bush to move closer to the cottage.

A flurry of flapping and whooshing noises erupts behind me. I turn back to Beau as an enormous pair of wings stretches from his shoulders. My beautiful bay horse rears onto his hind legs and flaps his wings forward, cupping the air with their feathers. A thundering clap rings in my ears just before the wind knocks me flat on my back and forces the air from my lungs as if he'd thrown a brick wall at me.

I stare at Beau from the ground, clutching my chest and gasping for air. He's still my stunning horse and best friend, but I'm unsure how to react as he folds his wings and steps toward me. He pauses just out of reach and allows me another moment to collect myself.

"What are you doing here?" a voice barks behind me.

Snorting, Beau throws his head as I scramble to my feet. He steps closer, and I latch onto his mane to face the newcomer. Beau curls to shield me, but I can still see the man dressed in leather armor stomping toward us. The long sword hanging from his belt clinks against the buckles on his tall boots. His brown beard and hair are thick and neatly trimmed.

"Well, there's no hiding her now," he grumbles, stopping before us. His blue eyes are soft as they scan me and then flick over to Beau. "Been a long time, old friend."

Beau nods and shoves the man with his nose.

"Still an ass, I see," the man snaps, turning to me. "I'm Kalstrop, keeper of the gate. You must be Ember." He reaches toward me with his palm facing upward, as if to take my hand, not shake it. I stare uncomfortably at it until he retreats. "Okay," he starts, raising his eyebrow, confused. "You're awkward."

Scoffing, I narrow my eyes. "And you're just the picture of grace?" I spout.

I turn my attention back to Beau. His wings tuck neatly against his body but ripple with his muscles as he follows my movements. The feathers appear to be made of leather and glisten in the light as if they are wet. I reach gingerly for the edges of the left wing, and my breath catches at the silky sensation.

"You are so beautiful," I whisper, not wanting the strange man to hear. I move further along his body and run my hand over the top of his wing. They are larger, but still feel like those of the turkeys and pheasants I've shot while hunting. "Can you fly?"

Beau curls around to rub his nose over my cheek, making me smile.

"Does this mean unicorns are real, too?"

"I don't know what the hell a unicorn is, but it's against the law to fly," the armored man barks as if I were speaking to him. "Come on. We have a long way to go, and the old man still hates you for tearing up his fields when you left, Beau. We gotta go around the farm."

Beau rolls his eyes and shakes out his mane.

"I thought you were the keeper of that gate," I say as he walks away. "Don't you have to stay here and, I don't know, keep the gate?"

Kalstrop stops and turns around. His crooked grin and lifted eyebrow give him an almost friendly appearance. "Hmm," he hums, waiting for us to catch up. "These orders come from a little higher up than those."

Unsure what he means, I stop and watch the armored man turn to resume his journey along a dirt path. Chewing on my lip, I turn to my horse and furrow my brow. Beau nudges my arm, but I don't move fast enough, so he roughly shoves me with his head against my back, forcing me to follow the quirky man.

"How do you two know each other?" I ask, jogging to catch up. "Do you know what he's saying? Can you hear him?"

"Beau and I go way back," Kalstrop answers. "Spent a lot of time together in the guard. He moved up the ranks faster than I did, though. I was sent to train a new unit in the mountains, and when I returned, he wasn't interested in mingling with us commoners."

"Still, it must have been nice to grow up together," I murmur, looking over the guard. He doesn't look much older than me. It's hard to imagine he'd have any rank 17 years ago.

Kalstrop scoffs and narrows his eyes. "Not really," he grumbles. "Beau's just a kid. I grew up long ago. He's spent his whole life trying to catch up to me. Haven't you, you ole nag?"

Beau spins to kick at Kalstrop in response.

"Bah," the armored man scoffs. "Nobody asked you." He shoves Beau away and lifts his arm out to me. "Why are you here anyway?"

I allow Kalstrop to link our arms as my face twists in thought. "We were attacked... I think," I start. My eyes stay locked on the path as we continue our journey, but I'm not really seeing it. I replay the events on the ranch, trying to make sense of them. "There was a lot of noise and smoke. Someone was bombing us with huge balls of fire."

"You didn't see who it was?"

I watch the eyes over the trees again. They were so still. I can't decide if their gaze was calm or if they were frozen in shock.

"No," I answer, recalling Alice's attempts to comfort me and how she ordered Beau to take me away. "It all happened so fast. My guardian said someone had found me and that I wasn't safe anymore. She said she would hold them off. Do you think she's okay?"

Kalstrop licks his lips and takes a deep breath as he narrows his eyes at the patch of trees ahead of us. "Yeah, kid," he replies quietly. "I'm sure she's fine." He rubs his fingers over mine before squeezing them and smiling down at me. "I bet she was glad to get rid of you. You look like you'd be a pain in the ass."

"Well, you're no walk in the park either," I grumble. "Where are we anyway?"

"We're in the northern highlands," Kalstrop answers. "Bad news travels fast around here, and it won't be long before trouble finds us. You don't happen to know your way around a sword, do you?"

"A sword?" I spout, laughing at his question. "Did we just step into the Dark Ages? Why would I need a sword?"

"The Dark Ages?" Kalstrop scoffs. "Kid, you're in Calisbrya. If you can't wield a sword, you're bloody worthless." He glances at Beau, who's been following closely. "Didn't you teach this kid anything?"

"I am not a kid," I bark, pulling my arm away from his. "How would Beau teach me to use a sword?" I kick at the soft dirt with my bare foot. "Alice and I have gone hunting for years. I'm pretty good with a crossbow and a rifle."

"Yeah, we don't have those here," the armored man snaps. He stops and scans me critically, making me feel incredibly uncomfortable. "There's not much to you. I don't have time to make you strong enough to swing a sword, but there's a bow over in the old armory. I can make you some arrows. It's better than nothing."

"Kalstrop," I start quietly, holding my arm out to the man. "Why do I need a weapon?"

Linking our arms, the strange man resumes our journey. "Because up until just a short time ago, you were dead, Ember," he answers, pulling me along and ignoring my stumble at his response. "If I'm going to get you to your grandfather alive, I'm gonna need help."

Kalstrop stops and waits for Beau to move beside us. After eyeing the armored man, my old friend lifts his left wing away from his body.

"Come on," Kalstrop urges softly. "Up you go. We need to reach the armory before dark. We can spend the night there."

Chapter 3

I'm still exhausted when I wake in the dirt beside a fire pit the next morning. It turns out that the armory is just a cave well-stocked with knives, swords, and armor. Kalstrop said he would stand guard, but now he sits with his eyes closed, leaning against the wall on the opposite side of the flames. He could only find one blanket, which Beau tore with his teeth when he pulled it from his hands before throwing it over me.

Yawning, I roll onto my back and am greeted by Beau's affectionate nuzzle. "Good morning," I murmur, scratching his cheek fondly.

Over the years, we've often napped in the afternoon sunshine after starting our days early on the ranch. Beau would normally stretch his legs and allow me to use his neck as a pillow. I don't remember him lying down last night, but it doesn't appear that he moved from where he dropped to the ground with his legs tucked closely to his body.

My eyes move to his wing, which spreads just enough to cover his hooves. "Can I see your wing, Beau?" I ask quietly, lifting my arm from the blanket.

He gently opens it to lay it over my body. Even in the fading fire's dim light, it's beautiful. I feel along the edge of a few feathers, lifting them away from the rest just enough to slide my finger under them. Underneath the long, leather-looking feathers are short, fluffier ones that appear to provide an insulation layer.

"These would've come in handy if we ever made it to the Olympics," I murmur, smiling. I smooth the top feathers and marvel at their silky feel. "That seems like such a stupid dream now," I add sadly, turning toward the sleeping keeper of the gate. "I wish these wings came with a voice. I'm scared, and he's not much help."

Beau rests his nose on the blanket against my neck, blowing a deep sigh. Although I wish he could speak, my old friend's presence offers more comfort than I could describe. In his silence, I'm able to consider all the information thrown at me over the past few days. Each new detail only confuses me more, and asking questions isn't getting me any answers.

"Alice knew about you," I say softly, leaning against Beau's nose. "She knew you were something special." I smile as a distant memory pops into my head. "Do you remember when she tried to convince me mounted archery was better than jumping?"

Beau lifts his head to nod.

"I should've listened," I say, scowling. "If you'd have shown me your wings back then, maybe I would've."

My horse huffs loudly and looks down at me, making me giggle.

"You're right," I say, pretending we're actually having a conversation. "I would've wanted to fly."

"What are you? 12?" Kalstrop grumbles from across the fire. "Or is this a mental breakdown? I always heard royals were crazy."

"What are you talking about?" I snap, turning away from Beau.

"Why are you talking to a horse?" the guard scoffs. He sits up and scratches his beard. "He can't answer you."

"But he's not a horse, is he?" I remark, twisting my face in thought. "A winged horse is a pegasus, right?"

Beau huffs and shoves me with his nose.

"Pegasus was the name of some God's winged horse," Kalstrop responds, annoyed. "That's not what he was. It was his name. Your name is Ember, but I don't see you burning anything. Besides, Pegasus couldn't change into a man. Beau can."

Frowning, I reach for Beau's nose. "I'm sorry," I whisper. "I feel like I offended you."

"He's a tragae," Kalstrop informs me. "They used to fly with the birds. It was something to see." Beau stretches his wing out to its fullest to show off his beauty. "That was before he was born. Maybe we'll see real change soon, and he can learn to take to the sky like his ancestors."

"My guardian made me sit through lessons every day," I start. "Geography and history were her favorite subjects. I've never heard of Calisbrya."

Kalstrop winces before he lifts an arrow from the dirt. "Well, you wouldn't, would you?" he replies, scraping a stone over the metal tip of the arrow. "You were in the human world. They think we're just fantasy, and we like it that way."

"But we're just across the woods," I spout, confused.

The guard stares at me for a moment before erupting into hysterics. "Across the woods?" he sputters, gasping for air. I scowl at him until he catches his breath. "Kid, you left that world behind when you went through the gate. You're in a whole new realm and, baby, we don't play by the same rules."

Something about Kalstrop's nonchalant attitude infuriates me. "Don't call me that," I snap, sitting up. "I'm not a kid, and I'm sure as hell not your 'baby.' I'm just trying to understand what has happened. I was attacked. My horse brought me to a land far, far away, and suddenly has wings. I think I have a right to ask questions!"

Although I'm nearly shouting at him, Kalstrop stares at me with complete indifference. His eyes shift from me to Beau before they roll. "Fine," he grumbles. "Ask your questions."

From the little I know of Kalstrop, I assume I'll only get to ask a few questions before I annoy him into silence. There are so many things I want to know. Very little has made sense since I woke to find myself on the floor surrounded by smoke from firebombs. I narrow my eyes, recalling that Kalstrop said I was dead until I came through a mysterious portal that connects our world to this strange realm.

"Why does everyone think I died?" I ask.

"Because your father told them all that you did," Kalstrop answers, looking up from the arrow. "Convince your nag to give me a feather, and I'll tell you why."

His wicked grin causes me to cringe. Sighing, I wrinkle my nose and turn to Beau. He's glaring at Kalstrop as only my majestic horse could.

"It's okay if you don't want to," I whisper, rubbing my fingers over his poll. "I imagine it would hurt, and you don't have to pay for my answers."

Beau bumps his nose against my cheek and stretches his wing over my head to lay it across my lap.

"Are you sure?"

He nods and lowers his wing, giving me access to the top. I frown when he looks away and presses his forehead to the ground. I must have been right about this hurting. I hate that he's braced for the pain I'll inflict, but rejecting his offer would be rude, and he's my only friend.

Taking a deep breath, I sift through his feathers to find one that looks older and carries a few splits along the flat edges. These would more likely be ready for molting if he were a bird. I wiggle it a bit until Beau begins to twitch from the pain and give it a hard yank. My friend's wing stays rigid in my lap as I smooth the feathers, hoping my apology transfers through my touch.

"He must think a lot of you," Kalstrop remarks quietly. "Beau hasn't given up a feather for anything his whole life."

"He's my best friend," I whisper, watching Beau slowly lift his head. "I would do anything for him, too."

"Yeah, well, give it here," the guard barks. "Pay first, answers second."

I rub the feather over my palm. It no longer feels like silk and now only resembles the leather it looks like. The edges are stiff and dry.

"You're gonna mess it up, and then he'll have to give us another," Kalstrop remarks. He smiles at my frown as I reach across the fire to hand him the feather. "Thank you."

"You knew my father?" I ask, urging him along.

"No," he answers, focusing on the feather. "I didn't know your parents. He did." Kalstrop nods toward Beau. "Made it all the way up the ranks to be Captain of the Royal Guard. He stood beside your father every day for nearly two years." The guard looks up, narrowing his eyes at Beau. "Hmm, I bet his mama was so proud."

Beau shifts around behind me, lifting his wing from my lap and holding his head high. Although his position displays a sense of pride, there is something in his eyes that I've never seen before.

"That all came to a crashing halt when your mother promised you to a dragon, though," Kalstrop continues, pulling my focus entirely away from my horse.

My mind spirals out of control as I stare dumbfoundedly at the guard. Air freezes within my lungs, and my mouth opens and closes a few times without producing a sound.

Grinning at my disbelief, Kalstrop snorts and shakes his head. "Yeah. You heard me. Much to your family's dismay, she wandered away unsupervised and promised her unborn child to the dragons."

"She was going to feed me to a dragon?" I spout, covering my mouth as my stomach turns.

Kalstrop laughs. "I don't know what they wanted with you, but you wouldn't be much of a meal for them," he sputters. "A tender morsel, maybe—no better than a snack. Your grandfather wouldn't have it anyway. Once he heard about the deal, he tried to have your mother executed."

"What?" I stumble through a few more noises, but my words won't come out. Beau rubs the soft skin from the side of his nose over my arm, attempting to calm me, but no amount of comfort could help me make sense of this. "You said Beau served my father. Where was he in all this?"

"In the thick of it all, protecting your father," Kalstrop replies, lifting an eyebrow. "He might not have agreed with your mother, but he hated his father. I don't know what happened within the walls, but he managed to keep your mother safe until you were born."

"You weren't there for any of it?"

"Some of us were too busy in the trenches to care what happened in the ivory tower," the guard grumbles, pulling a section of Beau's feather from its core. "I was sent off on a mission of the highest importance. When I came back, you were already dead, and Beau was gone. But we hear things. There are still whispers among the people. Some of the old court still talk about your father's trial."

"What happened to him?" I ask when it's clear he isn't going to continue on his own.

Kalstrop inhales deeply, placing his tools in his lap. "I was down with an injury by then and took some time off away from the castle. From what I'm told, the king could never tolerate such blatant disrespect of the crown," he says quietly. "Especially from his own blood. He was sentenced to death by hanging, but died before he made it to the noose."

I stare as Kalstrop rolls his eyes and flexes his jaw. "And my mother?" I whisper.

He shakes his head. "I heard she died giving birth."

I never knew my parents, but I always secretly hoped they were still alive and would take me away to a magical place. An amusement park or tropical island filled with wild horses was always where I thought I would go. Never in my wildest dreams did I imagine flying horses, ivory towers, armored guards, or a royal family would be involved.

My mind zips backward, rewinding to replay Kalstrop's answers.

"The king?" I mumble. "You said the king's 'own blood?' My father was the king's son? My grandfather is the king?"

"Hmm," Kalstrop hums, licking his lips. "Finally catching on there, huh, Princess? Life's not all rainbows and roses. Even princes and princesses fall when they cross the king in the real world."

I pinch my arm and slap at my cheeks, trying to wake myself up. Given the realism of my dreams, I struggle to believe that this isn't another one. Beau's wings are beautiful, and his presence and how he wants to help are a great comfort, but I want it all to end. I crave the safety of the secluded ranch in Montana. The endless winters and hopeless solitude would be a welcome experience.

"See? The royals are crazy," Kalstrop comments, staring at me. "You'll fit right in."

I lower my hands and surrender to my reality. "Why are you taking me to the man who killed my parents?" I ask.

"Those are the orders," he replies.

"But you said I was dead," I sputter, confused. "How could there be orders to bring me to him if everyone thought I was dead?"

"Princess, did I look surprised to see you?" Kalstrop scoffs. "You think anyone else will be? This whole damn realm is about to descend upon us with their eye on the prize. Your only hope is that we make it to the castle before one of them gets their hands on you."

"And how long will that take?"

"With no trouble? About four months," Kalstrop answers.

Assuming we've reached the end of our conversation, the guard returns to his work on the arrow. I slowly collapse against Beau's shoulder as my mind reels with all the insanity he just introduced to my life. My eyes narrow and lose focus as I try to grasp my backward fairy tale.

Alice read me stories about girls discovering they were princesses when I was younger. I never liked them, but she insisted that fairy tales can come true. I wish this were one thing she got wrong.

"Is this real?" I whisper to Beau.

My horse tucks his nose between my cheek and shoulder. The longer he stays there, the deeper our situation's sorrow fills my soul. It's obvious Beau doesn't want to be here either. I don't see how we have any other choice, though. There's no going back to the way things were.

"You said Beau can change into a man," I say to Kalstrop, holding my horse's cheek. "Why doesn't he change?"

"How should I know?" Kalstrop answers. "Maybe he likes the silver shoes." He lifts a bow from the dirt and begins stringing it. "You got one more, and then I'm done with your questions. Make it good."

I narrow my eyes at the fire, thinking over everything. Kalstrop has provided answers, but none that I wanted to hear. Nothing in my life has prepared me for this world that I'm apparently a royal in and will one day rule.

"If I'm a princess, why would everyone try to kill me?" I ask, wondering why my life would be in such grave danger, considering I've never lived here in the first place.

"They don't wanna kill you, Princess," Kalstrop chuckles, shaking his head. "No. You're much too valuable."

"Then what?" I shout, irritated with his stalling.

"Your status is what they want," the guard responds, grinning with his eyebrow raised. "Every man in this realm will stop at nothing to claim the next heir to the throne. You, Princess, are royal prey, and the hunt is about to begin."

Chapter 4

My muscles tremble as I pull back on the bow's string for the millionth time. Kalstrop hums quietly on the opposite side of the fire while he attaches another piece of the second feather he'd convinced Beau to give up on the end of an arrow. He's finished several and refuses to let me shoot any of them.

I lower the bow and lean on it, watching the irritating guard grin happily at his work. "Where's Beau?" I snap, making him jump.

"Standing watch," Kalstrop grumbles back. "He's rested enough. It's time he pulled some of the weight around here."

"When will he be back?"

"In the morning," he replies, rolling his eyes to glare at me. "You have more important matters at hand. Why are you so worried about the nag? I'm here. You don't need him."

"I trust him," I state. "I don't know you."

"Hmm," Kalstrop hums. "But do you really know him? For 17 years, he's been your horse. And, if I may add, a horse that didn't age. Yet you follow him blindly, trusting that his actions are for your safety and nothing else."

I scowl at him. I hate Kalstrop and everything that has slipped past his tongue since we met, but I can't deny he has good points. I've been lied to my whole life. I am in real trouble in Calisbrya, and he seems to be the only person capable of assisting me. Although I would never say the words out loud, I need his help.

Kalstrop narrows his eyes as he watches me crumble cross-legged in the dirt. "Get up," he barks. "You're not done."

"What am I even doing?" I whine. "This is pointless. I would need to hold an arrow to practice shooting one."

"You're building strength," the guard answers, watching me roll my eyes. "Princess, you are weak as shit, and I'm not guarding a damsel in distress across this land. You need to pull your weight around here just like the nag."

"Don't call me that," I mumble.

Kalstrop stares at me before taking a deep breath and straightening his back. "Princess," he starts in a more formal tone. "Your strength resembles that of a tiny baby who would only slow me down and cause havoc where we would need silence, cunning, and stealth."

I openly gawk at him, attempting to shoot daggers from my eyes. "You know what I mean!" I shout.

"Fine," Kalstrop huffs. "Ember, you are annoying as hell. I curse the day I received orders involving your existence. I want to rip you limb from limb, but instead, I have to keep you alive and chaste. If I have to tolerate you in my space, you will learn to defend yourself so that I can take a breath of fresh air away from you from time to time."

"Chaste?" I spout, standing to resume my training. "What makes you think I haven't been with a man?"

Kalstrop removes a twig from between his teeth as his face twitches. He sets the arrow down and stands quickly. I nervously back away, watching him march around the fire. Kalstrop grabs me by the hip and pulls me against his body. My breath catches as he pushes my chin with his thumb until our eyes meet.

The world stands still, giving me plenty of time to panic. I wasn't hot a few moments ago, but a bead of sweat rolls uncomfortably down my spine under the guard's gaze. He licks his lips and leans closer to mine. I want to pull away, but my body is stuck in this position, captivated by his attention.

"This is how I know, Princess," Kalstrop whispers. "You are easy prey." His eyes soften as he moves to rub his beard over my lips. "Hmm, King Kalstrop has a nice ring to it."

His wicked grin shoves my brain back into my head, and I focus on my hands, finding them tightly gripping his hips. I push Kalstrop away and step back. My arms stay stretched out between us, stopping the guard from coming near me again.

"That's enough," I snap.

Kalstrop stomps to his side of the fire. "I agree," he states, returning to his dry tone. "You need a bath. Get some rest, and I'll take you to the stream to wash up in the morning."

Rolling my eyes, I toss the bow into the dirt beside my blanket. Although I can't recall if this is true, I still snap back, "You're no bouquet of roses either, King Kalstrop." I flop onto my blanket while he chuckles at my frustration.

* * *

It's nearly a relief to find myself in a thriving garden when I close my eyes. I haven't had a dream since the attack. Warm floral fragrances and the gentle kiss of a soft breeze provide more comfort than words could describe. I don't know why I'm in a white cotton dress, but I can't find it in me to care at the moment.

The tall stone walls give way to towering hedges with light-green vines snaking throughout their limbs. The pink blooms on the vines throw a gentle scent as the petals blow in the breeze. My dress brushes against my legs with each step, tickling my skin.

A small clearing appears at the end of the hedge to my right. Water ripples over rocks in a shallow stream that flows through the center, and a family of peppered ducks gathers along its bank. I smile at the quiet quacking noises of the five ducklings nestled beside their mother.

"Well, hello," I say, moving slowly to avoid disturbing them. "Would it be all right if I sat with you for a while?"

The mother duck jumps to her feet and leads her ducklings to the other side of the stream. They lie in the grass and stare at me from the safety of the opposite shore.

"Okay, I'll keep my hands to myself," I whisper. "I appreciate the company just the same." I drop into the grass and dip my fingers into the stream. Little fish swim up to see if my skin is edible.

"Careful," a man's voice says, making me jump. "The local fowl are rumored to be hostile." I turn to watch a young man stride toward me from the opening in the hedge. "The ducks are said to be downright feral."

Standing over me, the man blocks the sunlight and smiles. His light brown hair falls along his face, cupping his soft blue eyes. I recognize him from many of my dreams. He was usually the only one not cheering for me in the stands, but sometimes he would be on my team.

I narrow my eyes at his attempted humor. "What are you doing here?"

"I'm not sure," he responds, sitting beside me. "I thought you would know. Maybe you missed me."

"Not likely," I scoff. "You weren't even a good rider."

"Oh, now that's just hurtful," the man says, grinning. "Where's your horse? I don't know that I've ever seen you without him."

I study the intruder before responding. "On watch," I grumble, turning away. "I wanted some time alone tonight."

The man breathes out a laugh before lying back in the grass. "Well, we can't always get what we want, huh?" He remains quiet for a moment before bumping his arm against my leg. "But, then again, it also seems we could get more than we bargained for. I heard you were upset about the crown."

I snap my head in his direction. "Who are you?" I bark. "What do you want?"

"Easy, Princess," the man says, holding his hands up. "I come in peace. This is your dream. I'm just along for the ride."

"Who are you?" I ask again, speaking each word slowly so that he won't miss any of them.

"My name is Durcarash," he responds. "Everyone just calls me Ash. I am but a humble messenger, here to guide you as you seem very lost, Princess."

"Don't call me that," I grumble. "And I don't need your guidance. I have a guard for that." I turn away from him and lie on my side, resting my head on my hand. "You can go now."

"Ember," the man starts.

"Ash," I spout quickly before he can list all the reasons he should stay. "I asked you to leave me alone."

My anger causes the air to become so still that I hear Ash take a deep breath behind me.

"I will leave as you wish, Ember," he whispers. "You may call for me if you should need my service. I will come back for you."

Narrowing my eyes, I roll to glare at him, but he's already gone. "I don't need an imaginary friend," I grumble, lying back and sprawling in the sun.

I lay still, soaking in the warm rays and listening to the creek. The sounds of nature settle my mind like the fields in Montana have for so many years. Out in the open, I felt protected and safe. Some of that might have been from Beau always being with me, but it was a comfort I needed to keep from spiraling out of control. I can't recall why I ever wanted to leave it.

* * *

"Woman, I hate you," Kalstrop barks, pulling another arrow from his armor. "I was nowhere near your target! We aren't leaving here until you can hit the broadside of a barn, so you better start concentrating!"

I wink at Beau as Kalstrop slaps the arrow into my hand. My leather sleeve extends over my palm and hooks on my middle finger. It's designed to protect my hands while shooting, but also shields me from the angry guard's would-be punishment. I've shot him several times over the past week, but my chest swells with pride this time as I purposely aimed at him and hit my target.

Grinning, I set myself up for the next shot. My shoulders relax as I roll them and drop easily into place when I draw back on the string. Kalstrop's craftsmanship is undeniable. The arrow couldn't be straighter if a machine made it. The tip is a three-sided prism that curls inward on the broad side. These will be nearly impossible to remove once they enter flesh.

I close my eyes and exhale deeply before opening them to set the arrow on the target. Letting it loose, I stand frozen and watch it slice through the air. My broad smile can't be contained when it finally sinks into the wood painted red with raspberry juice.

"It's about damn time!" Kalstrop shouts, clapping loudly. "Now do that a hundred more times. And a bit faster than a one-legged turtle would be preferred."

Scowling, I lower the bow to the ground and lean on it. "How about a bath, Kalstrop?" I suggest. "It would be nice to wash these rags. The sun's out today. I could hang them on the bushes by the creek while you are both there to guard me."

Kalstrop would fight me about this, but his pants are stained with mud after hauling our water in from the creek. His face twists a bit before he rolls his eyes. "Fine," he grumbles. "Get on the nag."

Smiling broadly, I throw my leg over Beau's back before he rises from his napping spot. Removing the dirt and grime caked on my skin is a beautiful thought, and I enjoy relaxing in the creek. However, I'm most excited about the space I get from Kalstrop while I wash.

It's a quick jog to the bend in the creek. My angry guard throws a bar of goat's milk soap at me and heads to the shore on the opposite side of the bend. Beau stays at a distance, but is never far. He kicked Kalstrop when he accidentally approached me before I finished dressing during our first visit to the waters.

I drop my clothes on one of the taller rocks near the shore and sink into the gravel-lined bowl in the center of the creek. Beau paws at the shallower water and lies down with his nose resting on a flat rock. I splash some water at him, making him glare at me, before resting my head on a log.

The springs in the mountains were always cold. The first time we visited, I was delighted by the warmth of this water. The soap, though, reminds me of home. While we drank the cow's milk, Alice spent hours painstakingly mixing and scenting bars of goat's milk soap. My favorite was lavender, but raspberry seems to be all they have around here.

"So, I'm getting better, huh?" I say, grinning at my lounging friend. "I guess I'm lucky Kalstrop didn't realize I hit him on purpose, though. He has a lot of anger in his heart."

Beau sighs and closes his eyes while I rub the soap over my leg. Kalstrop found a pair of boots among the armor deep within the cave. I'm thankful that they fit, but relieved every chance I get to take them off. Without socks, they create sore spots that boast various shades of red and blisters that will probably never heal. My guard forgot to act angry as he laughed at the idea of wearing something to shield his feet from his boots.

Because Kalstrop takes advantage of every moment of weakness I show, this is the only time I can let my guard down and voice my true feelings. My only friend has been an easy ear to bend when I need to talk. These moments make me glad he has chosen to remain a horse.

"What's going to happen when we leave here?" I ask, dropping my leg into the water. "That cave is well stocked with weapons that probably cost a fortune. I imagine something keeps it safe from being accidentally discovered. Is it another gate?"

Beau only ever responds to my questions by sighing. I've mostly asked about my parents and grandfather, but truthfully, I didn't really want the answer. However, I am pretty curious about how we have found safety within a cave that can only boast the security of a grove filled with trees and berry bushes. Beau looks away when I sit up to wash my arms and chest.

"I think my birthday was a few days ago," I mention, lathering my neck. "I thought I would gain my freedom at 18 like all the normal girls." I sniffle and roll my eyes to halt the emotions that are trying to come out. "I don't know what I'm doing, but I don't feel safe here, Beau."

My winged friend stands and pulls my clothes from the rock I'd left them on. He flings his head to throw them to me one at a time before stepping into the deeper water to rub his nose over my cheek.

I scratch his neck thoughtfully. "If I had heard the story from anyone else, I would think my grandfather was trying to protect me," I start, narrowing my eyes without focusing on anything before me. "But Kalstrop makes it sound like I am walking into something far worse than what my mother wanted."

Beau nudges my clothing again, reminding me I have limited time before my irritating guard reappears. I absentmindedly begin rubbing my soap over the thin fabric.

"My father didn't agree with my mother," I continue, still trying to piece the facts together in the correct order. "He didn't like my grandfather. He wanted to keep me away from whatever the king had planned so badly that he had you keep me hidden from the entire realm. He felt so strongly that he died to protect my life."

I mull over my thoughts as I scrub the articles of clothing together. The soft trickle of the water settles my mind, allowing me to focus on the facts and set aside my feelings about them.

"Here," Kalstrop barks behind me. "Since you think it's fun to put holes in my clothes, you can wash them."

Beau steps between us and lowers his wings to block Kalstrop from seeing me. My guard throws his shirt and pants over Beau's back, and they land gently in the water across the gravel pool.

When Beau relaxes, I know Kalstrop's gone. "I'm glad you're here," I whisper, collecting the guard's clothing. "I don't believe we have any other option, but I feel safer going to my grandfather with you by my side."

Chapter 5

"Again!" Kalstrop's bark echoes down the cave as I pull another arrow from the dirt and load it as quickly as possible. My sore fingers and aching shoulder complain when I draw the string back and take aim. The arrow cuts the still air and easily finds the center of my raspberry circle.

"Again," the guard snaps. "Faster."

We've been at this for days—several hours at a time. When my arrowheads started going too deep into the piece of wood Kalstrop had painted my bullseye on, he created a softer one out of straw and cloth so I wouldn't damage the tips. In my mind, I know he's trying to ready me for what we'll face once we leave the safety of this cave, but my body has had enough of his tyranny.

I lower my bow and rub my right arm. "I need a break," I grumble. "I'm pretty sure I'm having a heart attack."

"That's your left arm," Kalstrop sighs, rolling his eyes.

"Well, that one hurts too," I say, grinning.

The guard raises his eyebrow. "That only happens to men," he says. "What is wrong with you?"

Irritating Kalstrop has been my only entertainment, and I've gotten quite good at poking the bear. The more I talk, the more agitated he becomes, and he'll suddenly offer to tell me anything I want to know just to shut me up. It has been enlightening, but he still refuses to tell me what is hiding this cave.

"I'm hungry," I scoff. "Let's go hunting."

Kalstrop huffs a loud sigh. "Well, Princess, that's not happening," he spouts. "I'm not letting you shoot me again."

"Stop calling me that," I growl under my breath.

"Princess Ember," Kalstrop snaps, signaling I've hit his limit in record time today. "Great and powerful pain in my ass, what do you want?"

I smile broadly. "Tell me," I demand. I don't have to answer his question. He knows what I want. Nothing he tells me clears my confusion about my family or the realm, so I don't care to hear any more of his tales. "I'm not going to stop asking."

"Fine," Kalstrop huffs. "We're leaving in the morning anyway." He glances at Beau, who's quietly picking at the bushel of hay the guard had brought him. "That means you're standing watch tonight. I prefer to be rested when facing whatever awaits us out there."

Beau flips his head in response while I sink onto my blanket beside the fire, ready for the information I've wanted.

Kalstrop watches me settle across the fire pit from him. He throws me the rag coated with oil that he uses to rub my bow's wood to keep it from drying out. His information always comes at a cost. Today's price is labor.

"The highlands are sprite territory," Kalstrop starts with a sigh, lying back on his pack. "Not many would dare to come up here."

I narrow my eyes. "Sprites? Like little flying gremlins?"

"Careful, Princess," Kalstrop snaps. "You're protected by the sprite's magic up here. I told you we don't play by the same rules. When another being presents the danger of finding the armory, a sanctuary spell activates to relocate the grove, and all is saved."

"Why did it allow us to find it then?" I ask, wrinkling my nose.

Kalstrop stares at me for a moment. "I'm gonna let that sink in, Princess."

"Stop calling—wait," I spout. "You're one of them." I rest my bow across my folded legs and gawk openly at my guard. "But you're big. How is that possible?"

"We are not the little people you have running around in your mind, weirdo," Kalstrop scoffs. "I told you I would tell you about the cave's security. Now I have. I'm done talking."

"No," I say, shaking my head. "You can't just drop bombs and walk away. You need to clean up the mess you leave behind. I was wrong about size, fine. But where are your wings?"

Kalstrop's upper lip twitches as he stares into the fire. I get the feeling I've hit the part of the story that made him want to avoid talking about the cave. Even Beau pauses to watch our grumpy travel companion.

"You remember what I said about taking time away from the castle?" Kalstrop says quietly. "I told you I'd suffered an injury."

Pursing his lips, the guard shrugs his vest off and stands. I gasp loudly when he pulls his shirt over his head. The deep scars on Kalstrop's back have long ago healed, but the story they tell promises to forever bring him pain. His shoulder blades roll under them, highlighting every torturous inch.

My hand covers my shock as best as it can. "I'm so sorry," I whisper through my fingers. I sniffle and release tears that I can't explain. "That must have been very painful."

Kalstrop slowly slides his shirt over his head, leaving his back turned to me. "More than I could ever explain," he murmurs. "We can't fly, but our wings are part of our identity. Their absence is nearly as great as losing one's soul."

I swallow hard and release a shaky breath. "How did it happen?"

My guard pauses before sticking his arms through his vest. "It doesn't matter," he responds, shrugging it over his shoulders. "Our wings heal just like any other part of our body. But once they're gone..." He winces as his voice trails off.

"You are missing a defining portion of yourself," I whisper, shaking my head. "I really want to hug you right now. Would that be okay?"

Kalstrop rolls his eyes, scoffing. "That's because you're a fairy," he spouts.

Breathing out a laugh, I wipe the tears from my face. "There's no need to be mean," I say. "I just feel sorry for you, is all."

The guard stares at me until I'm no longer laughing. "No," he says, shaking his head. "You're a fairy—a water fairy to be exact." He pauses to let his words sink in, but then stands, reaching his arms out. "Here. Let me show you."

My chest heaves air as Kalstrop approaches. He holds his hands out and stops when I shy away from his touch.

"It's okay," he whispers. "May I?"

I would prefer for him not to touch me again, but I'm frozen as he gently pulls my braid forward over my shoulder. My hair became tangled while shooting my second arrow under Kalstrop's instruction. It wasn't bad, but it pissed my instructor off enough that I never wanted to hear him complain like that again. I've kept it braided, except to wash it, since then.

"Can you untie that?" Kalstrop asks quietly. He holds the end so the leather tie is visible. I pull it free and stare at my hair as he untwists the braid. "That creek is freezing, but it probably feels warm to you. Now that you're home, your powers will only grow. I can't help you with them. That's why we need to get you back to the castle."

He gently continues to straighten my braid. Thin strips of bright blue hair are embedded in the thick sections. I slip my fingers into them to pull the braid apart more, finding various shades of blue throughout. It is hidden and probably wouldn't be noticed unless someone was looking for it.

"Why?" I manage to mumble, my voice thick with fear.

"I don't have the answers you seek, Princess," Kalstrop murmurs. He rubs my shoulder, attempting to provide comfort, but his touch is too foreign to soothe my confusion. "There is one person I know who can help you. We'll surely find him at the castle. We will start that journey at first light. You should try to rest."

Just when I thought our conversation would finally end with an answer to satisfy my curiosity, Kalstrop hits me with another whirlwind of insanity. I barely notice Beau rubbing his nose over my cheek before leaving the cave to stand watch. I fall back on my blanket and stare at the jagged ceiling, but all I can see are the strands of blue hair that now hang from my head as if they were meant to be tangled in with the standard brown that I've always had.

* * *

After hours of wishing I would wake up from this nightmare, I finally fell asleep. The garden is a welcome sight after so many dreamless nights. I let my fingers trace over the large pink blooms as I walk along the hedges, looking for the little stream to hopefully visit with the duck family.

I smile when the end of the wall comes into view and turn the corner to find the mother duck sitting with her ducklings on the far side of the creek bed. "Not taking any chances tonight, huh?" I sit beside the stream and poke it with my fingers. Kalstrop's words about the warm waters echo in my mind. "I got some news today," I say, frowning. "I don't know if it's good or bad, but I don't like it."

The duck quacks, and her babies stir under her wing.

"Nothing about this world makes sense," I continue. "This can't be real."

In my dream, my hair is loose, so I flip some of it forward and study the colors. During the summers on the ranch when I was younger, my dark brown hair would give way to a mousy blonde by the end of the season. As I grew older, my hair settled into a light brown, rarely changing. Each strand of blue seems to be colored straight from the root as though it had grown out that way.

"I'm not safe here, am I?" I whisper. The ducks won't answer me, but I still look at them, wishing for a friend who would answer me honestly instead of a silent horse and a hateful guard. "Ash?" I say quietly, remembering his offer. "Are you here?"

"I told you I would come if you called," the man says behind me.

I spin to find him relaxing against the hedge near the opening to the clearing. I hate that my eyes instantly begin misting. Kalstrop's bombs about my identity and everything that I've learned since the attack have me reeling. Somehow, I'm supposed to be powerful and unyielding in this world of so many unknowns. But here in my dream, I just want to fall apart.

"I wish I could wake up," I whisper, putting my face in my hands to hide my emotions.

"I know you do," Ash murmurs before sliding his hands over my arms and pulling me to his chest. "Life can be a lot sometimes. We just have to take a deep breath and move forward until we find our place."

Following his advice, I breathe deeply and open my eyes. Ash is kneeling before me and leaning forward to cradle my head. His shirt is made of thin, rough material, and my hands clutch the dark green cloak draped over his shoulders.

"My hair is turning blue," I mumble, sniffling.

"Yeah, I see," he answers. "You might grow to like it, though. You should give it a chance." He rubs his hand over my head and leans back to look into my eyes. "At least it's not red. I heard those gingers are feisty."

I frown. "Not everything needs a joke."

Ash runs his finger along my jaw, wiping away tears I didn't know were there. "They don't require emotions either, Ember," he whispers. "You will be okay. All you need to do is make it to the castle. Your powers can help."

"I don't have any powers," I grumble. "I'm just a girl with blue hair."

Laughing, Ash sits back and leans on his hands. "Feeling sorry for yourself is allowed for now," he says. "But you will need to learn to control your powers. All fairies have a connection to an element, and your abilities will grow whether you want them or not."

Ash allows me to study him in silence. He doesn't appear to be much older than me, yet somehow seems ageless. Throughout every dream I've seen him in, he's never offered anything but silence until these past few.

"How do you know how to help me?" I ask.

"This is your dream, Ember," he reminds me. "I am what you need. I have been a teammate, a spectator, and now a teacher. I am yours to use as you will."

I stare critically at him before turning away. "You weren't a very good teammate," I scoff. "How could I trust that your teaching skills would be any better?"

Ash laughs. "I don't have many occasions to ride horses," he informs me. "You can't hold that against me."

"I appreciate you offering to talk to me when I need a friend, Ash," I say, scowling. "As you said, though, this is my dream. That would mean that I've conjured you up somehow and I'm making you into..." I narrow my eyes, trying to figure out how to describe the situation. "Whatever you are. I can't teach myself."

After a moment of silence, I turn back to Ash, and he puts his hand out to me. "Let me show you something," he says. "I'll prove it to you." When I just stare at his hand, Ash grins. "Come on. You're dreaming. What could go wrong?"

"Everything," I grumble, narrowing my eyes as the attack flashes through my mind. Gingerly, I reach my hand out to his and allow him to pull me to my feet. "Where are we going?"

"Nowhere," Ash whispers, turning me to face away from him. He presses his chest to my back, and I gasp when his hand covers my eyes. "And everywhere."

His breath blows over my ear. Ash's touch is gentle compared to Kalstrop's when his hand slides along my stomach to hold me against him by my waist. I latch onto his arm, attempting to pull his hand away from my eyes, but it's as stiff as stone, unrelenting in its grip on me.

"You're going to have to learn to trust me, Ember. Why not start now?"

Ash's whispers are slow and tranquil. As hard as it is for me to trust a stranger, I'm calmed by the fact that he hasn't tried to move me since covering my eyes. I relax my grip on his arm, but don't release it.

"There we go," Ash murmurs. "Picture a tree for me. Make it a tall one with long, thick branches. Hang a swing from the lowest branch—wooden with rope, not chain."

While continuing to remind myself that this is only a dream, I relax enough to let Ash's calm words filter through my panic. His even tone and gentle grip have me settled enough that I begin picturing the image he's describing. The tall maple tree looms over us. I've only seen a wooden swing in some movies Alice and I watched, so it resembles those with chipped paint and frayed rope hanging below.

"Perfect," Ash whispers into my ear. He lowers his hand from my eyes and reveals the tree standing before us. Everything is exactly as I'd pictured. "Your mind is a beautiful place. It must be wonderful in there."

The swing sways and the frayed rope flutters whimsically in the gentle breeze. When Ash releases my waist, I smile and step forward. The small stream has disappeared along with the ducks. We are alone in this grassy clearing with my solitary tree, surrounded by a tall stone wall.

"This is just as it looked in my mind," I breathe in awe. The rope feels rough under my fingers, but it provides a strange form of comfort. The paint flakes off when I touch it, so I reach under and pull on the rope's soft and flowy frayed ends. There are knots under the seat to stop it from falling off.

"We'll have to work on making your imagination more usable," Ash remarks, smiling. "For now, let's see if we can clean this off."

Using his cloak, Ash rubs the seat until most of the paint has given way to bare wood. He gestures to the swing, asking me to sit. I had a tire swing on the ranch, but never a standard one with a seat. I nervously turn and allow the strange man to guide me. He runs his hands along my arms and latches my fingers around the rope.

"Here we go." Ash's voice has changed to a tone I can't describe. I don't want to trust him, but his words are like a lullaby, easing every self-conscious thought I have. When he releases my hands to push my hips, his touch lingers, and the warmth of his skin blocks the breeze the swinging motion should create.

We silently spend hours in the green garden. The swing could have rocked me to sleep if I weren't already dreaming. Ash's touch and presence progressively become normal as he pushes me higher. The playful breeze on my face replaces the strangeness of his hands on my hips.

When Ash finally stops the swing, he leans over my shoulder to whisper in my ear, "I must go."

I take a sharp breath at his sudden nearness. "What did this prove, Ash?" I ask, remembering why we ended up with a swing in the first place.

Ash sighs and pulls away. He steps before me and kneels, placing his hands on my thighs and peering up at me. His face was always stern while watching me ride in competitions, but here in the garden, his expression stays soft and calm.

"You didn't know that you can control your environment," Ash starts, moving to catch my gaze. "I taught you how to change your dreams. Wouldn't it be possible that I could teach you how to control powers you didn't know you had?"

I shake my head and furrow my brow. "But this isn't real."

"Do you want it to be?" Ash asks, flashing a playful grin. He leans forward to brush my hair behind my ear, but something catches his attention behind me. "It's time to go, Ember. Until you call again."

I turn to see what has him spooked and roll over on my blanket to look at the mouth of the cave.

Chapter 6

It's late afternoon when we finally enter the forest again. Kalstrop had reached a new level of anger when he found out the cave had magically moved back to where we had passed through the gate. The irate guard attempted to strap packs to Beau and caught a hoof to the hip for his efforts. It's hard to imagine they were ever friends with how often they bicker.

Kalstrop has spent the day grumbling under his breath while slowly limping ahead of me on the trail. Beau quietly brings up the rear, pulling tall shoots of grass to munch every so often. This world offered nothing but confusion the first time we traveled through here. Today feels different. I've been grinning for hours, recalling my lesson from last night.

"What the hell are you smiling about?" Kalstrop barks. "We have even longer to go now. Stupid cave."

Sighing, I watch him slap at a tree branch as he limps past it. "Should you go see a doctor?" I ask. "That looks like it hurts."

"Do you see one around here, Princess?" he scoffs, glaring at me angrily. "Our healers live in town. That's where the people are, and the people pay them. You go where the money is."

"So, we're going to town?" I ask, lifting my eyebrow.

Kalstrop stops and stares at me in disbelief. "You're gonna die out here," he informs me. "No one can fix your amount of stupid."

After weeks in the cave and my lesson last night with Ash, I have a newfound appreciation for Kalstrop's foretelling of my death and the humor that lies within his words. I smile broadly at his display. "But if we were near a town, there would be a healer to help," I say as Beau stops beside me.

"Look around, Princess," Kalstrop growls. "We are alone out here. This is where you are at your safest. We cannot take you to town. Your stupidity would be a homing beacon for every male in the kingdom." He limps quickly to stand chest to chest with me. "They would claim your innocence, and the throne would be theirs."

Rolling my eyes, I push him away. "Kalstrop, you act like I'm walking around naked, just waiting for a man to fill a void," I scoff, pushing past him to lead the way down the trail. "Besides, your bitching will attract my killer long before they know I'm here."

After a few more steps, I turn to find Kalstrop and Beau stopped and staring at me. The angry guard's mouth opens and closes a few times before he furrows his brow. "You know, that might be the smartest thing you've ever said," he admits. "I don't like it, but it is true."

I cover my mouth to hide my triumphant smile. "Two can play at this game," I say, lifting an eyebrow. "Now get on the horse, broken one. We don't have time to waste, and I need you to heal. If I'm to make it to the castle alive and chaste, I will need your help."

Beau snorts and shoves Kalstrop with his nose.

"Shut up," the guard grumbles.

* * *

I wake from a dreamless sleep beside a low fire. It's not quite sunrise, so the stars still twinkle through the leaves on the branches above. Beau's deep breathing on my left distracts me from the tranquil nighttime forest sounds. I roll to my right and find Kalstrop cleaning his swords across the fire.

"Are you all right?" I ask softly.

Kalstrop sighs, looking across the flames. "You don't need to worry about me," he whispers. "Sprites are strong. That's our magical power. Strength." He flicks his eyes toward Beau. "You know how to get those shoes off?"

"Yeah," I answer. "I need a hammer and a flat piece of metal."

Kalstrop holds up his sword. "I think I got that."

Smiling, I breathe out a laugh. "You don't have to be an ass all the time," I tell him. "We're on the same team."

"No, Princess," he answers. "We're just on the same side of the sword. There are no teams out here. If you don't look out for yourself, you'll end up dead. That's not a price worth paying in the name of friendship."

"That sounds lonely," I whisper, frowning. "I've spent most of my life alone." I narrow my eyes and glance back at Beau. "Well, I thought I was alone." I rub my knuckles over his shoulder, but he stays asleep. "Why haven't we run into any other sprites?"

Kalstrop relaxes against his pack and lays his sword beside him. "The wings," he grumbles. "Elders say that I'm cursed, so my people avoid me. We have a few more days to enjoy the space my pain creates. You should rest."

I'd be lying if I said I didn't enjoy these quiet talks. Kalstrop has hinted several times that he's much older than Beau, though he looks like a man in his 20s. While typically filled with sarcasm and anger, he softens when we speak after Beau has fallen asleep, revealing a touch of tenderness. Sometimes I wonder if he'll tell me what happened to his wings if I ask during these times, but I fear losing our pleasant conversation by pushing him too far.

"Thank you for telling me," is how I end our nighttime chats. In my heart, I know that's what he needs to hear. Kalstrop doesn't have to open up to me or treat me with kindness. He has proven that every time he opens his mouth or looks my way in the daytime. But he chooses to be decent during the night, and for that, I feel the need to thank him.

Kalstrop bows his head in his customary way to end our conversation and closes his eyes. He won't sleep. This is his way of dismissing me without telling me to go away. He must have been a good friend before his ordeal.

* * *

The waterfall marking the edge of the sprites' territory is gorgeous. Although the water is clear, it's impossible to tell how deep it is with the amount of plants growing within its depths. Kalstrop shoves me aside and dives into the water, nearly taking me with him. He might as well have, because before I can turn around, Beau shoves me in after my guard.

Shielding my face, I break the water with my arms and drop well below the surface before I hit the foliage below. The depth is considerable, and everything shines in the midday sun. I smile at the little fish darting away from me before pulling myself back to the bank.

"You need a bath too," I grumble after spitting a mouthful of water at Beau. Pressing against the solid ground, I kick my legs and launch out of the water to sit on the bank. Beau steps back as I toss my bow and quiver into the grass. "Kalstrop's not gonna be happy about those getting wet. We'd better let them dry off while he's busy."

I take off my vest and boots and set them aside. Wet leather needs to be oiled before it dries. I dig through the pack Kalstrop dropped, looking for the tin.

"Get out of my crap," the guard barks.

His shirt lands in my lap, making me freeze.

"I am not your maid," I grumble at him. "Wash your own damn clothes."

His pants hit me next.

"Nah," he says playfully, making me look up at him. "Come here. I want to show you something."

I eye him carefully. This is only the second time Kalstrop has removed his shirt around me since telling me about his wings. I made the situation awkward the first time by staring at his back.

"What?" I ask suspiciously.

Kalstrop's smile instantly puts me at ease. It's the one he's reserved only for our nighttime chats. "You'll like it," he replies, swimming to me. "Come on." He slides his hands up my legs and pulls me into the water by my hips. "We'll be back, old friend. Watch my shit."

Before I can register what's happening, Kalstrop turns his back to me and wraps my arms around his neck. I instinctively latch onto him when he bobs a few times and swims forward.

"Hold tight, Princess," he says, looking over his shoulder. "Deep breath. Ready?"

I puff my chest, taking a larger gulp of air with each breath until I feel I might survive whatever he has planned. I love the playful smile he gives me when I nod. Kalstrop lunges forward headfirst into the pool. He swims straight at the violent cascade of the waterfall, pulling at the water until the current's rush is no match for his speed.

Once clear of the white wall created by the waterfall's splashing, a cave appears, teeming with vibrant colors and glowing rocks. I try not to interfere with Kalstrop's fast pace, but I can't help lifting my head to look around. The cave is alive with the excitement of a fireworks display.

I'm nearly out of air when we break through the surface. My head slams into the cave ceiling, causing me to duck back into the depths and inhale a mouthful of water.

"Sorry," Kalstrop says, helping me stay above the surface as I cough and gag. "Easy. Just try to get it out. We're almost there."

I look around to find we're in an air pocket barely large enough for the two of us.

"What is this?" I sputter.

"This is my home," Kalstrop whispers, brushing my hair from my face. "I haven't been here in a long time, but some things never change."

Wiping the rest of the water from my face, I narrow my eyes thoughtfully. "But you have," I whisper, grinning as I rest my arm over his shoulder. "You keep trying to be that mean, hateful jerk. It's getting harder, isn't it?"

Kalstrop scowls at my smile. "Shut up," he grumbles, turning to press his back to my chest. My guard lifts my right arm from his shoulder and wraps it tightly around his ribs. "Last leg, Princess. Deep breath."

We drop below the surface, and Kalstrop pulls at the water again, propelling us forward. The colorful rocks zoom by like streamers in a breeze. Ahead, I see a blue pool shimmering with the water's ripples.

Kalstrop aims at the surface and bursts out of the water, revealing a beautiful cavern lit by hundreds of glowing stones. Benches are carved into the walls, and white pillow tops line their flat surfaces. We swim to the edge of the pool and hold the rocks while catching our breath.

"Keep your voice down in here," Kalstrop murmurs. "There's an echo."

"You live here alone?" I ask, looking around the large open area.

"I don't live here," he answers. "It's just my home."

Confused, I watch him pull up on the ledge and leave the pool. "What does that mean?"

Kalstrop grabs my arms and heaves me from the water as if I were as light as his pack. He places me on my feet before him and brushes my braid behind my shoulder. "Sometimes a home is a reminder of events you'd rather not recall," he says quietly. "Walls never forget. You can't always go home, Princess."

I pull my lower lip into my teeth and look around the cavern again. "Did something happen here?"

"It doesn't matter," Kalstrop murmurs, walking away. He lifts a pillow to reveal a wooden plank covering a hidden pile of linens. "Here. Dry off." Kalstrop throws a towel at me before turning to a desk made of wood and stone with papers scattered across the top.

When he lifts a book, his scar highlights in the glow of a nearby stone. I dry my face and silently step toward my guard. He jerks when my fingers trace the reminder of what he lost. I flatten my hand and rub it over the uninjured skin beside the wound.

I'm unsure what holds Kalstrop still, but he allows me to inspect his injury. My fingers explore every inch as if the wound would give me clues as to how it happened. My soul wants to know how to fix it and make him whole again.

"I was tasked with finding the dragon your mother promised you to," Kalstrop murmurs, leaning onto the desk. "Ending his life would stop the dragons from claiming you. But what I found was a child. He couldn't have been more than two years old. I don't kill kids. I don't care who orders it.

"I was on my way back to report what I found when I received the news of your death. It was in the same story as Beau's disappearance, so I knew it couldn't be true. The nag would never willingly leave his post. I taught him too well."

Kalstrop slips from between me and the desk, creating distance between us.

"I went straight to the castle to learn the truth," he continues, staring at the pool. "I didn't find any answers. The king was furious that I'd failed him. I can still see his smug grin as they cut my wings off whenever I close my eyes."

My tears are involuntary, and my hand covers my open mouth. Words could never be enough in this moment. Kalstrop turns as I approach, and my arms latch onto his waist. I know I've given him what he needs when he folds over me and wraps around my shoulders.

"It took a long time for me to return to the castle after that," Kalstrop murmurs against my hair. "But I am a soldier, and duty calls."

"I understand now," I whisper, pulling away to look into his eyes. "I know why you hate me. My family did this to you, and for that, I feel shame. I'm so sorry."

Kalstrop's gaze is soft as he searches my face. I assume he's looking for any hint of the evil that seems to reside within my grandfather. He won't find any. I struggled to accept that we would need to hunt for food until Alice taught me to aim for the heart or head of our prey to take them down instantly. I could never cause someone a lifetime of pain.

"I will admit that the men who carried out the order died by my sword," my guard whispers, moving to cup my cheeks. "Until just now, your grandfather was the only other person alive who knew how I lost my wings. I vowed I'd never tell a soul what happened."

Kalstrop steps into me, erasing any distance between our bodies. Heat pulses through me just as it had in the armory, but I'm better prepared this time. My eyes focus on his lips when he licks them.

"Why did you tell me?" I whisper.

"There's something about you, Princess," he replies. His breath moves over my face in waves of hot and then cold. "You're different. You breathe light into the darkness."

My eyes stay fixed on his mouth as he speaks. Kalstrop has never been an object of my affection. I rely on him and trust that he will fight by my side. He will protect me when I need it and teach me to be strong so I can hold my own in battle. But I also feel safe with him. He will push the boundaries with me and never question my motives.

I raise my hand to slide my finger along his lower lip and lick mine, wondering what it would be like to feel another's. "Kiss me," I whisper.

"Princess," Kalstrop starts, shaking his head.

I let the back of my nails trace over his tidy beard. "Please."

My guard's jaw clenches, and his fingers tighten along my neck. His tension holds him firmly before me, but I'm desperate for this experience. I lean into Kalstrop and press my lips to his, feeling their soft warmth. He sighs and drops his arms around my shoulders to hold me against him.

I smile at the sensation of his beard tickling my skin before he pulls away. Kalstrop's eyes stay soft as I lick his flavor off my lips. He always has stalks and twigs hanging from his mouth. I could compare him to Beau with the amount of foliage I've seen him chewing on. But the minty taste of my lips explains his actions.

"Again," I command.

My guard stares into my eyes as he leans in, pausing just before reaching my lips. "As you wish, Ember," he whispers.

This kiss is different. I gasp at Kalstrop's forwardness, and he licks my lower lip, pulling it between his teeth. Folding against his chest, I surrender and allow him to give me the experience I'd requested. Kalstrop pulls away and reclaims my lips several times, giving me slow, meaningful kisses.

When he stops, I sigh and brush my lips against his. "Thank you," I whisper, leaving my eyes closed.

Kalstrop kisses me gently one last time before pressing his forehead to mine and pulling away from my lips. "Have you had enough?" he asks.

"Yes."

"Don't ask me to do that again," Kalstrop sighs. "You are not mine. You'll get me killed."

When we're alone, Kalstrop is very different from the man we met after passing through the gate. I believe he respects Beau in his own way, but only displays his brutish tendencies around him. I might not experience this version of him often, but I enjoy it every time I do.

"I would never let that happen, Kalstrop," I whisper, closing my eyes.

My guard breathes a laugh, pulling out of my arms. "It's cute that you believe you have power in the royal court, Princess," he murmurs. "I appreciate that you would probably try to save my life, though." He pulls a sack from under another pillow. "Hold that for me. We need to get a few of these for the trip."

I smile at how quickly he dismisses my awkwardness. I've watched plenty of movies with Alice, and she let me read a few romance books over the years. Not once did any of the characters ask someone to help them experience their first kiss. I assume it's not something one would normally do.

I touch my fingertips to my lips. Now that I've had my first kiss, no one can steal it. I watch Kalstrop move across the cavern in a new light. He didn't have to do that for me, but he cared enough to help me control something so important. I can't help wondering if my grandfather caused him to change into a gruff soldier. Perhaps he was a sweet man who might have made a good husband once upon a time.

"Why are you staring at me?" Kalstrop asks, snapping me out of my thoughts. I let my eyes focus and see that he's holding one of the glowing rocks. My guard lifts his eyebrow and shakes his head. "Last time I take you anywhere."

Smiling broadly, I hold open the bag to accept the rock.

Chapter 7

I've never been a morning person, so I grumble as Beau and I follow Kalstrop through the fog at daybreak. I had removed Beau's shoes as Kalstrop requested. It was easy for him to disguise how sore his feet were on the soft forest floor, but this morning, we are following a rocky trail along a cliff. I hang onto his mane and pretend he's moving slowly for my benefit.

"Let's go, Princess," Kalstrop barks without turning around to see how far we've fallen behind. "Clearly, we should have worked on your stamina, too."

Looking behind us, I glance at the highlands. We left their lush green colors behind before sunrise, and Kalstrop seems to feel their absence. Our only communication has been short and harsh. I frown as Beau stumbles, pushing me with his shoulder.

"We should stop," I whisper to my friend. "I know your feet must be sore."

Beau only shakes his head and continues down the trail beside me.

"I could wrap them," I offer. "Kalstrop might let me use his shirt."

The look I get tells me to drop it. Beau's right, of course. It's absurd to think that my angry guard would hand over his clothing to make Beau more comfortable. My friend would've been fine on the soft footing of the lush fields, but on this rocky terrain, he's struggling. I accept that this is my fault and hate that I've caused him pain.

I wince at every misstep and stumble throughout the day. Although I work hard to make our slow pace look like I'm to blame, Kalstrop's narrowed eyes have become more focused on Beau when we finally reach the bottom at nightfall. I try to distract him by tripping, but he's onto us when I push Beau toward a patch of grass.

"What are you hiding?" Kalstrop demands, pulling his sword.

He marches toward us, dropping his bag of glowing rocks. Beau extends his wings and lays one in front of me. He tucks it back to push me against him, but Kalstrop isn't looking at me. He stomps directly up to Beau and presses his blade to his throat.

"Tell me now!" the guard barks.

I try to push Beau's wing out of my way, but it's surprisingly stiff. "It's his feet," I shout, trying to see around the feathers. "They're sore. It's my fault. Don't you hurt him."

Kalstrop growls, but stays where he is, holding his sword to my friend's throat. "A hurt soldier is a worthless soldier," he grumbles. "Have I taught you nothing?"

Beau opens his wings, holding them high as if he were about to take off.

"Go ahead," Kalstrop sneers. "I dare you."

I take a deep breath and place my hand on Kalstrop's blade. His eyes are locked on Beau, but he allows me to push his sword down so it's pointed at the ground. I don't dare block his view, so I trace my other hand along his jaw, only gently moving the short hairs of his beard. The soft request for his attention soon eases the tension in my guard's expression.

"We can't fight among ourselves, Kalstrop," I whisper. "I promise not to hide things from you again."

Kalstrop lifts his top lip and growls in frustration as he spins away from us. I rub Beau's neck under his mane, watching my guard wipe his weapon clean. He rolls his wrist, flipping the sword, and lifts it to slide the blade into its sheath. Kalstrop marches forward, and once he's at a safe distance, Beau uses his wing to urge me to follow.

"It's hard to imagine you two were ever friends," I say quietly. "He gets so angry at you." I pause to think about our interactions and realize it's not quite as clear as I thought. "Well, I guess that's not exactly true, is it? He gets mad at me and takes it out on you. I'm sorry."

Beau doesn't react and lets me stay in my thoughts until Kalstrop stops ahead of us and drops his bag. I approach him, but Beau flips his wing over my head to stop me before I get too close.

Kalstrop narrows his eyes. "Knock it off," he grumbles. "I'm not gonna hurt her." He softens his gaze and watches me walk around Beau's outstretched wing. "I have some salts. If you'll help me collect wood, we can boil it down and soak his feet. You really should've told me right away. We could've been halfway through this forest by now."

I wince, thinking about the slow pace we kept all day. "I'm sorry," I whisper sadly. "I just didn't want you to yell at him anymore."

"You two have been close over the years," he remarks, nodding.

"I was so lonely," I admit. "He was my only friend."

Kalstrop waits for Beau to lie down before leading me further into the woods. "I get it," he responds, lifting a few broken branches. "I'm old. I've spent a lot of time alone. I kinda prefer it now." He places the wood in my arms. "Still, I wouldn't wish the lifestyle on anyone. If I died, no one would notice."

My eyes follow the thin log he places in my arms. "I would," I declare.

Kalstrop breathes a quiet laugh and grins. "I do appreciate your lies, Princess," he says. "I even wish some of them were true."

Shaking my head, I decide to change the subject. "Who taught you how to handle a sword?"

"Hmm," Kalstrop hums, turning away. "Once upon a time, I had a family, Princess. My mother was a member of the royal guard."

My eyes widen as I follow him through the woods. I'm barely paying attention to where I'm stepping, and just let him continue to pile wood in my arms. "Your mother was a guard?" I ask after a long pause.

"She vowed to leave once she and my father had their first child, my brother," he says, gently placing a log on the top of my stack. "But things happened, and she stayed with the king. Then I came along, and she vowed again."

Kalstrop lifts a larger log and lays it in the crook of his arm.

"That pull to do one's duty is strong, though," he continues. "Recognizing that she would never be able to stay away, she and my father began teaching us how to defend ourselves. They were both skilled in their own ways. My father was a blacksmith who crafted a wide range of blades, but he specialized in swords. My mother could sever a man's head before he even realized she'd moved."

"She sounds amazing," I gush, smiling when he glances my way. "And your father? Was he good with them, too?"

"Although he was excellent at crafting swords, he was far better at throwing knives." Kalstrop shifts his bundle and digs a short knife from his vest. He narrows his eyes and tips his chin toward a clump of birch trees behind me.

I want to look where he gestured, but I can't take my eyes off him. Kalstrop holds the blade between his fingers close to the hilt. He rolls his wrist and flicks his hand hard, releasing the knife. My guard tilts his head to the side and slowly pulls his lower lip into his mouth before turning back to me.

"What?" Kalstrop asks, raising his eyebrows. "You missed it."

Smiling, I finally turn to look at the trees. "I didn't miss a thing," I whisper, stepping toward where his knife remains lodged in the wood. "That was beautiful."

Kalstrop rolls his eyes, shaking his head. "Well, that's one I've never heard," he says, pulling the blade from the tree.

"It's like a dance," I tell him. "Beau and I practiced dressage. It's like dancing for a horse, and we would dance together across the field, doing flying lead changes and half passes. He hated the pirouettes but had a beautiful piaffe." I smile at Kalstrop's quizzical expression. "You had to be there," I say. "But you dance with blades. Even your long sword seems more like an extension of your arm."

"That's what my mother called it," he says, nodding. "Let's finish this and get back to your dancing nag. We're not in friendly territory."

"What happened to your family?" I ask, jogging to catch up.

"My mother was called up in the war," Kalstrop answers, grabbing a few more logs. "She didn't make it back. My father went next, trying to save my brother."

"I'm sorry," I whisper.

Kalstrop takes a few branches from the top of my pile. "I know, Princess," he says softly. "But you don't have to be. It was a very long time ago."

* * *

Although I've known how to build fires since I was a child, Kalstrop spends the rest of the fading daylight showing me where to find a special moss that helps to keep the flames low. He creates a thin layer over the wood before pulling a red rock from his pack. It's not glowing anymore, but I recognize it from his home in the cavern.

"What are those?" I whisper, glancing at Beau to be sure I haven't disturbed his slumber.

"Crystals," Kalstrop answers. "We could start this fire the regular way, but what would be the fun in that?"

I gasp as he blows on the red crystal, and it ignites in his hand. "Whoa," I breathe, reaching for the flames. "That's cool."

Kalstrop lifts his eyebrow. "It's actually hot," he scoffs. "Don't touch it."

Giggling quietly, I pull my hand back. "It's just an expression, Kalstrop," I say. "I've never seen anything like that."

"That's because you grew up in the human realm, Princess," he responds. "Imagine what life could be like in a world that believed in magic. The beauty within can only be seen when you look beyond the surface." Kalstrop studies me for a moment before sighing and turning back to the pile of wood. "Anyway, we'd better make this soak for your nag."

"Why do you call him that?"

Kalstrop hands me a small pot, shrugging. "We all need a title, Princess. I suppose I call him 'Nag' for the same reason you are called 'Princess.'"

"You've used my name," I murmur. "I wish you would again."

My guard looks up from his pack. "Princess is a title that deserves respect," he states, narrowing his eyes. "To call you anything else would be disrespectful." Kalstrop licks his lips with a sigh and returns his attention to the pack in his lap. "I'll not do that again."

I stare into the fire, lost in my thoughts, until Kalstrop dumps large salt chunks into the pot I hold. I jump and look up at him. "I don't want to be a princess," I declare.

"Then what do you want?" he asks, shaking his head.

I narrow my eyes at the woods beyond the low flames. Given what I've learned in the past few weeks, my old dream of riding in the Olympics would be a stupid answer at best. I can feel my cheeks flushing as I remember how strongly I felt about the event. I'd never wanted to be anything else.

"Plans change, Princess," Kalstrop says, briefly rubbing my shoulder. "As children, we find comfort holding a stuffed animal while we sleep."

He takes a deep breath and purses his lips.

"When you meet the one person you've needed your whole life, nothing will comfort you while you sleep until they're in your arms," my guard continues. "You can't hold on to childish desires when your future shows up. You have to move on and adapt. So, I ask again, what do you want?"

I may never understand how Kalstrop knows what I'm thinking, but I can't deny that he makes good points. I watch him rifle through his pack as I consider his words. I can't change the family I was born into any more than I could change the past.

His shoulders come into view when he leans forward, reminding me of his wings. I can't change what has already been done, but I can make sure his pain is never repeated. I can punish those who would harm others.

"I want to right wrongs," I decide, startling Kalstrop. "I'll replace what was taken and mend broken promises. I want a better world than the one we've inherited."

"Hmm," my guard hums. "From a dreamer to the overly ambitious." He pulls a blue stone from his pack and looks up at me. "Then I will turn you into a warrior, Princess. For that is what you will need to be to take on those who call themselves kings."

I smile broadly and eye the blue stone. "Another crystal?"

"It is," Kalstrop answers, nodding. "I wonder if this one would like you."

In general, it's entertaining that my grumpy guard always talks as though I have all the knowledge of his world. He proves any time I question him that he's utterly aware I have no idea what he's talking about, but he leads me into these situations so that he can scoff at me. I raise my eyebrow and wait for him to continue.

"Give me your hand, Princess," Kalstrop requests.

I place my hand gingerly in his and let him guide me toward the crystal.

"Nice and easy now," he murmurs, narrowing his eyes on the stone as it begins to glow. His quiet shushing noises stop me from pulling away when it suddenly liquifies in his hands. "Go slow, Princess. I've never seen this before."

With wide eyes, I kneel before him. My fingers break through the surface, but the crystal maintains its nearly sphere-like shape. Kalstrop rubs the top of my hand before sliding his fingers over mine. He kneels on the ground with me and laces our fingers to push his into the water.

"It's warm," he whispers, amazed. "Is this what it feels like for you?"

I smile and curl my fingers to tangle them with his. "There is only warm water in this realm," I respond quietly. "It's like it wants to be inviting."

Kalstrop pulls one hand away and studies his skin. "Dry," he says.

I remove mine to show him the water dripping from my fingers. "Wet."

"Interesting," my guard murmurs, rubbing my fingers. "This water feels cold." He reaches for the crystal again, but he's not touching me this time, and it won't let him break the surface. His fingers bump into it and knock it out of my hand. The solid crystal crashes to the ground and rolls into Beau's hoof, waking him.

"Sorry, Beau," I hiss, giggling. "We were experimenting."

Kalstrop scoops the crystal off the ground and slaps Beau's hoof. "I'll get you prancing like a pretty pony again, you ole nag," he announces. "I heard you know how to dance."

I click my tongue and swat at his leg. "Leave him alone," I scoff. "Let's see what that crystal does for you."

"It's not as grand," Kalstrop responds. He holds the crystal up and blows on it. A spiral of water forms on top like an upside-down tornado. It swirls several inches tall before collapsing and unceremoniously splashing to the ground. "See? It doesn't like me as much."

Giggling, I place the pot beneath Kalstrop's hands. "Do it again," I tell him. "This time, aim your splash."

Chapter 8

After hours of tossing and turning, I sigh in relief when the tall hedges of the maze garden appear before me. I've come to enjoy my time with Kalstrop while he trains and harasses me for not being good enough at whatever I'm learning. But these gardens are a beautiful treat when I get to experience them.

I round the corner to the enclosure with the creek and frown when I find it empty. The grass is still mashed where the mother duck has cuddled with her little ducklings, but there is no sign of them now. Remembering Ash's lesson, I close my eyes and picture my feathered friends, but they're still missing when I open them.

"Ash?"

I jump when hands slide down my arms.

"Sorry, Ember," Ash whispers, releasing his grip to let me spin around. "You looked like you needed comforting. I didn't mean to startle you."

"You were watching me?" I ask, blushing.

Ash smiles at my awkwardness. "I always watch you, Ember. You fascinate me." He slips his fingers through my hair. "You've been working with water." When I narrow my eyes in confusion, he flips a few locks forward to show me that more have turned blue. "The more you work with your powers, the bluer your hair will become."

"I was playing with a blue crystal today," I explain. "I turned it into water."

Sweeping my hair behind my shoulder, Ash steps into me and sighs. "Not quite, Ember," he says quietly. "Crystals have their own power. They will react to things that alarm them with their abilities. They are cold and unfeeling, while your touch is warm and inviting. You disturbed its natural element."

"It didn't like me," I say in sad realization.

"Don't take it personally," Ash says, rubbing my back. "They don't like anyone."

Allowing him to comfort me, I remember the crystals not responding to Kalstrop's touch. They didn't seem to mind him. Their only reaction came when he blew on them. I smile, thinking that they might be reacting to Kalstrop's breath. Now that I've experienced his flavor, I can understand why they appreciate the spices and herbs he chews on.

I rub my lips, recalling his mint flavor when I kissed him. "Not everyone," I murmur.

"What?" Ash asks, leaning back to look down at me.

"Nothing," I respond. I slip from his arms and step toward the creek. "Water always feels warm to me. I was told that was because I'm a water fairy. Can I make it cold?"

Ash waits for me to sit by the creek before joining me. "Fairy magic is not any one thing," he starts, leaning back on his hands. "You have the ability to bend the element to your will. The magic has no beginning or end, so your only limitations are the ones you create. It can be beautiful. However, left unharnessed, your power could also be dangerous."

I reach into the creek, but the water moves away from my hand. I lean closer, only for the ripples to jump over the bank to avoid me. "Do I disturb water's natural element now, too?" I scoff, rolling onto my hands and knees, desperate for this water to like me again.

"You need to calm down, Ember," Ash murmurs gently. "You are creating a limitation." He reaches out to me when I sit back to glare at him. "Give me your hand."

I've never been a good student and have no idea how to trust people. I don't want to give in to him, but I see no other option. Kalstrop says my lack of strength restricts me in his training, and now Ash says I'm creating limits in his lessons. Clearly, I need to shut up and learn from these men.

"Close your eyes," Ash whispers, pulling me to sit in front of him. He presses his chest to my back and guides my hand toward the creek. "Try to picture the last time you went swimming. Recall the water against your skin—how your clothing clung to you. Feel it moving over your body and creating a resistance."

As he quietly speaks in my ear, I recall swimming through the cave with Kalstrop. The crystals lit the way, making it appear magical and mysterious. Kalstrop's strokes pulled us both faster than I could ever swim alone. Memories are easy to get lost in, but I gasp and open my eyes when the water touches my fingers.

"Easy," Ash hisses when the water retreats to the opposite bank. "We wouldn't want to offend it." Sliding his hand under mine, Ash threads our fingers. "Let's see if we can encourage it to trust us." He leans us forward and cups our hands. "As if it were a little mouse," he murmurs. "Maybe it might like to climb into your hands."

Nothing about this makes any sense. I shake my head and lift away from Ash. He watches me walk along the creek, but doesn't try to follow.

"You spend a lot of time in your head, Ember," the young man says, keeping his eyes on me. "Elements are about the experience. It's more in the way they taste, touch, feel, or smell, and less about how you think things should be. Your mind is getting in the way."

"My mind is what creates this world," I snap, aggravated. "Shouldn't my mind be able to tell the water to knock its shit off and touch me?"

Ash smiles, laughing quietly. "Water's not a man," he says as though this information would make sense. "You can't command it into a frenzy."

Sighing, I lean against a tree. "What is that supposed to mean?"

"It's not an insult, Ember," Ash says, smiling as he stands. "You're a beautiful princess. Any man would be honored to touch you, but to hear you request their attention... I can't describe the pride one would feel." He brushes his fingers over my flushed cheek. "You could bend a man to your will with just a wink. Water will not be won so easily. Instead of actions, try emotions."

"Shall I be sad that it doesn't want to touch me?" I scoff.

Ash sighs and looks off into the distance. "This isn't working," he mumbles.

"Did you really expect it to?"

"Yes," he responds, rolling his eyes. "Come here." Ash doesn't wait for my hand. He abruptly grabs my arm and hauls me closer to the creek. "Lie down in the bed."

"What?" I say, narrowing my eyes. "No."

The young man closes his eyes and growls angrily. "You're impossible," he snaps. "Good luck."

In the blink of an eye, he's gone. I drop to my knees and rub my arm where his fingers dug into my flesh. I fought with Kalstrop until I finally gave in and started doing what he asked. When I did, things turned around. Not only did we begin to get along, but my strength and skills significantly improved.

I glance down at the water. The creek bed isn't deep. I would be in no danger of drowning if I lay among the gravel. I don't think anyone has ever died in a dream anyway.

Sighing, I step into the creek bed and frown as the water jumps away to run over the grass. "Don't be afraid of me," I whisper, sitting in the empty bed. "Perhaps we just need to learn to trust each other." I lie back and stare at the clouds. "We're in this together."

I try to relax in the quiet garden, but I can feel anxiety building within my nerves. I rub my hands over my pants, feeling the smooth green fabric sewn together at the seam. I try to focus on its soft sensation, but soon, I'm nervously tapping my fingers on my leg.

"Close your eyes," Ash whispers.

Air rushes from my lungs with a sigh of relief. I might have snapped at him and sent him away, but I can't deny my desire for his return. Although Ash's words are confusing and sometimes irritating, I need them. I'll never figure out how to work with water without him. Kalstrop already told me he can't help me, and Beau's incessant need to remain a silent equine has rendered him useless during my lessons.

"Rest your hands beside you," Ash murmurs. "Feel the pebbles under you. They are all part of the creek bed and belong to the water."

I stretch my fingers to flatten my hand. The stones are smooth against my skin, and I relax into their cool sensation. As I move over them, my mind assigns colors to them based on their shape and texture. I gasp when water reaches the tips of my fingers.

"It's okay," Ash says quietly. "Accept its embrace, Ember. Water will not harm you. It wants to be near you if you could find it in your heart to let go of the fears and harness your powers."

"But I don't understand them," I whisper. "I can't harness what I don't know."

"I will teach you," Ash promises. "You work incredibly hard to push everyone away. You could be unstoppable if you channeled even half of that energy into learning."

I exhale a deep, relaxing breath as the water swarms around me, filling the creek bed again and running along my body as if I'd never rejected it. Although the rocks are chilled, the water is still warm. "Can I make it cold?" I ask.

"Perhaps one day," Ash whispers. He slips his hand into the water to rub my palm, and I lift my fingers to thread them with his. "I have to go, Ember. You have a fight ahead of you. Take your lessons seriously, as they will be your only hope. Don't trust even the smoothest of voices. Danger doesn't always come at you from the front."

Furrowing my brow, I sit up to find myself beside the low fire in the forest. The sun is just beginning to rise, but it's still very dark within the canopy of the trees. I squint, trying to see into the darkness outside the fire's range.

Kalstrop leans against a tree nearby with his arms crossed over his chest. "Hey," he whispers. "You all right?"

I stand and join my guard in the darkness. "Where's Beau?" I ask.

He swings his hand to point to my left as another man appears. I reach out to Kalstrop, who takes my arm to steady me. I don't recognize the man approaching us, but I still know exactly who he is.

"Beau?" I breathe lower than a whisper.

The man is beautiful in all the ways my stunning equine partner had been. His dark hair and tanned skin are the image of perfection, and his piercing eyes shine even in the low light. He pulls a leather vest over the cream colored shirt I'd seen Kalstrop working on before we left the cave.

"Ember," he murmurs, smiling. "Come here, sweet girl."

I don't know if I told my body to move, but I quickly take the few steps needed to close the gap between us and fall onto his chest. Beau's arms wrap firmly around my shoulders, his muscles twitching as he attempts to remain gentle. As a horse, this man has been my best friend for my entire life. He may not have said a single word to me until now, but I know his soul, and the comfort I feel in his arms will never have an equal.

* * *

"Your archery has come a long way," Beau says quietly, breaking the silence. "Kalstrop isn't the most patient instructor, but you've done well under him."

"I don't think I had a choice," I answer, smiling.

We walk through the woods beside a well-worn trail in the midday sun. Kalstrop silently watches over us while we stroll arm in arm between the trees. My head has been flooded with a million questions, each more ridiculous than the last. I'm glad Beau finally broke the silence because I wasn't sure how.

"I have so many questions," I hiss, adjusting my bow. I've become accustomed to carrying it over my right shoulder, but my friend was adamant about escorting me with his left arm to free up his dominant right hand to pull his sword if needed.

Beau looks down and grins at my childish excitement. "I'm sure you do, Princess."

"Can you please not call me that?" I ask. "I get enough of it from Kalstrop. I feel we're closer than that."

"Hmm," Beau hums, nodding. "I have seen you at your worst."

I blush thinking of the long days we'd spent together at the ranch. "Oh, gosh, the things you have seen," I gasp. "I am so embarrassed."

"We will not speak of it, Princess," Beau says, chuckling.

"And Alice," I say, recalling her motherly moments. "She knew and still threatened to geld you every time I fell off."

Beau licks his teeth. "Yeah," he says, drawing out the word. "We'll not be speaking of that either."

Laughing, I squeeze his arm and lay my head against his shoulder. "Are we doing the right thing, Beau?" I ask, focusing my eyes on Kalstrop as he walks ahead. "Was he right about going to the castle?"

"You're the princess, Ember. You are the next in line for the throne regardless of the current monarch." Beau leans over to kiss the top of my head. "I know you don't want it, and I'm sure running away would be part of any plan you devised, but you are royal. You need to accept that."

I scowl, keeping my eyes on my guard. Kalstrop has a confident stride that rarely falters, but his shoulders are rounded, and his knees are slightly bent, making his footsteps lighter. I freeze, tugging Beau's arm when Kalstrop pulls his long sword to hold it before him.

Beau follows my gaze and shoves me behind him. When Kalstrop drops his pack, I instinctively draw an arrow and set up with my bow. We creep forward to approach Kalstrop. I study our surroundings, but nothing moves within the trees. The bushes and branches all stay still.

"What is it?" Beau hisses.

"Pixies," Kalstrop growls.

I lower my bow. "Like Tinkerbell?"

"No, Princess," Kalstrop snaps. "Tinkerbell was a fairy. Are you tiny? Do you make jingly noises when you talk?" He sighs loudly. "Pixies are obnoxious, horrible people who probably eat their young so they don't have to hunt."

"Now, Kalstrop," a woman's voice barks through the still air. "Is that any way to talk about those who own the land you happened to be trespassing on?"

Rolling his eyes, Kalstrop straightens his back. "Murielle," he groans. "Long time."

"Yes, it has been," the woman responds, stepping from behind a tree. "I believe the last time I saw you, you were slinking out of my bed before sunrise."

"I'm prettier in the dark," Kalstrop replies, lifting an eyebrow.

"I agree," she sneers before nodding in my direction. "Take her. I have big plans for that little girl."

Beau reaches for me, and I draw back on my string, but someone grabs me from behind. My arrow sails through the air, nearly hitting Murielle, and my bow is wrenched from my grip. I kick out and jump around, fighting against the arms securely holding me captive.

My eyes search wildly for my guards. When they land on Beau, he's standing wide-eyed right where I left him. A sword swings around and presses under my jaw, cutting my skin and making me freeze. I reach behind me for the blade owner's hips and steady myself with them.

Kalstrop scoops his pack off the ground. "Fine," he snaps. "Don't hurt her." He drops his sword back into its sheath and glares at Beau. "Your incompetence brings me joy, nag," he growls.

Chapter 9

The pixie camp isn't far and quickly comes alive with people playing flutes and small guitars near a mounting fire. Although everyone stops talking as we approach, they quickly resume their excited chatter once we pass. The mixture of numerous voices makes it impossible to understand their conversations.

"Bring her to my tent," Murielle orders when we reach a clearing at the center of their camp. "Get her ready."

"For what?" I ask, jumping against the man holding me. "Ready for what?" I shout as I'm dragged away. I'm shoved into a grand tent and thrown onto a chair surrounded by basins, clothing racks, and footstools. "What is going on?"

A young man appears and drops a footstool before me. "Hello, Princess," he says, smiling. "I am Remi. I will be preparing you for tonight's festivities. You look hungry. Would you like some delicious pastries?"

He takes a plate from a woman beside me and holds the puffs of cream and frosted cookies below my nose. Alice didn't let me have many treats, but I have a sweet tooth. I smile at the fun swirls and fluffy pastries.

"Maybe just one," I murmur, choosing a small cake with a flower made of frosting. "Perhaps my guards would like some." I lift my eyebrows while licking the sweet cream from my lip.

"No, Princess," Remi answers. "They will participate in the festivities away from your prep." He hands me another pastry and smiles. "Eat up, Princess. The sweeter the better."

I smile and accept the treat. I take the first bite as Remi removes my boots. He hands them to the woman and takes a rag she offers. I barely notice their movements as I'm given another cake. I smile at the little duck, reminded of my small friends in the dream garden. The cream is yellow but orange-flavored.

"These are adorable," I whisper. "I hang out with a little family of ducks at night sometimes." I gasp and cover my mouth. I hadn't meant to say that, but I'm sure the words slipped past my lips.

Glancing around nervously, I realize that no one seems to be listening to me. They are fussing over my skin and pulling at the fabric hanging from the racks around us. A woman hands me a cup as she passes by on her way to a bench nearby.

"What's going on?" I slur. "What are you all talking about?"

Remi steps forward and hooks my armpits to pull me to my feet. The cup of liquid goes flying as he wrestles my vest off. I try to object, but the room is spinning, and every ounce of my concentration is reserved for remaining upright. The young man shoves a pastel green dress over my head and digs in the sleeves for my hands.

"Let's go, Princess," he urges, more forceful than earlier. "It's nearly time."

"For what?" I mumble, letting him pull my arms through the holes. "I think I should lie down."

"You will," Remi answers, twisting my hair away from my face. "You! Come get her pants off. I'll hold her up."

They seemed so nice when I first met them. I'm having trouble putting my thoughts in order, but I feel myself being lifted. Someone digs under the dress, looking for my waistband. *Don't trust even the smoothest of voices.* Ash had warned me this was coming.

"What are you doing?" I slowly growl, ensuring all my words come out loud and clear.

Remi releases an exasperated sigh, dropping me onto the chair. "We're prepping for your wedding, Princess," he announces as if the answer were obvious. "You will be allowed to sleep once you've been bedded."

My breath catches, and my eyes widen. I remember feeling woozy when Alice let me drink champagne on New Year's Eve one year. This is so much worse.

When my lungs release the trapped air, I scream, "Kalstrop!"

"He's out there," Remi tells me, placing a bundle of wildflowers in my hand. "He'll have a front row seat. Did you know we get to watch? The consummation must be witnessed."

I swallow hard, and my stomach lurches. "I think I'm gonna be sick."

Remi grabs my wrists and pulls me to my feet. "That's probably just your nerves," he says dismissively. "I'm sure it'll pass." He smooths the yards of fabric cascading over my body and sighs heavily, eyeing me with a grin. "Stunning. I have truly outdone myself."

I'm led to the tent's flap, and Remi sticks his head out. I look down at my bare feet and narrow my eyes, trying to remember them moving to walk here. The sweet flavor of frosting covers my lips when I lick them. I can't even imagine what they would have put in the food, but it's clearly the cause of my current state.

Remi drags me through the tent flap and presents me to a large group of excited wedding guests with a grand flourish. Women stand with flowers and ribbons twisted through their hair and cling to men with puffed chests and proud gazes. There's a hushed murmur throughout the crowd as the women whisper to each other.

I scan the top of the crowd looking for my guards. The gathered spectators move aside as I'm ushered forward, but there is no end to them. The bobbing heads trying to get high enough to glimpse me extend far into the surrounding forest. My chest heaves from panic, helping to clear my thoughts with the added oxygen.

"Oh," I exclaim when I find Beau. His wrists are bound together over his head and tied with a rope hanging from a tall branch. Kalstrop isn't far from him, with his back to the same tree and his arms folded across his chest. His head is raised with a sword pressed under his chin, but his eyes remain on me.

I can't look away. Remi holds my arm and pushes me by the small of my back. Although I'm moving forward, Kalstrop's eyes are all I can see. My legs take each step, but I can only feel my chest rising with every deep breath.

Once I'm close enough, Kalstrop lowers his arm to brush his hand over his sack of crystals, which is still slung by its long strap across his body. His eyes flick to his right. When I follow them, I find Murielle standing on a raised mound of dirt with a middle-aged man whose decorative clothing matches my dress.

I dig my heels into the dirt and pull back against Remi. The man with Murielle narrows his green eyes and tightens his jaw. Even angry, his features are handsome. His muscles ripple under his shirt. I assume any of the women around me would feel blessed to be in my position. But he couldn't hold my attention the way my guard is now.

Kalstrop slips his hand into his sack, waiting for my display to pull more focus away from his direction. I drag Remi a few steps backward toward the tent and bump into some of the crowd that had closed in behind us. He tries to latch onto me with his other hand, but I swat it away and hit a woman beside me.

"Princess, you look hungry," Remi spouts hurriedly. "Quick. Someone get her some cake."

I lean forward and jam my finger down my throat. My stomach retches at the sensation, and the sweet treats that were so delicious going down revisit us in the form of a pile of mush at my feet. They don't taste as good this time, which makes more come up.

I spit the remnants in my mouth toward Remi's feet, and he jumps away, releasing my arm. Backing away from my mess, I look around for Kalstrop. The crowd is closer and blocks my view, but I find Beau's hands still tied and look below them just in time to see Kalstrop punch the man who had held the sword to his throat.

There's a shrill whistle, and the blue crystal suddenly flies through the air. Without thinking, I jump and snag the stone to clutch it tightly against my chest as it liquefies. I have no idea what a ball of water could possibly do to save us, but Kalstrop has a plan, and I need to trust him.

Looking back in my guard's direction, I watch him hold the red crystal before his lips. He blows on it to produce the fire as I'd seen before, but then scoops it off the top with his other hand. He hurls it into the crowd and watches as it explodes upon impact.

As Kalstrop repeats his actions, I scoop a handful of water out of the blue crystal. Following his example, I hurl it at a group of pixies, but my explosion differs dramatically. An eruption of darkness detonates, and a tidal wave of mud crashes over the top of us, knocking me back.

I clamor to my feet quickly, cupping another handful of water. I spin around to throw it toward my guards to give them the chance to escape, but Kalstrop is nearly at my side. Although his mouth is moving, I can't hear anything over the thunderous screams of the pixies surrounding us. Beau latches onto my waist and propels me toward the large tent.

With Kalstrop beside us, I hurl my water bomb at the closest pixies, sending them tumbling in a swell of mud. My guard throws a fireball, providing us with cover to disappear into the tent.

"If there were ever a time to swallow your pride," Kalstrop growls, jogging around the racks of clothing. He reaches the back of the tent and jabs a short knife into the canvas. After a quick peek, he turns back to us. "Beau? We could really use a ride."

I snatch my pants off the floor. "What's the big deal?" I ask. "You're fast, Beau. We need to run."

My oldest friend winces as I dig around for my vest.

"We are a very proud race, Princess," Beau says apologetically. "Tragae are not... ridden."

"I've been riding you for years," I spout, jamming the water crystal into my pocket. "We've both been on your back since being here." I hold my hands out in wonder.

"No one was around to see that," Beau growls. "And we'll not speak of it again."

Kalstrop draws his sword and steps around us to stand between me and the tent flap. "You've lost your tracking skills," he grumbles. "You're barely a soldier. Are you going to let them have her?"

With narrowed eyes and a clenched jaw, Beau pulls his shirt over his head. Kalstrop guides me to the back of the tent when my friend reaches for his waistband. Clothes are thrown in our direction, and when I look back, my beautiful winged horse stands tall, glaring down at us as though we should burst into flames from his anger.

"Come on," Kalstrop hisses. "Up you go."

He flings me onto Beau's back and slices the rear of the tent open.

"My bow," I call to him.

"I'll make you another," Kalstrop promises, leaping onto Beau's back behind me. "Go, Beau."

***

With his unrivaled stamina, Beau carries us for hours at a grueling pace. When he slows, the woods are dark and silent. Kalstrop remained quiet for the ride. His only movements were to check behind us until he was sure we weren't followed. He pats my leg and points to the ground when Beau stops.

"Seems our ride is over, Princess," Kalstrop snickers. "Why don't we let him retain some of his dignity?"

I click my tongue and sigh. "Beau might be out of practice, but your social skills need work," I grumble. "I could teach you how to be pleasant while you retrain him as a soldier."

"I'm pleasant enough," Kalstrop huffs. "I believe you have something of mine."

Kalstrop steps into me in a way I've become accustomed to. He licks his lips and looks down at me. I smell cinnamon when he exhales on my face, making me smile. I raise my hands to Kalstrop's chest and feel around his pockets while staring into his eyes. I like how they soften when we're this close. It makes me feel like we're almost friends.

"Ah ha," I shout when I find what I'm looking for. I dig in the pocket and pull out a few short cinnamon sticks. "Thought you could hide these, huh?"

Sighing, Kalstrop snatches my hand. "You can have one, woman," he growls. He digs into my pocket and pulls out the blue crystal. "That was... something."

I jam the cinnamon stick in my mouth and twist my face. "It was weird, right? The mud?" I turn to be sure Beau is following us. "Why did it turn to mud?"

Kalstrop shrugs. "I don't know," he scoffs. "I threw fire and produced an explosion of flames. You threw water and created an eruption of mud. How am I supposed to make sense out of that?"

I giggle and scratch Beau's neck. "I have no idea," I whisper. "Are you okay?"

My old friend bows his head and flips his nose to the trail ahead.

"Yeah, I agree," I respond. "Let's keep going. It's probably best we get out of the pixies' reach."

"Yes," Kalstrop spouts. "I'm sure the next land full of hopeful grooms will be better."

Although his words have an angry bite, I've come to know Kalstrop well, and he's become more than just my guard. I can hear some relief in his words. He holds his arm out, and I don't hesitate to accept it.

"So," I begin as he resumes our journey, "you can throw fire. I thought you said strength was your only power."

"I said it was a sprite's magical power," Kalstrop answers, lifting his eyebrow. "I come from a very long line of Sentinels, Princess. We protect the crystals within the cave, and I've handled them for many years." I open my mouth to press him further, but he puts his hand over it. "I've never let another hold them. I don't know why it reacts to you."

Laughing, I press his hand to my cheek before moving it away from my face. "Okay, fair enough," I say, leaning against his shoulder to settle back into our walk. "They were well prepared, Kalstrop. The dresses, the people, and even a tent set up."

"I told you everyone knows you're here," he answers quietly. "That was pretty tame compared to what I expected, though."

I recall what I had heard of Remi's ramblings. "They were going to watch... the thing," I mutter. "With me and that guy. Who was he?"

"Murielle's brother," Kalstrop answers. "He's actually pretty nice—compared to his sister anyway."

"I've never done that," I whisper, staring thoughtfully at the trail before us. I snicker and feel my guard lean toward me as he looks down. "You were the first boy I ever kissed."

Kalstrop sighs deeply. "I'm not a boy, Princess," he murmurs. "I haven't been for a long time. Regardless, we will not discuss that again."

"You sure do keep a lot of secrets here," I grumble. "Why were they going to watch?" I look up as Kalstrop turns away, wincing. "What? Tell me."

"It's royal tradition," he answers with a huff. "The marriage must be consummated for it to be valid. As you say, we keep secrets. We also lie. It has to be witnessed by multiple people of many ranks."

I can still recall the numerous times I'd tried to show Alice something Beau and I were working on, and how embarrassed I was when we got anything wrong. "That sounds horrible," I whisper.

"The right man would captivate all of your attention, Princess," Kalstrop says. "You wouldn't notice anyone else was there. He would be all you could see in that moment."

"Have you ever been in love?"

Kalstrop remains quiet for a moment, making me look up to find him staring at me. "Once," he answers, tucking some loose hair behind my ear. "It just wasn't meant to be."

"What happened?" I ask.

Sighing, Kalstrop turns back to the trail ahead. "She wasn't mine."

Chapter 10

I enter the secluded section of the garden to find the single tree standing in the center with its wooden swing. I smile at the little duck family, happy to have them back. I don't like my velvet green dress, but the supple leather vest over the top fits me well. My bare feet splash in the creek as I cross it to reach the swing.

My mind is instantly comforted by the garden's serene sanctuary, as it can only be disturbed by the occasional rustling of leaves. Sitting on the seat, I slide my hands over the ropes. I've only felt them once, yet they are still familiar. The gentle breeze caresses my face as I push off with my feet and lift my legs. I lean back, closing my eyes and letting my body increase the swing's momentum.

"You've redecorated a bit in here," Ash comments, disrupting my tranquility. "I like it."

I open my eyes to find Ash leaning against the wall in his usual place. "How do you know I did it?" I ask, grinning. "Maybe it was the ducks."

"Yes," Ash says, returning my grin. "I've heard stories about the waterfowl in these parts."

"Ash, have you ever worked with crystals?" I ask, slowing the swing.

The man twists his face in thought before pushing off the wall. "Sure," he responds. "When I was younger. It's been a while. Why?"

"How do they react to you?"

Ash steps behind me and pushes my hips to start the swing back up. "They don't," he answers. "I told you, they don't like anyone."

I narrow my eyes. "You said they were reacting to me because of my warmth," I start.

"Ember," he barks. "Stop reading too much into things. Crystals are just stones made of the elements. Water, fire, earth, and air. You can't turn this into something personal."

Giving Ash a few minutes to calm down, I focus on the hedge and recall the pond Kalstrop found for us to camp by tonight. The guys remained on the bank with their backs to me while I washed the pixies' memory off my skin. After spending time with Beau as a man, it felt weird letting him see me even as a winged horse.

I was frustrated, trying to change the water's temperature, but I smiled when I stopped focusing on myself. Kalstrop was talking to Beau much like he does with me at night. Their conversation was more one-sided than ours, but it was still cute to see them acting like anything other than enemies. I suppose they were great friends in the past.

"What have you been working on?" Ash asks, pulling my attention back to the garden. He moves beside me and pushes the small of my back as I swing past him. He chews on his lower lip before continuing. "I'm sorry for being cross. I will work on my temper."

I smile at his attempted sincerity. "I tried to change the temperature of a pond," I respond, avoiding the subject of crystals and mud bombs.

"Did it work?"

"No," I answer, scowling. "To be fair, though, I got distracted."

"Harnessing your powers will take hard work and focus," Ash says, pressing against my back to slow my swing. He kneels and looks up at me when it stops. "As I've said, danger is before you. You don't have time for distractions."

After the day I just had, I need the distractions he's desperate for me to avoid. My mind is still racing with what Remi said and Kalstrop's explanation. Bringing any of it up would require me to tell Ash about the crystals because he would want to know how we escaped.

"I think I just need a break," I suggest, drained by the day's events. "Would that be okay? Can we take a walk?"

"Sure," Ash answers, rising to his feet. He pulls me from the swing and turns my body until my back is against his chest. "I can't wait to see where you'll take me."

I breathe sharply as his hand covers my eyes.

"Just like before," Ash murmurs. "Relax your mind and picture where you want to be."

Home is where I want to go—the beautiful summer fields with dots of cattle over the hills. The goats would bleat every morning when we delivered their grain. I never understood why they beckoned for it when they always had access to hay and grass.

The horse fields are what I most want to see again. Beau didn't spend much time there, but we rode with the herd often, and I would love to relive that experience. I understand now why riding my beautiful stallion around the mares was so easy, never worrying about him getting caught up by one in season.

"Beautiful," Ash whispers, lifting his hand.

I hadn't been picturing anything, so I don't recognize the field we're in as I open my eyes, but I agree with his statement. The tall grass is accented by soft, pastel-colored daisies that sway in the breeze. Long grass would normally feel stiff, but this is soft under my hands when I stretch to skim the tops and touch the petals.

"Perfect for a walk," I respond, stepping away from Ash. "Will you join me?"

Although I've learned more about my powers from Kalstrop, Ash has proven helpful in other ways. Quick temper or not, he's useful. Alice once told me to "play the hand I was dealt." It would appear I've been dealt a handful of grumpy, unpredictable men, and I should learn how to handle them.

"Sure," Ash says, smiling. "A walk might be nice." He extends his arm and waits for me to give him mine. "What's on your mind?"

"I wanted to try working with water again, but I seemed to have imagined it all away from the garden," I answer.

"Water is never really gone, Ember," Ash says. He starts forward, escorting me through the lush green field. "Even rocks have some moisture to them."

I watch the flowers sway and smile at a bird hovering over us. "I suppose they would all need water to survive," I remark. "But they've hidden it from me."

"Remember I told you that the only limits to your powers are the ones you impose on yourself," Ash reminds me. "You can command water from anywhere. If you focus enough, you can call water from anything around you. You could pull water in a desert."

"But if it's in the ground, how do I find it?"

"It would find you," the young man whispers, patting my hand. "Consider the possibilities, Ember. If you pulled sulfur-rich water or hard water thick with calcium, think about what you could do with a mixture like that. You would be able to create something different."

"I don't think I understand, Ash," I respond. "What would I create with other types of water? Regardless of what's in it, it's still water."

"Oh, Ember." Ash smiles down at me, wrapping his arm around my shoulders. "It could be so much more. Calcium is a hard mineral. Sulfur is liquid when hot and solid when cooled."

"There was a sulfur spring on the far side of our ranch," I recall in a whisper. "It smelled bad, but my caretaker said it was supposed to be good for people to soak in." I wrinkle my nose. "It stunk so bad that I couldn't bring myself to go in that water. I hated just going near it."

Although I'm sure Ash would prefer I work on my powers and become better acquainted with them, we spend the rest of our time strolling through the long, flowering fields. I try to pay attention to his lesson on different elements that could mix into water, but find myself distracted by the bird coasting on the breeze. Ash filters into the background as I smile up at it.

The black bird is large, with broad wings that transition to white at the tips. It rotates from flying ahead to circling back to stay behind us. I wait to see if it will land, but it never does.

* * *

"Princess, come here," Kalstrop shouts, calling my attention away from the creek. "Just for a minute. You can go back to whatever you're doing when he gets this."

Sighing, I stand to join the men. Beau gracefully swings his sword, rolling his wrist and widening his stance, preparing to fight for my life. Kalstrop's grin makes me shake my head. He's enjoyed making me play the damsel in distress for the past week.

"Come on, fair maiden," Kalstrop purrs, grinning. "You know you wanna be in danger."

Lifting my eyebrow, I curl the corners of my mouth and approach him. His short blade is hidden just inside his vest, but Kalstrop is easily distracted when I'm this close to him. I pull it from its sheath and press it under his chin, making him suck air through his teeth.

"Call me 'fair maiden' again," I growl. "We'll conduct a spontaneous sharpness test on your blades."

Kalstrop's eyes narrow as Beau erupts with laughter behind me. "Show off," my guard grumbles. He snatches the knife and slides it back in his vest. "You're the one who told me to teach him." Kalstrop spins me to press his chest against my back and holds his long sword to my throat. "What were you doing anyway?" he whispers.

"Trying to hold the water," I murmur, watching Beau advance on us. "Like when I held the crystal."

"That's not how it works," Kalstrop breathes in my ear. He moves toward Beau, bending us forward, and rolls his sword toward my friend. Knocking the opposing blade away, Kalstrop catches my waist before I can escape and swings me around to press against his back. "She's mine now," he growls at Beau.

If Kalstrop had done this with any other woman, he might have gotten the upper hand and won the fight. But he has been training me too, and I refuse to be a pawn in this game any longer. I jab him hard in the ribs with my elbow and kick at the back of his knee. He groans and falls forward.

I step over him and pull his head up by his hair. "I belong to no one," I hiss in his ear.

Kalstrop looks up at me from the corner of his eye with a playful grin. "Yes, ma'am."

Leaving them to train, I wander back over to the creek. Although it hasn't moved away from me since the dream where Ash had to help me make peace with it, I have yet to get water to do anything for me. I lower my hand into the creek and attempt to slow its speed or make it rise along my arm, but it just babbles by at an unnaturally warm temperature.

I slap my hand against the surface. "Why won't you do anything?" I grumble.

"I don't think yelling at the water will help," Kalstrop says, startling me. He sits beside me and pulls off his boots. "Beau's hunting for dinner. You want to talk about it?"

"I should be able to do something, right?" I scoff.

Kalstrop sighs and sets his boots aside. "There's no right or wrong when it comes to magic and using your powers," he starts. "You can take things too far and perform terrible deeds that will leave you scarred and force you to carry unbearable guilt. But if you reject that path and follow your heart, you can accomplish incredible things."

I glance up at him, frowning. "What if I never learn to control it?"

"Then we'll all die," Kalstrop answers, grinning.

"Do try to be serious," I huff, turning away from him.

"Princess," my guard begins, moving to sit behind me. "You spend so much time in your head that you can't hear anything else." He presses his chest to my back and lifts his knees. "Close your eyes."

My eyes roll closed as I sigh, giving in to his lesson. Kalstrop lifts my elbows to his knees and tucks my hair behind my ear. He leans over my shoulder, unbuttoning the top of my vest to press his hand against the skin on my chest.

"Listen to your heart," he whispers. "Hear how steady it beats and take slow, deep breaths to calm it."

I can't hear my heart, but follow the instructions until my body relaxes into Kalstrop's. His warmth soothes the pain in my back from long mornings on the trail and even longer afternoons training with knives and the new bow he made for me. Every muscle aches, but he's trained any hint of fat out of me, and my clothes loosely drape over my body.

"Call your senses to the front," Kalstrop murmurs near my ear. "Feel the breeze, taste the forest, smell the flowers' nectar, hear my voice." Kalstrop slides his fingers under my arm. With my hand resting on his, he leans forward and places his hand in the water so that mine barely touches it. "With your eyes closed, see what you want the water to do."

I let go of a deep, raspy breath and lay my head on his shoulder. It's easy to lose myself in Kalstrop's lessons. He doesn't care about formality or boundaries, reminding me of my carefree life at the ranch. He may still refer to me as "Princess," but it has become more my name than a title with him.

I imagine the water flowing around us as we carelessly swim in a river. The water babbles over rocks and downed trees nearby before rushing in our direction. We soak in its soothing pressure and let it take the day's grime and sweat away. I thread my fingers with Kalstrop's as warmth travels up my arm.

"Open your eyes." My guard's beard rubs over my ear as he moves his hand from my chest to my waist. The warmth continues its journey up my arm, and I turn to tuck my face against Kalstrop's neck. "Princess, you're getting us wet."

I open my eyes to find the water traveling up our arms. It swirls like a whirlpool, only releasing drops at the bottom that land on Kalstrop's knee. I smile at the large wet spot forming on his pants. The swirl playfully splashes over our arms, almost like rolling waves.

Urging the water to stay with us, I lift our hands from the creek and hear Kalstrop gasp when it remains swirling around our arms instead of falling back into the current. My cheeks hurt from the breadth of my smile as it continues to tie us together.

"What are you doing?" Kalstrop whispers, rubbing his thumb over mine.

I turn back into his neck and rub my face against his skin. When I lick my lips, I taste the salt of his sweat from this afternoon's training session. "Hmm," I hum, smiling. "You need a bath."

Releasing the water, I let it wash over us.

Chapter 11

We stay beside the creek for a week, following its slow crawl through a thin forest. Kalstrop says the area is controlled by someone he knows, and we're safe since no one would dare to set foot on their land. My guard slept for a few days and is noticeably more pleasant now that he's rested.

While relaxing by the fire one night, it dawns on me that we might not be the landowner's only friends. "Kalstrop," I start, confused. "If we're safe, wouldn't other friends be safe too?"

My guard chuckles. "I said that no one would dare to enter her lands," he replies. "Not that we were friends. I don't believe she has any of those."

"She?" I spout. "A woman creates that much fear?"

Kalstrop groans. "Not exactly," he says. "She's a tigress. You don't want to cross her claws."

"She lives out here alone?"

"Last time I checked, yeah," Kalstrop answers, lifting an eyebrow. "Why?"

"I want to meet her," I declare, a smile playing on my lips. "This realm is filled with men who want to claim me. A woman rules this land. She can't marry me, and she is strong enough to hold control over quite a bit of land." I gesture to the woods surrounding us. "That is someone I need to meet."

I allow Kalstrop to continue listing all the ways my idea could end in disaster. Many end in my death, but there are a few where the tigress claims me. I find these hardest to believe and point out that our marriage could not technically be consummated.

"Oh, she'd find a way," Kalstrop scoffs, looking up as Beau joins us with three rabbit carcasses. "The princess has come up with a brilliant plan. You ready for this dumbass idea?"

Beau lifts his eyebrow.

"She wants to meet Precious," Kalstrop announces.

"You know she doesn't like to be called that," Beau snaps, sitting beside the small fire.

"That's her damn name."

"She goes by Percy," Beau says, turning to me. "I don't know that you want to meet her, Princess, but you are why she hasn't chased us off her land."

"Have you seen her?" I ask, pulling Kalstrop's knife from his vest. "What's she like?"

Beau hands me one of the rabbits to skin. "She's beautiful," he responds. "And deadly."

I mull over their words for a moment and consider all of Kalstrop's warnings. Beau seems to have a different opinion of her, but said the most intriguing part. "Why has she allowed me on her land?"

"Percy won't attack royalty," Beau answers, looking over my head. "She doesn't respect the crown, but wouldn't draw the attention of the royal guard by attacking those who wear it."

"But I don't have a crown," I say, confused.

"You do now," a woman's voice startles me from behind, just before something is placed on my head. Kalstrop tries to jump away, but stops when she grabs his throat and presses the tip of a thin dagger under his chin. "Kalstrop," she snaps, rubbing her lips over his cheek. "You never called."

"Man, you get around, don't you?" I laugh, turning to study the woman holding my guard captive. I'm unsure why she's naked, but she is absolutely justified in her confidence. Her muscles are long and sleek, covered by flawless skin and well-proportioned features. "You must be Percy. I'm Ember."

"Yes, Princess," Percy responds. "I have been following you." She presses on Kalstrop's jaw. "Planned this one's murder a few times."

"Precious, you know why I didn't come back," Kalstrop murmurs, trying not to puncture his skin with her blade.

"Boohoo," she snaps, pulling her dagger and releasing his throat. "You're still alone, so I assume that ship never came ashore."

"Enough, you two," Beau barks. He turns to me after rolling his eyes at them. "Percy and I go way back. She's almost as old as Kalstrop. Percy, the princess has asked to meet you. Although, for the life of me, I have no idea why."

Smiling, I reach for Kalstrop's pack. "You are beautiful, but would you like to cover up?"

"I prefer fur," Percy answers, winking. "However, I will dress if it would make you more comfortable, Princess."

"Please don't call me that," I request. "Beau says you don't respect the crown. Would you please call me Ember?"

"I will do as you wish, Ember," she responds, nodding.

As she dresses, I remove the twisted twig crown she'd placed on my head. It's primitive yet still beautiful, with tiny blue flowers threaded throughout. I imagine Percy sitting close by, watching my guard's training sessions and planning his death.

I glance at Kalstrop to see he's settled back in beside me. He's closer than he was before Percy arrived, and his long sword is now resting on the ground behind me, right beside his hand. His tense muscles and clenched jaw are clear signs that he's reaching his limit. This is how I knew I'd only get a few more answers out of him before he got tired of my inquisitions.

My eyes narrow as I sort through my questions to find the most important. The first fact I recall is that Beau said they were nearly the same age.

"How old are you, Percy?" I ask.

"Oh, Ember," she responds, lifting her eyebrows. "Did they not teach manners in your human realm? One does not ask a lady her age."

Switching tactics, I try to pry information out of her before Kalstrop stops me. "Do you know why my mother promised me to the dragons?"

"Princess," Kalstrop hisses.

"It's a fair question, Kal," Percy says, stopping him.

"I like my name, Precious," he growls.

Rolling her eyes, she flicks a hand at him. "You have this nasty habit of keeping secrets, Kal. The girl has a right to the truth," Percy scoffs with a wicked grin. Her expression lightens as she turns back to me. "Your mother didn't promise you to all dragons, Ember. She promised you to one."

"Do you know who?" I ask, intrigued.

Percy smiles. "His name is Leif," she responds. "A very, very long time ago, this land was ruled by dragons. There have been many battles between your kind over who should hold the crown. I suspect your mother was trying to end the feud."

"Do you know anything about him?"

Beau and Kalstrop begin to interject, attempting to halt my interrogation. I raise a hand to both of them before gesturing to Percy.

"I know he's blue," the tigress tells me, smiling apologetically. "I live a solitary life, Ember. I only know what I hear."

"Hmm," Beau hums, watching us from across the fire. "What have you heard lately?"

Percy laughs and begins filling Beau in on information that she's learned. Kalstrop works with me on the rabbits, but glances in the tigress's direction several times as she mentions names and places. My guards stay quiet, absorbing all the details she's willing to give.

"We all heard about her, though," Percy says, leaning back on her elbows to look me over. "And the boys on the playground are all drooling, wanting to get their mouths on her flesh."

My face pulls into a look of disgust. "They want to eat me?"

Percy lifts her eyebrow, but Kalstrop bursts out with a laugh heartier than I've ever heard from him.

"What?" I ask. I may be confused, but I can't stop smiling at Kalstrop's laughter.

"It's just an expression," my guard spouts, shaking his head.

Percy slides Kalstrop's sword from behind me while he's distracted. "Has he taught you to wield a sword yet?" she asks, slinging my guard's blade around with a bit more grace than he does. "I would guess not. Ole Kal has a habit of underestimating the fairer sex."

"I am not the fairer sex," I scoff, jamming a long stick through the rabbit I skinned.

"No, I dare say you are not," Percy murmurs. "Eat your dinner, Ember. And then get some rest. You begin training in the morning."

I shake my head, confused. "Training? For what?"

Percy stands, taking Kalstrop's sword with her. "Weapons training, dear girl," she tells me. Percy rolls her wrist, swinging the blade to the back before bringing it forward. She adjusts her stance and braces her palm against the pommel of the hilt.

I follow the blade to where it is resting against Kalstrop's neck. He rolls his eyes in Percy's direction.

"Woman, give me my sword," Kalstrop growls.

Percy laughs and flips the weapon to present Kalstrop with the handle while holding its blade. "I'll be back in the morning," she says, winking.

I watch her undress and catch the clothes as she tosses them to me. With one last wink, Percy lunges forward onto her hands and transforms seamlessly into a tiger. My eyes widen painfully as I stare at this large, beautiful cat I'd only seen on TV.

She strides over to slide the top of her head against my face and stops beside Kalstrop to roar in his ear before bounding into the forest. I stare after her, but the rest of my party moves on as if this were normal.

"She really is a tiger," I whisper.

Kalstrop clicks his tongue. "Yeah, she's a spitfire," he grumbles.

"What did you do to her?" I ask, grinning. "She hates you."

Huffing loudly, Kalstrop pulls one of the rabbits off the fire and hands me the skewer. "It was a long time ago, Princess. She'll get over it."

"I'd kinda like to know what you've been up to," Beau interjects. "Your escapades have already gotten in the way twice, Kalstrop. And we've only come across two clans. Once is a coincidence, but twice is a pattern. Who else have you slept with?"

Beau is serious. His face is stern, and he's glaring at Kalstrop, expecting an answer. On the other hand, my guard ignores Beau and focuses on his rabbit. He turns it a few times to brown the meat evenly and leans back to gaze upon me.

"How's your bunny, Princess?" Kalstrop bumps his rabbit into mine. "You'll need your strength. Precious is just as deadly with a blade as she is with her claws."

Glancing from Kalstrop to Beau, I lift my eyebrow. "He might explode if you don't answer him," I whisper, turning back to my guard.

"He'll get over it," he whispers back. Lying with his head on his pack, he pulls a strip of meat and pops it in his mouth. "I'm pretty tired after all that excitement, Beau. Why don't you stand watch tonight? Percy won't be far, so you shouldn't have any trouble."

I make quick work of my rabbit meat and smile when Kalstrop holds up a thick strip from his. "Why didn't you go back to her, Kalstrop?" I ask before biting into the meat. "She's beautiful."

Kalstrop nods, smiling. "She is," he agrees. "I had my reasons." He sets aside his skewer and pats his shoulder. "Come here, Princess. It's chilly tonight. Keep me warm."

Laughing, I roll onto his shoulder and look up at the stars through the canopy of leaves. "I think you hurt them when you don't come back," I say quietly. "They miss you."

"They only want the idea of me, Princess," Kalstrop answers, sighing. "The reality is a little different."

"No, I think you want people to see the bad in you," I say, rolling away to press my back to his side. "That way, you don't have to worry about them expecting anything good. You can't let them down if they're already disappointed."

Beau approaches us with his vest. I smile when he smacks Kalstrop's outstretched hand and kneels to place the smooth leather over my arm. Beau winks, brushing some hair behind my ear, before backing away.

"You'll agree with them soon enough," Kalstrop whispers, slipping his hand under the vest to rest it between my arm and ribs. "Goodnight, Princess."

* * *

I pull myself from the water in Kalstrop's cavern under the waterfall. Scowling, I tug my tank top into place. Alice said tankinis were cute, but I always found the tops annoying. My hair gushes water onto the floor when I twist it before throwing it over my shoulder.

The pool glows as if I were standing in a tropical lagoon, and the lines it throws over the ceiling dance to a steel drum's beat in my head. I smile at the crystals embedded in the walls. I hadn't touched them while here with Kalstrop, and I'm not sure I want to try it without his guidance.

Approaching the desk, I slip my fingers over the papers. Under the pile is an open book. I lift it from the mess and flip through the pages to find them all empty. The only markings are gold letters on the cover saying, "With Love." Finding nothing else written on it, I place the book on the desk among the dust.

To my left is an opening in the cave wall. I don't recall seeing it while I was here with Kalstrop, but I step toward it, finding two lit rooms down a hallway. I glance back at the cavern, sure someone is watching me. I hold my breath and stand perfectly still, but there is no other movement besides the water.

I follow the hall and look into the first room. It's a lovely bedroom with two smaller beds. Wooden swords and shields hang on the wall among the crystals. A bookshelf stands tall between the beds, filled with books of all sizes and colors. I smile at the quaintness and imagine brothers sharing this room until I notice one mattress has been stripped of its linens.

Backing out of the room, I move to the second. This room is much larger, containing a grand bed with beautiful curtain veils draped from each post. Adult-sized armor stands in the corner near a wardrobe bursting with strips of silky fabric. I move to the bed and slip my fingers over the thin fabric shrouding it.

Alice and I used canopy nets while camping under the stars to keep the bugs away. This is much more beautiful and would make any woman feel like a queen while she slept within its folds. The thick velvet blanket over the mattress would ensure she stayed warm if the night turned cold.

I step toward the wardrobe, but a noise echoes down the hall. I pause and narrow my eyes when I hear it again—a pebble dropping or maybe a footstep. Tilting my head curiously, I slowly tiptoe back to the doorway and peek out. No one is in the hall, so I continue toward the front cavern.

When I see Kalstrop standing over the desk, my jaw slackens, and I tuck back around the corner. Attempting to settle my heart rate, I take a few slow, deep breaths before peeking into the cavern. Kalstrop hasn't moved. He's rustling through papers, avoiding the book I'd closed.

Nervously pulling my lip between my teeth, I step out of the hallway. Kalstrop's chest swells when my fingers reach his arm and slide over his shoulder. He remains still, allowing me to lightly touch his scars. My fingertips follow each jagged line left behind by his wing detachment. I step forward and softly rub my lips over the damaged skin.

Kalstrop takes a deep breath when my hand slides up his back, and my fingers slip into his hair. I proceed around his body to sit on the desk in front of him. I watch my hands travel up Kalstrop's chest, smiling at the gentle brushing of chest hair over my skin. His touch is light when I feel his arms close around me, resembling a memory more than a current sensation.

My fingers reach for his lips, pulling them apart and tracing them with my nails. I lick mine and straighten my back to press them against his. Kalstrop tightens his grip on me and pushes his tongue into my mouth. He's more forward than he was when I asked for this, but still gentle. He tastes like cinnamon and feels so warm and soothing that I melt into his embrace. My hand cups his cheek while my fingers brush against his neck.

Kalstrop slowly massages my tongue with his, pulling back so I miss him and advancing to give me more. He threads his fingers into my hair and pulls me away to tuck close to my neck. His beard tickles my skin, and I breathe out a laugh until his mouth opens to allow his tongue and teeth access to me. I've never whimpered before, so the sound is as foreign as it is exciting.

I pull on Kalstrop, hoping to urge him on, but he lifts off my neck just as he reaches my shoulder. He looks away as I search his face for any indication of how to reclaim his attention. I risk turning the entire situation incredibly awkward by grabbing his face and pulling it toward me.

"Stop, Ember," Kalstrop whispers, turning to look into my eyes. His lips are warm and gentle when he presses them to mine one last time. He licks my lower lip before pulling back just enough to breathe into my mouth, "You're not mine."

Kalstrop scoops the back of my knees and lifts me to his chest. He carries me down the hallway to the larger room and places me on the grand bed. The colored veils drape around us as he tucks me into the thick velvet blanket.

"I can't make you leave, but you need sleep," Kalstrop whispers.

I pull him until he's on the bed beside me. I throw my arm over him and snuggle into his chest. "Thank you, Kalstrop," I whisper, looking up at him from my comfortable spot.

He looks down at me, confused. "For what?"

"For always being my safe place," I whisper, nuzzling my face into his skin with a sleepy groan.

I'm pretty tired after the long days and the unexpected exhilaration of my experience with Kalstrop. My eyes close and refuse to open. However, before I drift off, I hear Kalstrop's deep sigh. He murmurs something I can't understand while I'm sure I feel him roll to wrap his arms around me.

Chapter 12

Kalstrop has remained close to watch over us while I train with Percy. When I woke from my night with him, his arms were wrapped tightly around me. My movement startled him, and he jumped away. He's been cold ever since, making me somehow regret my dream.

"Ember, think about the blade like a paint brush," Percy says, reminding me that I'm in the middle of a lesson. "Over and under in fluid strokes. Strike with the edge of the blade, not the side."

I glance down at the wooden practice sword and watch it slap the tree with its broadside. "I'm sorry," I say quietly. "Maybe I'm just tired."

"You're distracted," Percy replies. "Come practice your water trick and tell me what's on your mind."

Sighing, I lean the wooden sword against my sparring tree and follow her to the river. Percy has a long flat rock that she stretches out on while I practice guiding the water up my arms. I haven't gotten it to do anything else, but she insists that I'm getting better.

"How long have you known Kalstrop?" I ask.

Percy groans as she rolls to face me. "Not long," she answers. "I think it was a little over ten years ago when he sought me out. He was pretty broken back then. Seems to be doing better now, though."

I look up the ridge to where he stands, leaning against a thick tree to watch us. "Why was he looking for you?"

"I don't know, Ember," Percy answers, following my gaze. "One night, he told me he was trying to right a wrong. Said he had to sacrifice everything for a love that wasn't his."

I let the water fall back into the river and sit upright with my legs crossed. "There's never anything for him, is there?" I narrow my eyes at my guard. He's staring back at us with a steely gaze as unfeeling and cold as the day I met him. "No one is ever his," I whisper.

"Guards' lives are generally lonely, Ember," Percy says quietly. "There are a few soft beds here and there, but they walk their path alone. It's a life they choose. Duty over family."

I recall Kalstrop's tale about his relatives and how war had torn them apart, leaving him as the sole survivor. "There's more to him than just a soldier," I say, turning away from my guard. "He's shown me a different side."

Percy rubs her hand over my arm and smiles sadly. "I, too, saw a softer side," she reminds me. "It doesn't last long, young one."

Looking up at the ridge, I frown when I find my guard's tree vacant. Kalstrop is gone, his hardened gaze and watchful presence left only as a memory. "Have you ever been in love?" I ask, twisting my face in thought.

"When you live this long, Ember, there's no telling when the love of your life will appear," Percy answers, rolling onto her back. "Has he? No. But there is the hope that one day he'll show and I'll have a powerful man to share my land with."

"And he would be a tiger like you?" I like talking with Percy. She doesn't get irritated with my questions like Kalstrop or look incredibly uncomfortable like Beau. She seems to understand my cluelessness and doesn't mind helping me understand.

Percy squints in thought. "He wouldn't have to be," she responds. "That's probably why there aren't many of us left. It would take somebody pretty special to win my heart, though." She glances back at Kalstrop's empty post. "He didn't want it."

I reach for her hand and squeeze it. "I'm sorry he hurt you."

"He's a difficult man with a long history," Percy responds. "Even if he doesn't know where he belongs, he knows where he shouldn't be, and that was with me." She sits up and winks. "That doesn't stop me from holding it against him."

I giggle and stand, pulling her with me. "I suppose we should get back to it so we can get out of your fur," I announce. "I wouldn't want to scare away the right man or bring war upon your land with my presence."

"Yes," Percy growls. "I may have to kill you for that."

We find Beau sitting on a stump near my sparring tree, holding my wooden sword. "This is heavier than it was," he remarks, lifting his eyebrow.

"You noticed, huh?" Percy says, laughing.

"Why don't you try this, Ember?" Beau holds out his own sword.

Taking the handle, I'm surprised by how easily I lift it before me and swing it in the graceful X Percy has been teaching. My wrist rolls effortlessly with it, allowing the blade to slice through the air smoothly. Mimicking Percy's stance from the day we met, I spin it behind me and take a step back, bracing the hilt with my palm and aiming it at Beau.

"Beautiful," Percy whispers.

"I agree," Beau says, knocking his blade away. "Now let's fix your stance."

He steps behind me and presses his chest to my back. Beau sets his legs wide and pushes my thigh to adjust my position. He reaches for the other, but I've already begun moving it, figuring out the plan on my own.

"Percy, if you wouldn't mind being our sparring partner?" Beau requests, straightening his back. His arms lie over mine, and his hand provides a protective layer over my fingers on the sword's handle. "Nice and easy, Perce. Don't injure the princess."

Her smile spreads like I imagine it would on a cat. I lean back into Beau and press my legs against his as he guides me through the movements. Every step and swing of the blade is choreographed to perfection like a ballroom dance routine. I can nearly hear music as we lunge and retreat in a slow-motion battle to the death.

Beau pulls me backward and rolls the sword in our hands to face the opposite direction. His fingers thread mine to control the handle for us and yanks it forward until the blade rests against Percy's throat. He steps into her, mashing me between them, and presses his elbow against the sword. As they regard each other, our only movement is my chest as I heave air from the excitement.

"Do you yield?" Beau asks.

I can hear his smile and laugh with Percy as she pulls back. Beau lets the sword swing around in our hands and bows to our opponent when the blade rests safely in his sheath.

I face Beau as he steps away. "Can we do that again?" I ask, smiling broadly. "That was amazing."

"It's easy with you," Beau says. "You're a pocket-sized princess."

I click my tongue and swat at him.

"I'd call her fun-sized," Kalstrop says, appearing beside a tree deeper in the woods and causing me to lose my scowl. "She's got this way of fitting where she doesn't belong."

I approach Kalstrop and place my hand on his chest. Where I would experience kindness and a gentle glance, I now find walls and steel. "I hurt you," I whisper. "I didn't mean to."

Kalstrop inhales deeply and flexes his jaw. "Go back to your lessons, Princess."

I reach for his cheek, but Kalstrop snatches my wrist.

"Don't," he whispers.

* * *

"I think I'm going to miss having you around, Ember," Percy says, smiling. She swings her blades out by her sides, waiting for me to advance. Percy surprised me with a set of medium-length swords of my own a few days ago, and we've practiced nonstop since. "Not getting tired, are you?"

"You wish," I reply, grinning.

These blades are about two feet long and feel half the weight of Beau's sword. We started with them dulled, but have since sharpened them. Beau has remained close and throws sticks and rocks at Percy when he thinks she's too rough. I, of course, take advantage of the distraction and advance on her while I can.

"Ha!" Percy shouts, spinning and catching me off guard. One blade jabs my side while the other sits against my throat. "You're dead."

"Give it a rest, you two," Beau grumbles. "You've been at it for four days. Let the princess eat."

Percy takes the plate he holds out. "I'll miss having you around, too, Beau," she says, winking.

Rolling his eyes, Beau shakes his head. "Come here, Ember."

I sit beside Beau and bump our shoulders. "I'm getting pretty good, right?" I smile broadly as he hands me a plate of meat and a mashed pile of green stuff. "Okay, what is that?"

"It's a vegetable close to a pea," Beau answers, lifting a bowl. "When boiled, it falls apart, so it's best to mash it up like potatoes." He smiles at my wrinkled nose. "You'll like it." He tucks close to my ear before adding at a whisper, "It's Kalstrop's favorite."

I smile and shake my head, but look up to where he's pointing to see my guard walking toward us from the river. Beau notices everything, so it shouldn't surprise me that he's noticed something off about us lately. I move over to make room on the log beside me.

"I made this for you," Kalstrop announces, coldly glaring down at me without sitting.

Putting my plate aside, I take the leather belt he offers. It's thick with matching sheaths on the left side. Their lengths are perfect for my blades. A beautiful design is etched across the back, and there is a single, solitary thin leather loop hidden behind where my swords will rest.

"What is this for?" I ask quietly.

Kalstrop takes a plate Beau offers and sighs. "It doesn't matter," he growls. "It's nothing for you to use."

Beau rubs my back, watching Kalstrop leave us to sit among the trees. "Give him some space, Ember," he whispers. "He's been angry for a long time. Change is hard."

* * *

I haven't had a dream since the night in Kalstrop's cavern, so I'm nearly startled when the gardens appear before me. The sun is bright, the breeze is soft, and the floral scents are more inviting than ever. I jog forward with my arms outstretched, allowing my fingers to trail over the leaves and vines.

I turn the corner to find my little garden haven occupied by not only the duck family, but Ash is here too. "Have you been waiting long?" I ask when he looks up from the empty swing.

"I have," he says softly, beckoning me to join him. "Where have you been?"

I sit on the swing and wait for Ash to push me. "I made a friend, I think," I answer, smiling. "We have been working with swords. She says I'm getting pretty good."

"But, Ember, that is not what I told you to work on, is it?"

"I've also been working with water, Ash," I add, grinning over my shoulder. "I have made progress."

Stopping my swing, Ash walks around to look into my eyes. "Show me."

I childishly pout, but allow him to pull me to my feet.

"Ember, I told you this was important," Ash states knowingly. "You must practice."

When he stops by the creek and turns to face me, his hair falls over his cheek. Smiling, I brush it back behind his ear. Ash's eyes have a kindness to them as he looks over me that I can't recall seeing before.

"I have missed you," he whispers, wrapping his arms around my shoulders. "I don't mean to be cross. I was worried, and I'm not very good with emotions."

I breathe out a quiet laugh as Ash kisses my forehead. "So, we both have new skills to learn."

"I suppose," he responds, stepping back. "Show me your progress."

Taking a deep breath, I relax my chest and kneel on the bank. I lower my fingers into the creek and sigh happily when the water begins to swirl up my arm slowly. I lift my fingers and disconnect from the gentle rapids while still carrying the water that had joined me.

"It's like a wet hug," I say, grinning at Ash. "It seems to want to be with me."

Ash lifts an eyebrow. "Cute," he says, eyeing the water. "Now you need to learn to command it."

I frown, watching the swirling water slow its pace. "How do you command water?"

"You tell it what to do," Ash answers. "Be the leader."

Bringing my arm closer to my face, I study the reflection in the ripples. "What would I tell it to do?" I whisper.

"Anything," Ash spouts, frustrated. "Ember, you're just playing. You need to control it, not simply carry it around."

I bite my lip in thought, but then remember the crystal and the water balls that turned into mud. Standing tall, I move my hand carefully out to my side. I reach back, ready to throw the water when it releases its grip on me and falls to the ground unceremoniously.

"Well, that was disappointing," Ash huffs. "All this time wasted, and you've learned a parlor trick."

I didn't figure any of this out on my own. Kalstrop was instrumental in obtaining the few skills I have with water, even after he told me he couldn't teach me. I narrow my eyes at Ash. Something makes me think I should avoid the subject of my guard altogether.

"Can you show me?" I ask.

Ash rolls his eyes. "No, Ember, I can't," he growls, jamming his hand out between us. He keeps it flat as if holding a platter before curling his fingers into a circular shape. "I don't work with water."

I gasp and step back as his hand bursts into flames. My excitement grows in steady waves as the small blaze builds to engulf his skin and hide the appendage altogether. I tear my eyes away from the dancing fire to see Ash staring at me. His gaze is hard and unfeeling.

"If I can control fire, you can control water," Ash says pointedly. He shakes his hand, and the flames instantly disperse. "You need to work harder."

I step forward and reach for Ash's hand. It surprises me that he willingly offers it for me to inspect. "It didn't burn you," I whisper. "Can you feel it?"

Ash moves closer and pushes my chin up. "It feels cold," he murmurs. "You're warm."

He licks his lips, and without telling my body, I reach up to press mine against his. Ash tastes of earth and wood, bringing an air of calmness as he steps forward to close his arms around me. One wraps around my waist while the other drapes over my shoulder. His fingers thread through my hair and hold my head, stopping me from retreating.

My first kiss was sweet, the second more heated, but this is different. I would call it commanding. Ash wants me to take charge of water, and this is him controlling me. I reach for his cheek, hoping to settle him into allowing me to move away. Instead, I urge him on, and his tongue searches for mine.

I hadn't meant to experience Ash this way, but getting lost in his kisses is easy. My eyes roll closed at his flavor and warmth. I soon find my fingernails softly trailing over his neck, permitting him to take of me what he wants.

Ash pulls my hair and presses his forehead against mine when a moan releases from somewhere in my throat. "Why did you do that?" he heaves.

"What?" I ask, confused.

"Why did you kiss me?"

I shake my head. "I don't know."

Ash licks his lips, making me exhale deeply and reach my lower lip out, desperate to feel his again. "Don't come back until you do."

My arms flail as he shoves me away, and I begin to fall into darkness without hope for a safe landing.

* * *

Time passes, and I panic while descending into darkness. Eventually, I am pulled back to consciousness by strong arms enveloping me in warmth. Kalstrop catches me as I wake, screaming and covered in sweat. I latch onto him, gasping and crying.

Thankful to have a light source, I stare at the fire and heave deep breaths. Kalstrop remains stiff with a solid grip on me, keeping my body from falling away from him as I crumble with exhaustion. My fingers firmly grip his favorite linen shirt and threaten to rip it if he tries to move away.

"Easy, Princess," Kalstrop whispers when he finally speaks. "It was only a bad dream."

I rub my face against his chest. "I don't have those."

He takes a deep breath and rests his chin on my head. "Well, now you do." He leans back on the log that Beau and I had sat on a few hours ago, pulling me with him. "I'll be right here. I won't let anything hurt you."

I realize that Kalstrop is trying to get me to go back to sleep, but I can't let that happen. Too many horrible things could arise if I drift off again. Ash was mad enough to send me spiraling out of control for what felt like hours. He wants to know why I kissed him, but I don't have that answer. And if I fall asleep, Kalstrop might leave despite my death grip on his shirt.

We silently stare at the fire together until the sun begins to shine through the trees. His steady breathing and rhythmic finger swipes over my back keep me grounded and calm.

"Everything okay?" Beau asks behind us, making us jump.

Kalstrop sighs and stretches his arms. "Yeah," he says, yawning. "The princess had a bad dream. I was just keeping her company."

"Has that ever happened?" Beau sits on the log and rubs my back. "Did you get any sleep?"

"I'm all right," I whisper, catching his hand as he tries to feel my cheeks for feverish temperatures.

"I hope so because we need to leave," Beau announces. "Percy said someone breached her northern walls, and there's only one reason anyone would come on her land."

I roll my eyes and slump back into Kalstrop. "Me."

"Yep," my guard agrees.

Chapter 13

Within hours, we're running through the woods with the clan of my next suitor hot on our heels. I don't have the same stamina as my guards, so Beau presses his hand to my lower back and pushes me along while Kalstrop isn't far behind, throwing small fire bombs.

"They're gaining on us," my guard growls. "Can't you move any faster?"

"She's doing the best she can," Beau snaps.

I trip over a root, nearly falling on my face. "I need to stop," I spout, grabbing my chest.

Beau pulls his sword and turns to face our hunters, holding me against his back as I heave deep bursts of air. Kalstrop glares at me when he reaches us before joining Beau. The clan is running, and their footsteps sound like distant thunder, but the ground vibrates, alerting us to their proximity. I pull my short blades and move to Beau's other side.

"What are they?" I whisper, looking up at the men.

"Imps," Kalstrop murmurs, focusing on the forest before us. "Thousands of them."

They come into view as a blur of small men, approximately waist-height. Surprised laughter bursts from my mouth, but I quickly stifle it when my guards move into the defensive stance Percy taught me. I brace my legs and steady my blades—one held up across my body at chest level, while the other in my left hand is held backward and braced for an upward strike.

From the moment they reach us, it's clear that Kalstrop had been right about our last encounter. The imps are small, but fierce in every way. They are thick with rippling muscles and wielding large swords sharpened to slice easily through any flesh they might encounter.

As fast as my blade stops one, another is there to take his place, and bodies pile up in front of us. Imps of all ages come at us with the full intention of ending our lives. None of them is here to marry me. They want my blood. It's not long before my arms are just as tired as my legs. My chest can't pull enough air, and my blades slide around in my hands from the blood covering the handles.

The imps jump off the bodies of their fallen comrades to attack us from all angles. Beau and Kalstrop flank me as our attackers begin to win this battle and push us back. Despite our clear disadvantage, my arms continue their fluid motions imprinted on my muscles by my trainers. Every swipe is a new body, but another is behind it without skipping a beat.

"Beau, we gotta run," Kalstrop shouts. "Come on, man. Swallow it!"

I glance up at Beau just as he looks behind us. He takes a deep breath with widening eyes. "I don't think that's gonna help."

I chance a peek and stumble in disbelief. The imps have backed us to the edge of a cliff. The speed of their attack and the varied directions from which they approached now make sense. No matter how hard we fought, they were driving us to our slaughter site.

"Screw the law, Beau," I shout. "You need to fly us out of here."

Beau's silence causes me to pause with my blade deeply embedded inside an imp's head and look up. "I can't," he spouts. "I don't know how."

I gawk at him as he kicks the imp away from us and nearly yanks my sword from my hand. "You have wings," I shout, swinging at my next attacker. "You just flap them. Birds do it."

"They also fall out of the nest first," Kalstrop scoffs. He looks behind us at the cliff. "That's a long way down." He steps back as another man jumps off the pile of bodies and barrels into him. "We gotta try something. Do the flap thing at least!" He kneels to catch an imp running straight at him and flings the man over his head off the cliff.

I step closer to the ledge to watch the short man fall until I lose sight of him. "I don't want to do that," I declare.

Beau groans and throws his swords down. Kalstrop and I move aside as he lunges forward. His hooves paw at the air between us and strike at the imps. Without a blade to stop them, Beau is hit a few times with their weapons before he squares his feet and stretches his wings.

I mimic Kalstrop, squatting by Beau's haunches. The leather feathered wings fully extend back before scooping a tremendous burst of air down and forward, blasting the imps away from us. My guard and I stand to advance on our attackers, but another wave is already before us, taking the fallen imps' place.

Growling, I wipe my hand on my pants, trying to clean off some of the blood, but my clothes are covered, too. "What about the crystals?" I shout as an imp slams into me, knocking me against Beau's shoulder.

"Great idea, Princess," Kalstrop growls. "We'll burn to death instead of falling."

Side-stepping, I press my back to Kalstrop's and lift my eyebrow at Beau. "This is it," I tell him. "Now or never. We're out of options."

Beau glances once more over the cliff and blows out his nostrils. Smiling, I grab Kalstrop and pull him back with me. My guard crouches, allowing me to step onto his knee and slide onto Beau's back.

"You better be ready to run!" my guard shouts, rising to his feet.

Kalstrop hasn't missed a beat. It's clear to see why he was such a fierce soldier. I can't imagine him losing a battle against any enemy. His arms have been slinging his long blades for at least an hour and have yet to appear tired. His strength has no equal in any realm.

"Now!" Kalstrop shouts. He turns and launches onto Beau's back, latching onto my waist and throwing one of his swords to knock the closest imp back.

Beau lifts his wings from our legs and charges at the cliff's edge. Out of habit, I count his strides. Three, two, one—he launches into the air as if to throw all of his effort into an impossible oxer. The gorgeous brown and black wings stretch out beside us, and for a moment, the world stands still as we glide through the air, feeling the wind and freedom of hawks and eagles.

Then the moment is over.

Beau's mane flies freely through the air before me while his body falls from underneath us. Kalstrop screams something behind me, but the rush of air and my blinding panic won't let his words filter in. Beau's wings move erratically, twitching, flapping, and bending.

Kalstrop tightens his grip on me while I release my swords to free my hands. I tangle my fingers in Beau's mane and pull with all my might, trying to stay on his back while we free-fall to our deaths. Kalstrop joins in my efforts, finally drawing us together so I can feel Beau's muscles under me.

Blocking out all my fear, I squeeze my eyes shut and recall the past 18 years. "Come on, Beau," I start gently, opening my eyes to focus on my friend. "You were born for this. You can do it. If you try for me this one time, I will prove to you that this is where you should be."

Beau's ribs extend between my legs as he takes a deep breath. He hated all the Olympic training I put him through, but I had a way of convincing him to try anything. I always thought he just needed encouragement. Now I know he wanted to feel like I believed in him.

Kalstrop sits up, pressing his chest against me as Beau's back stops attempting to fall away from us. The sleek wings steady in their battle against the turbulence and remain outstretched in an effortless glide. I lock my knees behind the wing joints and guide Kalstrop's legs to rest directly behind mine.

Now that we're out of Beau's way, he begins to test some of his moves. He creates tight circles to stay against the cliff wall. Kalstrop murmurs into my ear that we are still breaking the law and need to use the wall as cover. I doubt we're hiding from anyone, but I just nod and continue to smile at my beautiful friend, finally doing what he was born to do.

Besides the occasional imp falling to his death, our descent is silent and undisturbed. Beau circles the bottom a few times to allow Kalstrop to look for enemies before finding an area with fewer trees. He arcs his wings and stretches his legs as the ground rushes toward us.

Although I'm braced for the impact, nothing could've prepared me for the force that threw me onto Beau's neck. Kalstrop releases my waist and rolls over my shoulder to land on the ground before us. Beau stumbles in an attempt to avoid him and crashes into a clump of trees, knocking me off his back.

I scoff as I climb out of the mud he'd thrown me into. "You might need to work on the landing," I grumble, picking leaves out of the sludge caked to my legs. "Kalstrop!" I shout into the trees behind us.

"Yeah," he groans. "I agree."

I suppose Kalstrop might have been furious when he emerged from the trees if it weren't for the deep gash in his thigh, causing him to limp and grimace. Blood cascades down his leg from the fresh wound. As I rush to his side, I'm relieved he avoided the slop that Beau and I landed in.

"Got through that whole battle without a scratch and the nag had to throw me on my own damn sword," Kalstrop grumbles, glaring at Beau as he pauses to lean on a tree.

Kneeling beside him, I pull the sliced edges of his pants from the wound. "That looks deep," I murmur. "You need a doctor."

Kalstrop swats my hands away and pushes off the tree. "Doctors aren't an option with you around, Princess," he snaps. "I need a few herbs, and then you're gonna help me sew this thing up."

I wince at the thought. "Oh, yeah, no," I stammer, shaking my head. "That's not... No, I can't stitch up a wound." I stand and watch him approach the mud-caked Beau. "Don't start with him. It's your own damn fault you fell off."

Kalstrop whispers something I can't hear, and Beau nods before turning away and galloping into the trees. "We need tracks, Princess," my guard grumbles. "There's a flower that grows within the rotted stumps around here. When it dies, it causes a fungus that will speed healing. Even with that help, we will still move slowly for a few days. Beau's tracks will confuse them."

"Okay, where do we find these stumps?" I ask, pulling Kalstrop's arm over my shoulder. My eyebrow lifts when he tries to protest. "You need help. I'm the only one around."

I appreciate Kalstrop's scowl as he sighs and relaxes into me. "Fine," he grumbles. "Just look for a fallen tree. We'll start there."

My guard can only be described as hard as nails. Even injured, he pushes himself to the limit while we move slowly through the forest. We come across several downed trees within the first few hours, but only a few have flowers, and none contain the fungus we need. Kalstrop's weight on my shoulders gradually increases until I'm forced to stop.

"This would be faster if I searched on my own, Kalstrop," I say, lifting his arm off me to help him rest against a tree. "You should be riding Beau."

"I am not getting on that nag ever again," he grumbles, latching onto my arm. "And you are not wandering off on your own. Get over here and rest with me."

We shouldn't stop, but I'm thankful for the break. I'd never admit to Kalstrop how exhausted I am because that would only fuel his sarcasm and move me further away from the guard I wish he'd turn back into. I relax beside him and take his pack from his other shoulder so he can sit and rest his injured leg.

"Why did they want to kill me?" I ask once he's settled.

"I suspect that was more about the balance of power than anything," Kalstrop says, wincing. He moves aside to give me a spot beside him against the tree trunk. "They would probably prefer to leave your grandfather on the throne than hand it back to a fairy."

His words twist around in my head until they make sense. "My grandfather's an imp?"

Kalstrop snorts, grinning. "That's probably why you're so fun-sized."

"I am not that short," I scoff. "How is my grandfather an imp?"

"He's half fairy, half imp, Princess," my guard responds, taking his pack from me. "Rarely will you find blood that is purely one thing or another. When you mix it, it's sort of like combining colors. You can blend red and blue a few times, but each mixture will produce a different shade of purple."

I chew on my lip and stare at him, confused.

Kalstrop rolls his eyes. "He's heavy on the imp side and never got his fairy powers," he says, annoyed. "So, the imp world views that as having an imp on the throne. Even if marrying you would see another imp as king, there is no promise that their heir would be of their kind."

"But my parents were fairies, right?"

"Your father inherited his powers from your grandmother, and your mother was a pure fairy," Kalstrop responds, softening his tone. "I believe that's why your powers are so strong."

It's my turn to roll my eyes. "What powers?" I scoff. "I barely learned a parlor trick. I haven't figured out how to do anything useful."

"Do you know why soldiers spend so much time alone, Princess?"

"Because you're always in battles," I answer.

Kalstrop hums, lifting his eyebrows. "That would be a very valid reason," he responds, surprised. "However, we actually spend our time alone because emotions are distracting and get us killed. You must learn to shut off your emotions and focus on your tasks."

I watch him close his eyes and rest his head back. Percy had said something along the same lines, and their words made sense, but only to a point. Kalstrop uses my emotions in my lessons, and they've triggered the only ability I've acquired so far. If I had pushed them away to only use practical thoughts, I would be without any skills at all.

"Kalstrop, I—," I start, but cut myself off when I glance up, finding him asleep.

He didn't spend the final evenings in the camp with us, but I know he didn't sleep last night after my nightmare. My guard never showed any sign of tiring throughout the hours of fighting, even when it was clear Beau and I were struggling. When his body is done, he has no choice but to succumb to the exhaustion and let it shut down.

Kalstrop licks his lips and grumbles incoherently when I adjust his leg to jam his pack under his knee, but doesn't wake. I tiptoe away to search the woods nearby for a rotted stump. This part of the forest is thick, so I can't venture far without losing sight of my sleeping guard, but I'm excited that the second stump I find holds the fungus Kalstrop described.

Green spikes protect its pink skin. Although the stump is rotted, the unyielding wood around the fungus prevents me from accessing the area below the thorns. I look around for a thin rock to use as a knife since Kalstrop has our only blades.

I crouch behind the stump when a stick breaks nearby. The ground is thick with moss and damp earth. My steps have been silent without even trying.

Focusing my eyes toward the sound, I smile as Beau appears, carrying my swords. Although Alice ensured that I studied the anatomy of both humans and animals, this is my first time seeing a naked man. I had no expectations for how they looked or how I would feel, but Beau is gorgeous.

"Well, I did not expect to see so much of you," I whisper, standing. My eyes refuse to blink as they travel over his body, drinking him in. I can feel my skin sear with the blush spreading across my face, but I can't look away. "Jesus, Beau. You're beautiful. I can't decide if I prefer this or the horse."

"This is highly inappropriate, Princess," Beau grumbles, holding my blades out. "Take these so I can change, please."

"You went back for them?" I ask, taking my swords.

"Kalstrop asked me to," Beau replies. "He doesn't want you to know, but he made those. Don't tell him I told you. He might actually kill me."

Narrowing my eyes, I hold the blades out before me as Beau changes back into the winged horse. "Why wouldn't he want me to know?" I ask, then pout, realizing my friend can't answer me now. I shake my head and sigh. "I will never understand you two."

Chapter 14

With the ground so easily hiding our tracks, we spend a few days in the moss-covered grove. Admittedly, I've spent more time studying Kalstrop than anything, but he doesn't seem to notice as he tries to teach me how to make the poultice he needs for his wound. I catch him sneaking glances at me while I pulverize the fungus to mix it with the moss and grin when he pretends to scrutinize my work.

I'm horrified when he pulls a needle and thread from his pack on the third morning and hands it to me. "Kalstrop, I can't stitch you," I say, grimacing.

"Come on," he answers, shoving my hand away. "It's like clothes, only it bleeds."

Beau has stood guard over us while Kalstrop's wound healed with the help of the poultice. He nudges my shoulder, encouraging me to follow my guard's instructions. I swallow hard and sit beside Kalstrop. His wound is on the outside of his thigh, toward the back. I'm sure he could've found a way to do this himself if he were alone, but it would've been complicated.

I release a deep, shaky breath. "Okay," I start, glancing up at Kalstrop's face. "What am I doing?"

Kalstrop rolls to his side and stretches his leg over my lap. "The poultice has drained out anything bad," he starts, laying his head on his pack. "I just need you to close it up. Loose stitches, Princess. Don't rip my skin."

I feel every flinch of Kalstrop's muscles in my throat as I slowly close his wound. Each new piercing of the needle brings fresh blood to mop up, and my guard's leg shakes more violently as I progress, making this procedure increasingly difficult.

After painstakingly placing 12 sutures in my guard's thigh, I sigh and sit back. "I think I'm done," I announce. The stitches are as evenly spaced as I could manage with Kalstrop's flinching and his body shaking from the pain. I hated every moment of it. "Are you okay, Kalstrop?"

My guard rolls his face away from the pack and breathes deeply. "Yeah, Princess," he answers quietly. "I wish we had a sharper needle."

Kalstrop closes his eyes, and I dab the rag over his skin once more to clean off any remaining wet blood. Turning to my right, I relax against the tree Kalstrop had been leaning on for days to rest his injured leg. He's been sleeping a lot these past few days, so I assume he needs more after what I've just put him through.

Having never sewn a person, I hadn't thought about the state of the needle while I forced it through Kalstrop's skin. I lift it and squint at its tip. Thinking of how painful the procedure must have been causes me to frown. The needle's tip is as dull as a well-used pencil's lead. There is no denying that if I had experienced it, I would have been screaming for hours.

I slip my hand into Kalstrop's shirt, rubbing it over his back and ribs. I haven't noticed any other scars besides those on his back, but I'm sure there are more. None of them would've equaled the pain of losing his wings, including this new injury.

As we lie there, I let my mind wander from Kalstrop to Ash. I haven't had a dream since he kicked me out of my garden. He asked me why I kissed him. *How should I know?* He licked his lips, making them look delicious, and I thought, "What the hell? Might as well try kissing this guy, too, since he's just a dream."

I roll my eyes and huff loudly, disturbing Kalstrop. I rub my fingers lightly over his skin until his breathing evens out. I kissed Kalstrop because I trust him. I gave him an order, and he obeyed, giving me control over that pivotal moment in my life.

Ash enjoys power. He seems happiest when showing me things I didn't know, thus proving his ability over mine. I twist my face as I realize why he was so angry. I took that moment from him. Ash doesn't want to know why. He wants an apology.

* * *

A soft lapping of water echoes through the darkness, making me open my eyes. Confused, I look around the large bedroom at the end of the hall in Kalstrop's cavern. My body relaxes into the soft, warm mattress covered with the velvet blanket. The colorful veils sway in a nonexistent breeze, and the glowing crystals provide a gentle illumination.

I glance down at the pressure against my skin to find Kalstrop lying on my arm, wearing a slight grin. After a few months on the trail, his hair has grown out and now gently touches the corners of his eyes. I brush it away before sliding more of my arm under him to press my chest against his back.

"You shouldn't be here," he whispers.

"I know," I answer quietly. "But I think you need me right now."

Kalstrop sighs. "I don't need anyone."

"Tonight, I will pretend I don't want to be here," I whisper, sliding my other arm around his waist. "And you can pretend you don't need me."

My guard doesn't answer. I'm sure he's fallen asleep until he rolls to lean against me. Kalstrop slides his hands over my arms and threads his fingers with mine. I close my eyes and relax with a smile when his beard rubs over my palm as he kisses it.

"Thank you," Kalstrop whispers.

* * *

Kalstrop's injury continues to heal with each passing day as we move through the forest. He cut the shirt I used to wear under my leather vest into pieces and made slippers for Beau's hooves so he wouldn't leave behind tracks. Kalstrop explained that it is incredibly inappropriate for me to see my friend in less than full dress, and since his clothes were destroyed on the ridge, he'll have to remain a winged horse until we find more.

Finding water takes three more days, but it feels worth it as we drop to our knees in the shallow river. Beau pauses beside us to allow Kalstrop to remove the fabric from his hooves before wading far enough to lie down and let the water cover his back. I wait for the dirt he'd kicked up to flow downstream before sticking my face into the tiny rapids and pulling large gulps.

Once satisfied, I sit back on my heels and smile at Kalstrop. "You need a bath," I say, shoving him over.

"I hate you," he growls, splashing water at me. "You need one too." Kalstrop stands and leaves me to dig through his bag on the bank.

I watch him for a moment, but then turn my attention to the river. I hold my hand out over the water and try to visualize it rising to me. I twist my face and hold my breath as I angrily stare at it. A growl creeps from my throat, and I swat uselessly at the ripples.

"What are you doing?" Kalstrop asks from behind me.

I turn to see him standing on the bank, watching me curiously. "Trying to command water," I declare, furrowing my brow. "It's not listening."

Kalstrop blows out his lips. "Have I taught you nothing?"

"Well, you did say you couldn't teach me to use my powers," I remind him. "I have to learn somehow."

Sighing, Kalstrop licks his teeth. "All right," he grumbles. "Come here, Princess."

I slosh through the water in my boots until I reach the bank, and Kalstrop pulls me onto dry land. I try to protest, but just end up laughing at him when he spins me around to face the river. He growls playfully in my ear, only making it worse.

"Woman, stop laughing," Kalstrop grumbles. "Close your eyes."

Wrapping his arms around me, he latches onto my ribs with one while the other reaches up to cover my eyes with his hand. I take a deep breath and relax against him so he can guide me.

"Clear your mind and listen to the water," my guard murmurs.

But I can't clear my mind. Kalstrop's injury had been horrible, but I'm thankful for it since it is why I have him back. He's sworn since the beginning that he couldn't teach me. Yet, somehow, he's taught me more than anyone else.

"What do you hear?" he asks.

"You," I answer without thinking. "I've missed you."

Kalstrop remains silent for a moment before sighing. "I'm never far, Princess," he responds. He widens his stance, making our shoulders level with each other. Kalstrop slips his hands under my arms and stretches them out to my side. "Lay your arms on mine. Let them feel weightless as they float over the water."

"I can't float on the water if I'm not in it," I murmur, laying my head on his shoulder to stare at the clouds. I watch them drift by momentarily before closing my eyes and resting my cheek against Kalstrop's jaw. "I'm floating on you."

"Focus, Princess," my guard growls. "Listen."

Releasing a deep breath, I give in to the lesson. The noise of the forest dwellers fades into the background as the cascading ripples of the shallow river flow in. The sound resembles that of static. It erases all other vibrations and settles into a beautiful symphony of silence.

Kalstrop's chest moves with his deep breaths against my back, and I begin to feel as though I'm floating. The pressure my weight puts on the bottom of my feet is no longer part of my story. My leather vest is snug, yet a breeze finds its way between my skin and the animal hide.

My body burns in the heat from the sun, begging to be cooled. Hair sweeps across my face in a building rush of hot air. I lick my lips, wishing for relief from the heat swirling around me. I want to open my eyes, but they aren't responding.

I gasp when something lands on my face, quickly followed by more. It's warm, yet still refreshing. My body tenses with panic, and I take several deep breaths, attempting to settle my heart rate.

Kalstrop moves to remind me he's still there, and I focus on the noise, trying to find his voice. "Open your eyes, Princess," he whispers when I locate him.

I lift my head from his shoulder, and my eyes widen as they open. Kalstrop gently moves my hand so that I can reach forward and touch the water as it lifts from the river and falls over us in a personal rain shower. Smiling, I turn to face him and catch the mini rainbows surrounding us.

Dirt and blood streak down Kalstrop's face as he grins at me. "You did good," he whispers.

I cup his cheeks and wipe the grime away with my thumbs. "You are my friend, Kalstrop," I whisper back. "You are more than a soldier to me. I will always miss you when you forget that."

Kalstrop laughs quietly, shaking his head. "Old habits, Princess," he murmurs. He sweeps his hands over my face and pushes my wet hair back. "Now, if you don't mind. I'd like a shower."

Scoffing, I step back to watch him pull his belt from his pants and toss it over by his pack. Kalstrop pulls his shirt over his head and lifts his eyebrow while throwing it after the belt. I realize I'm staring when he pauses after loosening his pants.

"I did ask nicely," Kalstrop says.

"Right," I respond, furrowing my brow. I turn away and look out over the river, finding Beau still lying near the center, watching us. The rain shower tapers off when the smell of Kalstrop's soap hits my nose.

"Princess, a little water pressure, please?"

Giggling, I focus back on the water and release a deep breath. The rain shower builds back up, and I lift my gaze to allow it to fall on my face. It's still not cool, but warm water is best for removing imp blood and days of mud from the forest trails.

The droplets land gently on my face but harder on the rest of my body. I can feel our battle washing off my skin. The river carries it away to cleanse my soul of the lives I took. Relief washes over me with each drop, like a fresh beginning and escape from what I've done.

* * *

"You're getting better," Kalstrop says, snipping a stitch from his wound. "You should probably leave some of that in the river, though."

I smile when he stops to look up at me. "But there's water everywhere, isn't there?" I ask. "The plants and animals thrive even when away from the rivers and streams. So there's water elsewhere under the ground or in the roots of plants. How do I access that?"

"Why do you think I know everything?" Kalstrop scoffs.

"Because you do," I respond, frowning.

My guard narrows his eyes in thought. "Hmm," he hums, turning back to his task. "I don't know what it is about you that annoys me so deeply. Clearly, I don't know everything."

I click my tongue. "Kalstrop, do you remember your dreams?"

"I don't do that."

"Everyone dreams," I state, snatching his blade. "It's part of sleeping." I kneel beside his leg and squint at the stitches. "I used to love my dreams. I went to the Olympics every night with Beau. We were unstoppable. I couldn't wait to grow up and leave that ranch so we could show everyone what real talent was."

Kalstrop's eyes are calm and caring when I look up.

"We were gonna conquer the world," I add. Sighing, I turn back to his wound. "Now I'm afraid of my dreams, and the world is trying to kill me."

"They don't all want to kill you, Princess," Kalstrop grumbles. "Some of them wanna impregnate you."

My jaw slackens and my eyes narrow as I turn to stare dumbfoundedly at him. Kalstrop's chuckle starts small, but the sensation of my eyes boring holes into the back of his head gets the better of him. He turns and ducks as I swat at him.

"Princess, there are far worse monsters in this world than you will ever encounter in your dreams," Kalstrop says quietly. "Your dreams can't hurt you. They aren't real."

I cut a few of his stitches while thinking about his words. "But they feel real."

"Did you ever win the Olympics?" Kalstrop asks. "Were there medals hanging in your room when you woke? Was your name known far and wide?" He studies my face for a moment before continuing. "I'm sure you would've been amazing, Princess. But it wasn't real."

I wince as I pull the rest of Kalstrop's stitches. He doesn't seem phased, but the suture gripping the skin when I pull it looks like it would be painful. "Beau was the real star," I tell him, rifling through his bag for the salve. "The medals would've been in his stall."

Kalstrop snorts and looks over the river where Beau is messing with his wings. "That old nag," he says, chuckling. "Flying was fun, though, wasn't it? 'Til the end anyway."

Chapter 15

I run barefoot through the hedges until I reach my secluded garden. I wouldn't have picked the white satin dress, but it's comfortable and even feels fun as it brushes against my legs. It fluffs a bit when I suddenly stop in the archway to study my sanctuary.

The mother duck sits alone in her grassy bowl, her ducklings nowhere in sight. The creek still babbles through, but something about it has changed. My chest tightens when I glance at the tree and find my swing broken in half.

"Do you have something to say to me?" Ash whispers into my ear, making me jump.

I swallow hard, my heart pounding. "I'm sorry," I murmur.

"I don't think I heard you," he says more firmly.

My chest lifts to pull deep breaths as he turns me to face him.

"I'm sorry," I repeat, looking into his eyes.

Ash scans my face. "For what?"

This is a test I can't fail. I don't care what Kalstrop says. Falling for hours into that black abyss felt real to me, and I don't want to do it again. I can't give Ash the chance to do something worse.

Since I still have things I need to learn from him, I need to ensure I don't anger him further.

I recall my first kiss. Kalstrop gave me control over that moment, guaranteeing no one could steal it from me. "I took something that wasn't mine," I say with more conviction.

Ash steps into me with a soft gaze. He cups my cheek and lifts me by my jaw. His lips remain just out of my reach as he breathes into my mouth. "You've improved," he whispers. Ash brushes his lower lip against mine, making things come alive within me that he should not be able to affect. "Show me."

My brain is in a fog as Ash steps sideways and pulls me by my hand. I'm unsure what he's referring to until he stops by the creek. Typically tied to stay out of my face, my loose hair floats whimsically in the breeze, showing off the blue streak. The hue is brighter, and the colored section is bigger.

Taking a deep breath, I relax and extend my hands over the creek until its rapids lift. The water rises in small streams and releases droplets to touch my palms before falling back into place among those who remained. I smile and turn my palms upward, asking them to rise above me and fall as rain would. I look at Ash and open my fingers. The water responds by turning to mist, like a thick fog.

Ash grins, watching the water swirl around us like a personal storm. "Good," he responds. "Can you direct it?"

I narrow my eyes quizzically as he unties his cloak and lets it drop from his shoulders. It's heavy from soaking up the water I've allowed to fall on him. I become distracted as my gaze travels back up his body.

I don't recall Ash ever wearing a shirt without sleeves. The only mark on his skin is a burn on his left bicep. He extends his arm and follows my gaze to see what has captured my attention. I slide my hand along his forearm, resting his wrist on my shoulder.

"I thought fire didn't burn you?" I murmur, sliding my fingers over the damaged skin.

Ash snatches my wrist, startling me. The water gently falling around us drops like a bucket dumped over our heads. "Once upon a time, it did," Ash snarls. "I ended that."

I push against his grip until I can brush the tufts of hair falling in his face behind his ear. "It looks like it hurt," I say tenderly. "I'm sorry it happened."

"I don't feel pain," Ash responds abruptly, stepping back. "Start again." His hand sweeps toward the water.

We spend hours beside the creek, testing my abilities. Each new failure causes Ash to huff loudly or roll his eyes. My determination to impress him pays off when I finally form a ball of water in my hand and throw it against the tree.

"Good," Ash murmurs. "Do it again."

I hold my hand out for the water to flow into. It circles and swirls until it forms a perfect sphere. Pulling his lower lip into his mouth, Ash rubs the underside of my hand and studies my result. He pulls his hand away to reveal that it is dry despite the ball of water above it in my grip.

Ash curls his fingers and creates his ball of fire. His curious gaze remains fixed on the water. As he draws his hand closer, my ball begins to tremble and pulse, but the moment Ash's fire touches it, the water drops through my fingers and retreats to the creek bed.

"Hmm," Ash hums. "Interesting."

"What was that?" I ask, equally surprised and curious.

"An elemental argument," Ash answers, narrowing his eyes at something over my shoulder. "I think it's time for you to go."

Glancing behind me, I only find a magpie sitting on the hedge. He's calm and beautiful, with black-and-white feathers. His wings spread, showing a pretty blue streak where the different-colored feathers meet.

"Isn't that the bird that was flying in the field?" I ask, turning back to Ash.

The young man steps into me, making me gasp as his chest lands against mine. "Maybe," he whispers. "Does it matter?"

I feel like I should answer him, but I'm frozen now that his face is so close to mine. My chin is delicately braced between fingers of silk, and Ash's breath moves over my skin in hot waves. His eyes are gentle, but there's something else I don't recognize in them, adding to the tension in the air.

"You keep practicing what I taught you," Ash whispers, brushing his lips against my cheek. He hums as my breathing speeds up and moves to sweep the tender touch over the rest of my face. Ash pauses just beyond my lips' reach. "I will be here when you return."

"Ash," I beg through raspy breaths. Every nerve in my body trembles, wanting to feel his lips again. The part of me that had to apologize for kissing him a few hours ago is ready to take that plunge again. His desire for control makes me want to surrender to him.

"No," he whispers. "You haven't earned it yet."

* * *

The bow feels foreign in my hands after weeks with the short swords. Kalstrop worked tirelessly on it while we walked along the river until it was ready for tonight's hunt. He's tired of fish and wants red meat. The buck before me calmly chews the grass in his mouth, not detecting our scent since we're downwind.

"Are you sure that's not a person?" I hiss at Kalstrop. "Like Percy?"

My guard rolls his eyes, sighing. "Please just shoot the damn deer, Princess," he grumbles.

The sound of our voices causes the buck to turn in our direction, taking away my clean shot. "What now?" I ask. The bow creaks as I release the tension on the string and shrink back beside my guard. "I could try for the throat."

Kalstrop's annoyed with me. He remains crouched with his elbows on his knees and rubs his hand over his face. "You would die out here by yourself," he growls. "You know that, right?"

"No, I wouldn't," I scoff.

My eyes fix on the leather arm guard Kalstrop had gifted me a few nights ago. It fits like my first band had, but stops at my wrist and contains a few of the short blades he has been teaching me to throw. Since I'd never seen it before, I assume Kalstrop made it while I was sleeping to fill the long, empty hours.

I pull the longest knife and sling it to my right, causing the buck to dart in the opposite direction while I quickly set up with my bow and arrow again. His evasion technique provides perfect access to his heart, and he slides into the dirt, disappearing in the tall grass with my arrow planted deep within its chambers.

"I'd do just fine without you," I announce triumphantly, turning to my guard.

Kalstrop chuckles as he stands. "Maybe you would." He joins me at the edge of the woods and throws his arm around my shoulders. "Let's grab your kill and head back to camp. Your nag should be waking up soon."

I frown, thinking about his plan. "Do we really have to leave the river in the morning?" I ask. "I feel better having the water near me."

"We all like your little shower trick, Princess," Kalstrop grumbles. "But the castle is another month that way." He points toward the setting sun.

The river is flowing south. Kalstrop wasn't happy about it, but agreed to stay by the water this long. I have better control now and can easily direct the showers I create. Sometimes, I can make water balls, but thoughts of Ash and my self-doubt often disrupt my focus. Kalstrop's tired of watching me try.

We quickly work on my buck, clearing the gut and removing the head to make him lighter. Kalstrop ties its legs while I find a long branch to slip between them so we can hang it. The large deer still feels heavy as we lift him, but my guard doesn't seem to notice.

"You've healed well," I mention, tired of the silence.

Kalstrop glances back over his shoulder at me before responding. "I still don't wanna get back on that damn nag," he grumbles. "I have never cut myself before."

I cover my mouth to muffle my giggle. "That wasn't his fault, Kalstrop," I say plainly. "If I have to rule this place, the first thing I'll do is lift the ban on flying."

"I studied birds when I was young," Kalstrop says softly. "The idea fascinated me. I miss my wings, but they were never designed for flying."

"What did they look like?" I whisper.

"They were soft as silk and shimmered like wet, black satin," a woman's voice calls out, making me freeze. "Kalstrop has always been smooth. The view's a little different now, though."

I drop my end of the branch and pull my blades, looking for the voice's owner. My stance widens as she steps out from behind a nearby tree. Kalstrop slowly drops his end of the branch and sidesteps to stand between us.

"She's pretty," the woman purrs, looking me over. "Not really your type, sprite."

The woman's tanned skin is highlighted by her fitted leather top, which has been oiled to a reddish shine. Her black pants are tied with a blue ribbon around her waist, and her boots are stained as though they've seen many battles. She moves freely without a belt or satchel to hold a weapon.

I step around Kalstrop, not interested in his protection. "You must be new here," I scoff. "I'm everyone's type, sweetheart." I roll my right blade and rest that wrist over my left fist, ready for a strike.

Kalstrop sighs and pushes my blade down. "Easy," he whispers. "She's not here to fight."

Pausing for a moment, I narrow my eyes at Kalstrop. "How do you know?" I set my swords back on the woman when he only rolls his eyes. "So she's another one of your friends that's not a friend?"

"Stop," Kalstrop snaps, wrenching one of my blades out of my hand. "If she wanted you dead, you'd never see her coming."

"Then what does she want?" I bark.

"'She' is just passing through and wanted that buck," the woman says, fairly annoyed.

"I shot this for my guards," I spout. "We don't share."

"Princess," Kalstrop hisses.

The woman's eyes widen as she takes a sharp breath. "That's the princess?" she asks. "You found her." Her eyes travel over me in a way that makes me cringe. "His majesty will be pleased."

"Where is the kid?" Kalstrop questions, leaning to pick up his side of the branch.

"Not sure," she answers. "He's been missing for a while. You haven't seen him, have you?"

Kalstrop nods toward the opposite end of our branch, wanting me to lift it. "No," he responds. "You're probably in the wrong neck of the woods. It's peaceful here."

The woman lifts an eyebrow at Kalstrop before turning her attention to me. "I wasn't going to share that meat with you either," she says. "Perhaps we should both be willing to compromise."

"We'll feed you, Arica," Kalstrop says, heaving the branch over his shoulder. "But then you gotta go."

"Sure," she murmurs. "I'll take that, Princess." Arica lifts my end of the branch and holds her arm out to me. "It would be my honor."

Backing away, I shake my head. "No, thank you," I respond.

From the corner of my eye, I see Kalstrop nod slightly. I jog to his side and slide my hand around his arm. My guard takes a deep breath and calmly leads us back into the woods. I'm accustomed to his silence and typically find it comforting, but I wish he would answer the questions he knows I have.

"She has no weapons," I whisper, leaning my head against his shoulder.

The air is so still, I nearly hear Kalstrop look down at me. "She doesn't need them."

"Why not?" I hiss.

"Because I'm a dragon," the woman answers. "I also have impeccable hearing."

I swallow hard, but Kalstrop continues forward without hesitation. My grip nervously tightens on his arm, and my fingertips threaten to pierce his skin. We haven't discussed dragons since Kalstrop's tale of my family's history. I hadn't given them much thought.

Kalstrop leans over and uncharacteristically kisses my head. "Relax, Ember," he murmurs. "She won't hurt you."

Although his words would seem normal to anyone else, they trigger a memory for me. The only time Kalstrop has used my name in the past, since I learned I was a princess, was while we were in his cavern. He whispered it to me when I asked him to kiss me again. He was at ease, calm, and happy to follow my order, and I trusted him completely.

I relax my grip on Kalstrop's arm and let him guide us back to the river. This is his subtle way of telling me that I can trust him. Our quiet journey takes longer than it should as Kalstrop zigzags through the forest.

The sun sets when we stop just inside the trees beside the river. I follow Kalstrop's gaze and find Beau standing in the current with the water up to his back. It's a slow-moving section, but it could still be dangerous for my friend.

Kalstrop stops me when I try to approach the river. "Watch," he whispers. He leans against the tree to take some of the buck's weight off his shoulder.

Beau's wings are outstretched just under the water. He adjusts their angle, dipping one and then the other, testing how they react to the current. His body lifts and sways with each motion.

"I think he caught the bug," Kalstrop murmurs, smiling.

"What is he doing?" I ask quietly.

Kalstrop breathes a short laugh. "Flying."

"Is that a tragae?" Arica asks loudly.

Beau stumbles in the water and flaps his wings, slapping them against the surface, attempting to regain his footing. He jumps against the current toward the shallower water, braced for a fight.

"It's all right, nag," Kalstrop grumbles. "It's just us."

Chapter 16

We sit around a small fire for hours as we prepare and cook the buck. I curiously watch our dinner companion while she ignores my guards to trim steaks from the carcass. Beau stands tall behind Arica, staring at the back of her head, his distrust evident in his steely gaze. Kalstrop remains by my side, always keeping himself between the dragon and me.

The conversation stays light while we eat, and doesn't catch my attention until Kalstrop stiffens. "Arica, you don't even know where the kid is," he says, lifting an eyebrow. "How are you going to take her to him?"

I furrow my brow. "Who are you talking about?" I ask.

"Leif," Arica responds. "Your intended and the prince of this realm. He has been my charge since birth, but has a nasty habit of disappearing." She stops and narrows her gaze with a far-off look. "Although this time has been quite a bit longer than normal for him."

"I heard he was blue," I blurt out.

Kalstrop laughs, rubbing his face.

"What?" I scoff. "That's what Percy said."

Arica's eyes are kind as she studies me curiously. "His dragon is, yes," she responds. "But his other form..." She sighs noisily and smiles. "You two shall complement each other well."

I stutter through a few syllables, but Kalstrop clears his throat, coming to my rescue. "She's not going with you," he states plainly.

Arica hums in thought, lifting an eyebrow. "I don't believe that's up to you, Kalstrop."

"She's not leaving me," my guard snaps.

The dragon sits up, stretching her back. "She is not yours, sprite."

Kalstrop's face twitches, and his hand rests over his sword's handle. "Nor is she yours."

The two glare at each other, causing a tension that could be cut with Percy's wooden practice swords. Beau moves closer and triggers Kalstrop to take a deep breath. He opens his mouth to speak just as I realize they're arguing over me.

"I do not belong to anyone," I bark, shifting my eyes between all three. "You are fighting over me as though I were property. I am not a possession, and you will not be telling me where I will go."

"I fear you may be mistaken, Princess," Arica says sweetly. "You do, in fact, belong to Leif, and I will be escorting you home."

"You don't even know where he is, Arica," Kalstrop scoffs. "You're not taking her."

"I am not going anywhere with you," I shout. "Why is no one listening to me?"

"Not now, Princess," Kalstrop hisses. He reaches across my chest to push me back, solidly placing himself between Arica and me.

I jump to my feet and put my hand out, stopping him from grabbing me. "Then when? When do I get to decide who I belong to?"

"Please, Em—," he starts, but stops abruptly and falls forward.

Kalstrop's sword looks small in Beau's hands as he sidesteps to stand behind Arica. "You can't have her," he growls, thrusting the blade through the base of her neck.

The dragon had no chance to react as Beau leaped into action, terminating any danger she presented. Arica falls to the ground with wide eyes and blood pouring from her mouth. I can only stare in disbelief while Kalstrop holds her body down with his boot and pulls his sword free of her flesh.

"Are you insane?" my guard snaps, shoving Beau. "Look what you've done!"

"I'll admit that escalated ridiculously fast," I spout, ignoring Beau's nakedness as best as possible while waiting for an explanation.

"I ended the threat," he shouts back. "They can't have her."

"Why not?" Kalstrop growls through his teeth. "What's your claim in this?"

The ground begins to vibrate around us. Tuning out their argument, I look around to see rocks jumping in the dirt. Even the water in the river appears disturbed.

"What is that?" I ask quietly. Neither of the men is paying attention. They are still heated, arguing over who I belong to and which of them should be making the decisions. "Hey!" I shout. "What is that sound?"

They pause, listening to the rumble.

"Dragons never travel alone. That is the rest of her party," Kalstrop grumbles, wiping the blood from his blade. "Your dumbass nag just brought an entire clan of dragons down on us."

I watch Kalstrop slide his sword into its sheath, waiting for him to continue. "So, what's the plan?" I snap when he doesn't.

"We only have one choice, Princess," Kalstrop states, stopping to stare at me. The rumble grows rapidly. Distant thunder quickly escalates to a dominating storm that will soon be upon us. Kalstrop appears to be focusing on it and attempting to determine its direction. He grabs my shoulder and heaves me past him as Beau dives forward to change back into the winged horse. "Run!"

We're suddenly sprinting at full speed through the woods along the river. Trees whip past us in a blur, branches slap my skin, and vines grab my boots. Kalstrop's hand remains firm against the small of my back, propelling me forward and helping me keep pace with them.

The air turns cold as we lose the light. My lungs hate each sharp breath I take, and every muscle burns through their fluid movements. I keep my eyes on Beau to guide me through the dark forest of mist and shadows. The corridor of foliage is so narrow that his wings catch on branches even while folded tightly against his body.

When it seems we'll never escape the barrage of stinging branches and violent vines, we fall out of the forest onto a well-worn road. Kalstrop stops beside me, heaving air nearly as hard as I am. He releases my back and moves to see up the path.

"A bridge," he spouts at Beau. "We have to slow them down. Go!"

Without being able to ask what Kalstrop means, I'm shoved up the road, and his hand is on the small of my back once again, launching me toward a wooden bridge shrouded in fog. Just beyond it, short, dark buildings with tiny wisps of smoke flowing from their chimneys stand, sleeping comfortably in the night. They have no idea what is headed their way, and Kalstrop is forcing me in their direction.

"We can't lead them there," I shout through my raspy breaths. My words are barely audible over the rumble of the army behind us. "This isn't their fight."

"It's them or us, Princess," Kalstrop snaps.

Beau's hooves thunder over the wooden bridge, echoing against the tiny dwellings and waking their residents. Lanterns begin to glow, curtains pull back from windows, and doors open. These villagers retired tonight to enjoy a peaceful, quiet slumber, but will wake to die in a battle they were never part of. Their blood is on our hands.

Once off the bridge, Beau extends his wings and slows. Kalstrop guides me to run alongside our cantering friend.

"Get on," he yells, grabbing my waist.

I'm flung onto Beau's back before I can react. Kalstrop leaps behind me, and we take to the air. The rush of wind steals my breath. My guard leans forward, pushing my back until my chest is against Beau's neck. Our fingers tangle into the thick mane that stings our faces and place every bit of faith in our friend as he soars through the air on his second flight.

Beau's wings flap furiously, cutting the air and building speed. Glancing between my arm and his neck, I catch bright bursts of blue and white, followed by muted explosions. Torches carried by fleeing villagers scatter throughout the woods before extinguishing with their carriers. Bows and swords would've been no match against the elemental eruptions.

One burst of light is shot directly into the sky, revealing our presence against the blackened veil of night for a moment before Beau dives toward the treetops and uses them for cover. My exhausted muscles relax in the warmth of the bodies surrounding me. With Beau's flight surprisingly controlled, I close my eyes and block out the fading screams of the villagers.

Kalstrop slides his legs into the position I'd moved them to during our first flight and releases Beau's mane with one hand to wrap that arm around me. He lifts his head off my back to look around. I join him as he points to our right, signaling for Beau to turn.

The night is filled with the sounds of nocturnal animals and the buzz of insects. The absence of the rumbling army of dragons accompanied by the terrified screams of villagers provides an unsettling comfort. I take a deep breath and slowly release it, along with the rest of my tension.

I look over my shoulder at Kalstrop. "Do you think they'll be okay?"

My guard releases his grip on Beau and holds me tightly with both arms. I rest my head back on his shoulder and close my eyes when his beard rubs over my cheek. I feel the weight of his words long before he says them.

"I'm sure they're fine," he whispers.

My emotions begin to bubble, and a few tears slip out before I can stop them. I should feel something for those who just lost their lives to save ours. I want to honor them for their sacrifice, mainly because they had no idea why they woke up to a dragon attack. However, this response is rooted in the meaning behind Kalstrop's words.

"Thank you for lying," I murmur.

Other than his deep sigh, Kalstrop stays silent throughout the rest of the night. Beau remains as close to the ground as possible, traveling miles away from the dragons and steering clear of villages. Although he's not playing or trying tricks, his joy is obvious as he finally gets to practice the skills he's been learning in the water.

The stench of rotten eggs wrinkles my nose right at daybreak. "What is that?" I scoff. "It smells like sulfur."

"Yeah, great, ain't it?" Kalstrop grumbles. "Down by the caves, Beau. We'll be able to rest there."

"Ugh." I pull away from Kalstrop and gag with my tongue out. "Why do you hate me?"

Kalstrop chuckles, but reaches for Beau's mane as we descend. His body tenses, expecting the worst. Beau uses his wings to slow our approach, and, even though his hindquarters drop, he touches down with ease and gently trots a few strides before stopping.

"Well, that was better," Kalstrop remarks, looking around us. "I might have to start calling you 'the graceful nag.'"

Sighing, I reach back and shove him off Beau's back. "Can you try to get along?"

Beau tosses his head in agreement while Kalstrop jumps to his feet and yanks me down with him. He flips me onto my back, but braces my head so my landing is far more gentle than it would be for anyone else. He kneels beside me, and his sword is suddenly pressed against my throat.

"No," he answers, grinning.

I pull his short knife that he always leaves unguarded. "It was worth asking," I say, pressing the blade to the crease between his inner thigh and groin.

Kalstrop clicks his tongue and straightens his back. "I hate that Percy taught you that."

I take his hand and let him help me to my feet. "What are we doing here?" I ask. "We had sulfur pits on the west side of the ranch. I hated moving the cattle near them."

"Yeah, well, it'll hide us from Arica's clan while we rest," Kalstrop answers. "You've gotten good at hiding it, but I know you're tired. I'm exhausted just looking at you."

"I missed our banter," I announce, linking our arms. "Your grumpiness brings me joy."

Kalstrop scoffs and turns to lead us into the trees on the hill. "Stop stealing my lines."

* * *

The sun is high in the sky by the time we reach the mouth of the cave Kalstrop had chosen. Beau's hooves drag over the ground as I watch him trudge into the darkness. I'm exhausted, but I still drop my gear and head back out with Kalstrop to find firewood.

"What was your plan with the dragons?" I ask, breaking the hours of silence.

Kalstrop has unmatched stamina. It's rare to see him tired. The look he gives me is a different form of depletion. "I didn't have one," he answers. His heavy sigh says more than his words ever could.

"So, if Beau hadn't killed Arica..."

"I would've let her take you," Kalstrop finishes. "Going up against dragons is suicide, Princess." He places a broken branch over his woodpile and rubs his face. "Even I have my limits."

My head remains foggy as Kalstrop leads me back to the cave. I can't imagine anyone stronger than my guard. He places himself between me and everyone we come across without a second thought. Even after hours of running, he's the only one of us who isn't half dead.

Kalstrop builds our fire while I settle in the dirt beside Beau. Flying must be tiring work, because my friend is fast asleep and hasn't noticed we've come back. I stare at my guard as he works diligently to avoid looking in my direction.

"I don't believe you would've let them take me," I whisper.

"You don't know me, Princess," Kalstrop responds quietly, sitting on the opposite side of the fire. "When you've lived this long, the stains of your past don't wash away in the bath."

I chew my lip and recall our nightly chats. He's a different man when it's just the two of us. "Your past doesn't define your future, Kalstrop," I say. "I was a bratty teenager who thought I would rule the world with my riding skills."

Kalstrop breathes a laugh and graces me with a gentle smile.

"You've turned me into something greater," I continue. "I'm a soldier who will fight for her freedom because of you."

"There was always a warrior within you, Princess," Kalstrop assures me. "I only taught you how to control her."

"Maybe there's a good guy somewhere inside of you," I murmur sleepily. "I'll help you find him."

Chapter 17

"You look tired, Ember," Ash states, pulling me out of the darkness. He steps through the garden gate and reaches for my hand. "I will not keep you long tonight."

I look down at the silk pajamas brushing gently against my skin. The shorts expose various bruises along my legs, and the thin straps over my shoulders could never hide the multitude of slices and cuts from the tree branches. I'm accustomed to having sore muscles, but wince as each wound threatens to rip open whenever I move.

"It's been a very long day, Ash," I murmur, letting him lead me into the garden.

"I can see that," he responds. "Would you like to tell me about it?"

I consider the evening that had started with an innocent hunting trip. "Not really," I answer. "Can we just relax tonight?"

"Have you been practicing?" Ash asks, pulling at my hair, which hasn't changed much.

"I've tried, Ash," I say apologetically. "I'm sorry to say that my frustration gets the best of me too often."

Ash is clearly disappointed, but he's not blind to my situation. I'm in no condition to work on my magic. Each minute of running, every muscle that worked to keep me on Beau, and the many painful bursts of air I pulled into my lungs are taking their toll on me tonight. I'm useless and barely functional.

"Come here," he murmurs gently. Ash's tone is so sickeningly sweet that it causes me to pause, fearing the worst. I'm too slow to reach my hand out to him, and he snatches it, yanking me against him. "Do as you're told."

Ash turns me so that my back presses against his chest. One arm wraps around my waist while the other hand covers my eyes, making me gasp. My fingers dig into his arm, trying to pull him off my face, but he only tightens his grip. Ash tucks beside my ear and whispers, rubbing his lips over my skin. I have no idea what he said, but it doesn't matter as I drop my hands and turn my head, wanting to feel it again.

"Make a tub grand enough for two or three people," Ash whispers away from my skin. "Not very deep—just enough to lie within its warmth. There should be bottles of scented soap and a few pillows to rest your head on. Floral and fruit washes are okay, but make one of mint." Ash sighs, breathing warm waves over my neck. "Lovely."

When he lowers his hand from my eyes, he reveals a very different scene from our garden. There's a gazebo with a veil of ivy vines cascading from its roof. Steam rises from the tub set within the center. Large, fluffy white pillows lie against one side, while various colored bottles line the other.

"Let's get you cleaned up, Ember," Ash offers, stepping away and holding out his hand for mine.

Staring in wonder at the beautiful scene, I allow him to lead me. "Where did this come from?"

"I told you that you have control over your dreams," Ash says, smiling. "What you want will appear. I am only here because you want me."

He looks back as he steps up the stairs to watch me blush. I've never wanted anyone, so I'm unsure if he's correct, but I still feel weird about it. Once we reach the top step, Ash cups my cheek and holds me before him.

"Don't be nervous," he murmurs, brushing his lips over my forehead. "I want you too. However, it's not our time just yet." He smiles and kisses the tip of my nose. "Soon."

Ash ushers me to the pile of pillows. He stares into my eyes as he raises the sides of my silk top and gently pushes my arms up to allow him to lift it over my head. Ash drops the shirt and trails his fingers over my cheek before continuing down my body.

When his eyes leave mine, I watch his expression change from kind and caring to something I don't recognize. Ash pulls his lips between his teeth and slowly licks them while releasing a shaky breath. My stomach muscles tighten at the sensation of his fingers along my waistband.

I don't believe a blush can travel throughout a person's body, but I would be bright red from head to toe if it could. I should tell Ash to stop, and part of me wants to, but I can't. Against my better judgment, I am at his command.

My waistband is lifted from my hips, and the thin fabric falls to the floor. The air is not cold, but goosebumps rise over my fevered skin. I feel naked standing before Ash in my underwear, and it only gets worse when he steps back and eyes the lacy fabric.

Ash pulls his shirt over his head and waits while I appreciate his body. I realize that I am doing to him what he did to me, but I can't pry my eyes away. Ash is flawless except for the burn on his arm. His muscles flex beautifully under his gently tanned skin. Their strength promises protection as well as pain.

With a satisfied hum, Ash steps into me. My chest presses against his burning skin, and my body heats straight to the core. The sensation of his hands sliding across my back pulls long-forgotten air from deep within my lungs as I melt into him. I didn't tell my arms to latch onto his waist, but their grip is firm and unrelenting as my thoughts battle to the death inside my head.

"You are harder to resist than I thought, so you'll keep your bottoms on," Ash whispers, causing a sigh of relief to jump out of me accidentally. "I don't want to get my pants wet, but I want to join you. Close your eyes and change my clothes."

My lids drop firmly upon his command. However, my thoughts are more unsettled than ever. I know that a part of me is fascinated by Ash and all he has to offer. He's beautiful, mysterious, and wants me in every way that excites my body. His need for control and desire to rule over me are the traits that terrify even the warrior within my mind.

I haven't even considered Ash's clothes when he steps back and looks down at the bright pink shorts he's now wearing.

"Um... Okay," he says, lifting his eyebrow. "That's not really my color, but this is your show."

I don't believe I chose his clothing, but it's obvious he's not in control either. I stifle a giggle as he grabs a pillow and steps toward the steaming bath. Feeling more confident now that I know he's not interested in taking this further than I'm comfortable with, I accept his outstretched hand and allow him to guide me into the water. I wait while he sits and adjusts the pillow behind his back before lowering into the water and crawling into his open arms.

I'm positioned between his legs with my head against his chest. Ash lifts his knees to hold me in place as he reaches for some soap bottles. He settles back into the tub, allowing me to relax while he opens them to sniff their contents. Soft floral blends waft through the air. I take deep breaths and lightly rub my fingers over the soft hair on his legs.

"We'll begin with the mint," Ash murmurs, dipping a rag into the water. "It will soothe your muscles."

My arm is lifted from the water, and Ash gently rubs the thick suds over my skin. Although the mint stings my cuts, my muscles tremble at the tingling sensation it leaves behind. Ash drops the rag and uses his fingers to work the tension that's causing me to shake. The pressure starts soft but soon becomes firm enough to reach sore spots closer to the bone.

Time stands still as I fall under the spell of Ash's touch. The rhythmic rise and fall of his chest lulls me into a false sense of security, and my eyes roll closed as I groan from the deep massage. His attention moves up my arms to my shoulders, and my hands drop into the water to grip his thighs.

Ash tends to each muscle, slowly easing its ache before moving to the next. Once satisfied with my arms, he leans forward for my legs. I'm rolled onto my side, so I wrap my arms around him while he works on my left leg.

"These are some deep bruises," Ash comments, curling my leg to look at a particularly nasty one on my knee. He raises it to his lips and gently kisses the purple skin. "I wish to take away your pain, Ember."

"I fear my journey will only get worse, Ash," I whisper, sliding my hand to trace my fingers over his chest.

"There would be less need to fight if you would learn better control over your powers," he murmurs, slipping his hand over the length of my leg. "You could be a powerful force of nature with an element at your command."

Sighing, I close my eyes. "I think I should just get some sleep, Ash," I say. "I can practice more tomorrow. We are near water tonight."

"Sure," Ash responds, leaning forward and lifting me with his chest. He stands and reaches for me. "One last attempt."

I'm too exhausted to resist, so I let him lift me from the water. Ash is tender as he tucks me under his chin and allows me to cling to him, hoping not to fall. Soap bubbles pop over my skin while his hands brush them away.

"Perhaps we could end with a shower," Ash recommends.

Smiling, I lean away from his chest. "It would be my honor," I gush.

Everything about Ash is kind and gentle as I step back and lift my arms to my sides. His fingers stay light on my hips, and his eyes look over me curiously. I love when the water rises to meet my palms and know the joy is displayed across my face. The sweet grin Ash responds with is one I've never seen before.

I push the droplets over our heads and drop them to fall around us. Closing my eyes, I tip my chin to allow the water to wash over my face and push my hair back. The warm rain washes the soap suds and tingling mint from my skin, leaving behind a cooling sensation.

Ash's fingers brush over my cheeks while his hips press back into mine. His breath blows in tantalizing waves over my face. His fingers dig into my jaw, daring me to break an unspoken rule again.

I open my eyes to find Ash right before me. Water runs down his face, causing his hair to fall perfectly into his eyes. His gaze is no longer gentle, and his eyes warn me not to take what doesn't belong to me. My pride still stings from the apology Ash demanded, but everything in me wants to test his limits again.

Closing the nearly nonexistent gap between us, I test his command by rubbing my lower lip against his. I relinquish control of the rain and slide my hands over his back. Ash remains still as I taste his lip. I reach to brush the back of my fingers over his cheek, asking for more.

The muscles in Ash's face twitch, his jaw clenches, and he swallows hard. A whimper comes out with my deep exhale, causing him to come undone. Ash crashes into my lips and pushes his tongue into my mouth. Such forwardness should scare me, but his loss of control creates an excitement I didn't know was possible.

Ash pushes my chin up and curls over me, asserting his dominance. One hand trails down my jaw and rests over my throat while the other slides across my lower back and holds me firmly to his hips. My mind slips into a daze, drunk off his kisses.

I answer Ash's affection by dragging my teeth over his lower lip, unfortunately reminding him that this was not his idea. His fingers tighten on my throat, and he holds me just out of his lips' reach.

"Ash," I choke through his grip, clawing at his arm with wide eyes.

"I said no," he growls slowly, enunciating each word angrily.

I'm hurled backward into the water.

* * *

I jump awake in the sulfur-rich air of the cave and double over, coughing and sputtering as soapy water flows from my mouth and nose. The fire's flames are low, but I can still make out the bubbles along the edge of the tiny pools I create. I wipe my face with my hands and arms until they are fully coated with soap and saliva.

"Here," Kalstrop hisses, rushing toward me and pulling his shirt over his head. "Easy now. Are you okay?" He eyes the wet ground before me while wiping the mess off my hands. "What is that?"

The pressure of Ash's fingers still lingers on my throat. I'm not sure it could handle the vibration that words would create. I look up into Kalstrop's eyes, and he sits back, understanding that this is one thing he can't help me with.

"Come here," he whispers, holding his arms out.

I hesitate but eventually fall against him, drained. Although Kalstrop is muscled from head to toe and has incredible strength and stamina, his embrace is always soft, warm, and comfortable. I curl my legs onto his lap and slowly catch my breath.

"We're going to stay here for a few days," Kalstrop murmurs, leaning his cheek on my head. "I want to be sure we weren't followed." He rubs my arm and leans back on Beau's wing to cradle me. "Just rest, Princess. We have time."

Sniffling, I wipe away some water that's running from my nose. "You said a dream couldn't hurt me," I whisper hoarsely. I look up at my guard from his chest. "What happens when that's no longer true?"

"Dreams aren't real, Princess," Kalstrop answers, holding my cheek. "The occasional nightmare might sneak into the mix, but dreams are a fantasy our mind creates to escape reality. Although we may not know why the mind generates that world, it wants to be there, and while we sleep, we are at its mercy."

I lie back down on his chest and think over his words. I could never understand why my mind would want to experience drowning, but I know all too well why it wants Ash there. His need to control me creates a desire to hand it over and push his limits at the same time. When he looks at me, the hunger in his eyes sets my body on fire.

"My mind seems to have me on a path straight to hell," I grumble.

Kalstrop chuckles and squeezes my shoulders. "Bring some water," he whispers. "I've heard it's hot there."

Chapter 18

The sulfur pools are a milky turquoise under their veils of steam in the sunlight. Beau remains close daily and stretches his wings beside me while I study the white wisps. The sulfur is heavy and resistant, making it challenging to work with, and I struggle to keep the water in the air long enough to rise over my head.

"I want to find you some clothes," I tell Beau, plopping beside the closest pool. "I'm getting too used to you not being a person again."

Beau roughly shoves me with his nose, nearly pushing me into the water. My stomach clenches as the memory of my near-drowning resurfaces.

"I don't think I'm ready for a swim just yet," I say, narrowing my eyes at the water. "Kalstrop says we're leaving tomorrow morning. How are you feeling?"

Beau lies beside me and stretches a wing across my lap. Under the leather feathers is a thin layer of muscles that seem to help him hold different angles while flying. During an inspection on our first morning here, I discovered that he'd worked them very hard. They were sore and tender to the touch.

Over the years, I've hurt Beau many times. It was usually when I'd done something stupid, which I regret more now than I did then. He always enjoyed stretching out in the field while I rubbed salve into the strained muscles. Helping him feel better reminds me of easier times filled with long summer days, warm rain showers, and cool breezes.

My fingers pause, and I sigh, turning to Beau. "Do you ever wonder what would've happened if we'd run in the other direction?" I ask.

He peers at me thoughtfully before shaking his head.

"I do," I say, twisting my face. "We ran straight to a land filled with men who want to marry or kill me. No one knew me back there."

Beau nuzzles my cheek and motions toward the water.

"True," I say thoughtfully. "I do like working with water. I suppose regrets could go both ways." I glance down at the wing in my lap. "And you wouldn't have flown. I would've missed out on your joy."

He tilts his wing and rubs his nose over it.

"It looked like fun," I whisper, scratching his ear. "I could never wish that didn't happen." I look toward the cave and narrow my eyes. "Kalstrop will wake soon. We should finish your rub before he does. You know he'll have an opinion."

I can nearly hear Beau chuckle as we return to soothing his tired wing. After a while, I move to the other side and quickly slip through the feathers to find the sorest spots before my guard wakes.

Kalstrop stays awake for nearly a week, but once he's at his limit, he will sleep for two days straight. He made sure we were out of harm's way before succumbing to his exhaustion. I don't like to watch him sleep. He can't be woken, but his dreams seem to make him angry, and I never want him to look at me that way.

I haven't felt hungry since my nightmare, so Beau and I have stuck close to the cave. I didn't think it was possible, but I've become used to the smell. Although my hands are stiff from the many hours I've spent rubbing Beau's wings, I don't mind the sacrifice as I've realized they are the most important tools we have in battle.

Once I've finished Beau's wings, I turn my attention back to the water. Ash had mentioned something about minerals and how they would change how it works with me. The pools vary in color, which I assume is from different amounts of sulfur.

I stand beside one I haven't worked with before. Lifting my hand, I call the water up to me and watch curiously as thick globs slowly ascend to hover over the pool. The three separate sections vary in size from a baseball to a beach ball. I can't feel the weight, but the amount of concentration they demand drains me quickly, leaving me lightheaded and breathless.

I focus on the smallest blob and release the others. The little sphere moves away from the pool with me and gently settles in my open palm. I poke my finger at it, but it doesn't let me break the surface. I rub my free hand over the top and try to flatten it, smiling when it refuses to change shape.

"That's new," Kalstrop says, making me jump. The blob of water leaps into the air and splashes to the ground. "So was that."

Smiling, I turn and accept his outstretched arm. "I've missed these little chats," I say. "How did you sleep?"

"Meh," Kalstrop grumbles, shrugging. "With my eyes closed."

"You don't look like you enjoy your dreams, Kalstrop," I admit.

My guard winks, taking a deep breath. "I told you I don't dream," he reminds me. "Perhaps it's the standing still that makes sleeping so unpleasant." Kalstrop turns his attention to Beau and tilts his head. "What is that nag doing?"

Clicking my tongue, I turn him away from Beau and guide him closer to the pools. "It can't be easy lifting 1300 pounds of body weight plus us," I say softly. "He's only used his wings twice. They're tired."

"You're too soft on him," Kalstrop grumbles, patting my hand. He sighs loudly and grins at me. "Show me what you've been working on."

After everything we've been through, I enjoy these moments. Kalstrop watches while I work with the individual sulfur pools and show him how they react differently. It's my turn to be fascinated when a water ball allows him to reach beyond its surface, but still rejects me. I try to place one of the firmer spheres in his hands, but it bursts the moment I release it.

"You've been busy," Kalstrop comments after drying off his hands. "It seems harder to lift."

"It is," I agree, twisting my face. "Almost like it's solid." I rub my palms into my eyes. "It sounds so silly, but it's the difference between a cloud and a boulder."

Kalstrop narrows his eyes and stares into the distance. "As with elements, minerals have different compounds," he starts thoughtfully. "Liquefied metal moves like water, but is heavier. The sulfur affects the water, changing its properties and how it works with your powers."

"Well, it makes it smell bad," I say, laughing.

"Yeah, I think I've had about enough of that," Kalstrop agrees. "We should head in before it gets dark. Are you hungry?"

I shake my head. "No," I respond. "I think I'll just get some rest tonight."

* * *

My breath catches when I open my eyes to find the garden hedges before me. The simple white cotton dress and my bare feet are less than comforting. I enjoyed solid, dreamless sleep over the past few nights, but it seems it's time to apologize again.

I try to move slowly, not wanting to reach my destination, but each small step covers the same distance as if I'd leaped through the air. I stop when the entrance archway appears, but it continues to move closer even though my feet remain still. My hands tremble as I push my hair from my face, tucking it behind my ear.

"You've kept me waiting," Ash growls. He steps around the archway, grabs my arm, and pulls me against him. "I don't like waiting."

I stand frozen against his unrelenting grip on my neck and waist. My fingers dig into his hips while my palms rest on the bone, ready to push him away. Ash's breath blows over my lips as his face twitches with tension.

"I believe you have something to say to me," he states firmly.

I swallow hard and lick my lips to create moisture. "I'm sorry," I whisper shakily.

"Hmm," he hums, searching my face. "That's not it."

Ash's hand moves from my neck to my jaw. His touch softens, and he uses his cheek to push me out of his way. My lungs heave a noisy breath when his mouth closes on my neck, and I crumble against him. Ash's tongue creates steamy waves while his teeth remind me who's in control. He exhales over the wet skin, sending shivers of excitement throughout my body.

My chin is lifted, and Ash continues on the other side. His hungry teeth accompany each lap of his tongue. By the time he pulls my earlobe with his lips, I'm entirely at his mercy.

"You are mine," Ash whispers into my ear, letting his lips rub over my skin.

"Mm-hmm," is all I can manage through my raspy breaths.

"Say it," Ash growls.

Stuck in the euphoric daze and desperate for him to put his mouth back on my skin, I draw a deep breath. "I am yours."

Ash sighs, dragging his lower lip over my cheek. "Let's just make sure you never forget it," he breathes over my skin.

Before I can process his words, Ash pushes his tongue into my mouth and lifts my right leg, hooking my knee over his hip. His gentle kisses contradict the firm grasp he has on my thigh. Ash continues to pull away and reclaim my mouth, ensuring I stay right where he left me.

My attention is wholly focused on the hand sliding over my skin. Ash's palm presses firmly against my muscles on its incredibly slow journey up my leg. His fingers reach my underwear and tenderly brush along the elastic hem. As he follows it to the back of my leg, my body begins to shake, and my skin burns with fever.

"Easy, pet," Ash whispers, pausing his advance. "Not yet." He slips his hand into my underwear and holds me against him by my butt cheek. "Close your eyes and take me somewhere. Make it a beautiful place worthy of your first time."

My eyes close tightly. Images and thoughts race through my mind, nearly out of control. Ash makes me want to give him command over anything he wants, but the moment I cross invisible lines, he finds a way to punish me. His discipline somehow managed to escape my dreams last time. I would never survive a mistake during an intimate moment with him.

Water quietly laps against something, echoing around me and silencing my thoughts. I breathe deeply, finding the air warm and soothing as it enters my lungs. Ash's hands aren't on me anymore, allowing my leg to drop slowly and my foot to rest in the dirt.

I open my eyes to find I'm back in the underwater cavern filled with glowing crystals. My white dress is gone. In its place are my fitted leather vest and green pants. I shake my head at my bare feet, but appreciate that my swords hang from my belt.

Nothing about Kalstrop's home has changed. I approach the desk and smile at the book I had closed last time I was here. Carefully lifting it from under the papers Kalstrop had placed on it, I rub my hand over the cover and flip through the pages. I freeze when I catch something written on one of them.

Frantically thumbing through the pages, I search for the only one marked. My lungs push short bursts of air as the words stare back up at me:

Turn around.

The water sloshes behind me. My eyes widen, but the rest of me becomes paralyzed with fear. The book shakes as I tremble and drops onto the desk when hands land on me.

One rests over my hip while the other slides around my throat. Fingers push my jaw up, and a mouth lands on my neck. I want to scream, run, or at least fight in some way, but something keeps me here. There's something different.

I focus on the tender way the mouth caresses my neck. Only the tongue and lips reach my skin, while teeth are notably absent from this experience. The fingers move in sweet, gentle circles, tickling my jaw to encourage it to stay lifted rather than holding me out of the way.

My eyes roll closed, and tears leak from their corners as I notice the most crucial detail. This face rubbing against me has a beard. The merciful grip on my body allows me to slowly turn and face my companion. "I wanted it to be you," I whisper, brushing my fingers over Kalstrop's cheek.

"I know you did, sweetheart," he says softly. "That's why I'm here."

Kalstrop reaches for my leg but also braces my back to lift me to his hips. I wrap my legs around his waist and cling to him with my face buried in his neck. Kalstrop carries me down the hall to the large room and kneels to lay me on the veiled bed.

Everything about my guard is warm and inviting. His gaze is caring, his touch is gentle, and his every movement is slow and cautious, ensuring he's invited to proceed. When he lifts off me, I smile at his bright pink shorts.

Clicking his tongue, Kalstrop sighs. "Yeah," he grumbles, grinning. "That's cute." He lies beside me and brushes some hair from my forehead. "Why don't we change some of this? Close your eyes."

Although I happily do as I'm told, Kalstrop still lightly drapes his fingers over my eyes. He rests his head beside mine and whispers in my ear. He describes a beautifully decorated room with candles and a bed covered in silky sheets. He dresses me in a soft cotton shirt and lacy panties.

"Just take my clothes off," he murmurs. "I don't need them. You may wear your clothes as long as you wish, Ember. This moment is yours."

I roll to my side and lock onto his lips without opening my eyes. I didn't bother to dress myself. I don't need clothes either. Until I turned around and saw him, I didn't know why I was in his cavern. But as I lie in this man's arms, everything seems so much more transparent. The only beautifully safe place worthy of my first time is in my guard's arms.

Kalstrop's touch is sweet and innocent as his hand slides along my exposed skin. He's patient while I explore his body, getting acquainted with how he feels without the leather and armor in my way. Our tongues meet on equal ground, and our lips smile into each other's kisses.

I could happily drown in Kalstrop's affection, but I'm ready for the next step when he rolls over me. I lick his flavor off my lips and stare into his eyes as he lifts my leg to twist my hip. When Kalstrop searches my face, his expression is one of care and concern.

I reach for his cheek and guide his mouth back to mine. My guard's weight fills me with a sense of security that could warm me on the coldest nights. With each brush of my tongue and pull of my lips, I permit Kalstrop to take what I offer and accept him while he gives me the only first experience that will ever truly matter.

Chapter 19

When I wake, my eyes remain closed. The memory of Kalstrop's warm body wrapped around me is so vivid that I can still feel his arms. Every movement was a perfection of tenderness and grace. My guard ensured I was comfortable and cared for every moment of our evening.

Kalstrop's words echo in my mind, making me smile. "I will always come for you, Ember," he had whispered. "You've been in my heart since I first saw you. Never doubt my devotion."

I couldn't think of a response that would've been worthy of his declaration, so I just placed my head on his chest and listened to his heart thump while his fingers slipped through my hair. Besides, it was just a dream, and none of it really mattered anyway.

My body stiffens as the vivid memory under my head breathes deeply. My eyes widen when I open them and they rest upon the front of Kalstrop's armor. I slowly lift off him and untangle our appendages while he remains asleep. I sigh in relief that I'm still fully clothed, but that is little comfort after what I just did in my dream.

I've never seen Kalstrop smile while he sleeps, so I try to focus on that as I slink away and quickly leave the cave. The sun is just peeking over the horizon, illuminating the foggy pools in its glow. I crouch beside the closest pool and swirl my finger in the water until it begins to climb up my arm.

"At least I'll always have you, right?" I ask the thick turquoise fluid curling around my hand. Water remains the same whether I'm dreaming or awake. I narrow my eyes at the liquid still steaming as it winds up my arm. "I get the feeling you're important, though. I wish I knew why."

"Now you're talking to water?" Kalstrop says, yawning.

I jump and accidentally throw the sulfur water back into its pool. "It's better than talking to myself," I respond, turning to watch him stretch in the mouth of the cave. I have no control over my eyes as they slide down his body. I lick my lips, recalling his flavor, and my cheeks flush at the memory of his skin beneath my fingertips. "We should get going."

Kalstrop watches me curiously until I turn away. "Are you all right?"

I press the back of my fingers to my cheeks, attempting to relieve my fevered skin. "Yeah," I answer, nervously racking my brain to find an explanation for my strange behavior. "I just had a weird dream last night." I release a deep, calming breath and turn back to my guard. "But it doesn't matter because dreams aren't real, right?"

Kalstrop's brow furrows. "Sure," he murmurs. "I suppose."

Packing up the cave and covering our tracks doesn't take long, and we soon leave the sulfur flats to resume our journey. Before reaching the forest, we cross a vast grazing field, which takes a few hours. To appear occupied, I stretch Beau's wings and brace them while he twists them into different angles.

"They're moving better than they were a few days ago," I comment as he tests the second wing. "How do they feel?" He stares at me for a moment before continuing his stretches. "Yeah. I'm not sure what I was expecting."

"We're gonna start hitting villages," Kalstrop says from the edge of the field. He stops, waiting for us to catch up. "By now, everyone should've learned that you're traveling with a tragae. We need to find him some clothes."

"I've missed his voice," I think out loud. "Won't they recognize you?"

"Princess, no one is looking for me," Kalstrop grumbles. He holds his arm out and lifts his eyebrow when I only stare at it. "What is wrong with you? I'm not gonna bite."

I force a small laugh and link our arms. "I'm just nervous," I lie, twisting my face. "I'm worried about everyone's plans for me now that we're getting close to the end."

"Getting drugged and nearly marrying a stranger, meeting a tigress, and murdering hundreds of imps didn't hit your nerves at all?" Kalstrop asks, raising an eyebrow. "What kind of ranch did you say you lived on?"

I shrug. "Those were all unexpected," I say thoughtfully. "I'm about to meet the only family I have left. He's been looking for me. What do you think he has planned?"

"I don't know, Princess," he answers. "However, I don't believe you have any need to fear the castle. Your safety has been assured, and I'll be with you every step of the way."

I hate that his words make me blush, but they remind me of my dream and the pretend Kalstrop's vow. "Thank you," I whisper.

* * *

Kalstrop wraps his fingers around my belt to hold me behind a tree while he watches a village from high atop a ridge. I sigh and rest my head back, tired of fighting him. Every time I start to ask a question, he shushes me. Even Beau got bored and wandered over to a patch of grass.

"What are you doing?" I can't deny being excited to get all of my words out for once.

"Watching," Kalstrop mumbles. He leans back to look at me. "Nothing is as it seems out here, Princess. Peaceful people can kill you faster than a guard unit because you never see it coming."

"So, we'll be careful," I respond. "I'm hungry, and someone is cooking down there."

"Yeah, me too." He breathes deeply and glances at Beau. "Will you stay up here with the nag while I find him some clothes?"

I narrow my eyes in thought and look down at his pack. "Yes," I answer, "but I want all the fabric in your bag."

"Why?"

"I want to talk to Beau," I say firmly.

Kalstrop shakes his head. "Good luck." He pulls a short blade and a small pouch from his pack before handing it to me. Kalstrop holds it open and points to the blue crystal. "In case you get into trouble."

Smiling, I hold the pack to my chest. "I'll guard it with my life."

Once Kalstrop leaves, I move deeper into the woods and sit against a tree while Beau changes to his human form and dresses. His grumbling makes me giggle as I pull the water crystal from the pack. It liquefies and swirls in my hand.

"Hello, my friend," I whisper. "It's been a while, hasn't it?"

"This is not dignified, Ember," Beau grumbles, sitting beside me. "And as far from proper as we can get."

I lean my head against his shoulder. "I know," I murmur. "I'm sorry. It's just been so long since we've been able to talk."

"I'm sorry about Arica," he whispers, putting his arm around my shoulders and pulling me to his chest. "The idea of her taking you to him." He pauses and takes a deep breath. "I couldn't let that happen."

I replay my conversation with my guard about his thoughts regarding the dragons. "Kalstrop didn't have a plan either," I tell him. "He said he would've let her take me."

Beau rubs his fingers over my arm while considering my words. "During my time in the royal court, I learned that no one is as they seem on the outside," he starts. "They all wear their costumes and play their roles, but behind closed doors, monsters turn into pussy cats and docile puppies become wolves. Spoken words are often the ideas of fools. Their actions, however, are far from what you might expect."

I look up at him from his chest and furrow my brow, confused.

"When a stranger looks upon you, they see a pint-sized, lost princess," Beau says, petting my hair. "You may be small, but you are mighty. I could not be prouder of your sword skills, and your arrow finds its target consistently now. You will exceed anyone's expectations. I would venture to guess that you wouldn't need our help to escape the dragons if they had taken you.

"Kalstrop has been around for a few centuries," Beau continues. "No one will ever meet who he truly is. It has taken a long time for him to become the cold-hearted man you know. He's never allowed a door to remain open behind him for anyone to see what he changes into when his guard finally comes down."

Turning his words in my head, I recall the talks Kalstrop and I had late at night after Beau had gone to sleep. "So you think he would've come after me?"

"We will never know, Ember," Beau answers. "But we could never truly comprehend what we are capable of until we find ourselves in a situation that requires action."

"What about my grandfather?" I ask, recalling what I wanted to discuss in the first place. "What are we expecting when we reach the castle?"

"I'd heard the rumors about your grandfather's heritage, but he was not my charge, so it wasn't important," Beau says thoughtfully. "There are very few among us with pure blood. You can't help who you love. Your grandmother wasn't, but thick on the fairy side. Your mother, though. She was a pure-blooded earth fairy."

I recognize the change in subject, but I've never heard anything about my mother. "Did she use her powers?"

Beau chuckles a bit before squeezing my shoulders. "She made the most beautiful gardens," he murmurs. "The castle grounds were filled with tall hedges and long corridors of separated gardens. She erected elaborate archways at each of their entrances. Your grandmother was a water fairy who created little streams to water the trees and flower bushes."

"That sounds lovely," I whisper, smiling.

"It would all depend on how you looked at it," Beau grumbles, making me look up. "She would be in one of her crazy woman moods, and suddenly, the entire garden changed. The hedges created a maze, and as soon as I memorized them, she'd change them around."

"'Crazy woman moods?'" I repeat, lifting an eyebrow.

"I'm a soldier, Princess," Beau says, laughing. "I fought in wars, covered in blood and surrounded by shouting orders and screams of dying men. But that has never compared to the hormones of women. You ladies will forever baffle the minds of men."

Straightening my back, I sit up to kiss his cheek. "But I bet she adored you," I gush. "You have always been the best part of my day."

"Naturally," Beau says, smiling broadly. "Seriously, though, what's on your mind?"

"I don't want to be a queen," I admit, tucking my forehead under his chin. "I don't even want to be a princess."

Beau sighs and lifts his chin to look around. "I had hoped that you would have a life away from this," he starts. "That's what your father wanted for you."

"He didn't want to be king?"

"Hmm," Beau hums thoughtfully. "He believed royalty was a game better suited for men. Your mother had many freedoms that angered your grandfather. The worst of which was her ability to travel unsupervised. Your father certainly regretted that decision."

"Do you know why my mother promised me to a dragon?" I ask.

"No," Beau whispers. "Her family was very old, though, so I'm sure she had her reasons. It didn't sit well with your father. His fear for your future is why he sent you away with me. He wished you to grow up free of these pressures to be whoever you wanted."

My vision blurs as I revisit the past. Our carefree days in the cattle fields of the Montana ranch seem so long ago that they could be someone else's memory. I recall the exhaustion of a long summer day and how I thought it would be the end of me. Those lazy days are gone now, and I have become accustomed to the depletion caused by endless days on the trail since coming here.

"I did have a charmed life, didn't I? I miss the soft beds," I say, muffling my giggles. "And pasta. I would kill for a plate of spaghetti and meatballs."

"You used to sneak some rolls out to the barn and share them," Beau says, joining my laughter. "I liked the flaky cheddar ones."

Sighing, I sink against him. My smile turns into a frown as I return to the present and look to the future. "We can never go back there," I whisper. "That chapter is over, and I have to try to survive long enough to rule a world I know nothing about."

"I'll be here," Beau says, rubbing my shoulder. "I won't let them continue to shut out the voices of women."

I had meant to ask Beau about my grandfather and what to expect from him, but he changed the subject, causing many more questions to flood my brain. My father had given my mother the freedom she needed to make this pact with the dragons. He must have trusted her to make decisions, but drew the line at the dragons. Yet he still shielded her until she gave birth.

He sent me away to protect me from this deal, or perhaps my grandfather, who was furious about the pact my mother had made. From what Arica had said, the dragons were only after the crown. She mentioned Leif liked to take off on her, unguarded. He seems more like me than anyone we've met so far.

I curl my legs over Beau's lap and wrap my arms around him. As my horse, he was my best friend. It's easy to allow him also to occupy that role as a man. I could be angry with him for keeping the truth from me all these years, but what would be the point? I agree that it was for my safety after our months in this realm.

"Well, this looks cozy," Kalstrop barks, approaching from the town. He throws a few robes in our direction. "I got you some clothes, Beau. And Princess, you need to cover up. They all know you're near."

Taking a deep breath, I look up at Beau. "What were their names?"

"Your father's name was Emory, and Timber was your mother," he answers, smiling.

A matching grin spreads across my face. "They named me after them?"

"Your father did," Beau responds. "He loved your mother very much."

I sniffle from tears I didn't think I had. "Thank you."

Chapter 20

The small village appears to be in a permanent slumber while we sit together at a table under a canvas canopy. With ten tables, they could seat perhaps 40 people at the most, and that still seems like too much for a town this small. On the outside of the canopy, two steaming oversized vats are stirred by a large, tan-skinned man with marks covering his body. In the human realm, we call them tattoos, but these appear more like they were painted on him.

A few women sit at the only other occupied table. They both look tired, but steadily scoop something from their bowls and nod to each other as they chat. When they drink from their cups, I glance into mine. If the light were dimmer, I might not notice the murkiness of the water. The little piece of wood floating on top is a nice touch.

"I know I said I was hungry, but what is in those vats?" I hiss as Kalstrop adjusts my cloak again.

"Boar stew," he answers, tugging the sides of my hood down so they lie against my cheeks. "Don't look so disgusted. They don't have running water here. They cart it in from the creek. Try to be grateful."

I narrow my eyes at the women sitting together. Their weary appearance makes me wonder if they brought the water this morning. "Maybe I could help them," I suggest.

"No," Beau states firmly, raising an eyebrow.

"But if the water were right here, it wouldn't need to be carted," I say. "It would be cleaner and healthier."

Beau sighs and rubs his face, rolling his eyes upward.

"We cannot draw attention to ourselves," Kalstrop hisses.

I stare at him for a moment. "I'd say we're failing miserably at that with these large cloaks," I scoff. "We look like we're casing the joint."

Kalstrop's face twists, and he points to my other side. When I look where he indicates, I find a couple walking arm in arm, wearing similar cloaks. The woman is carrying a basket of flowers, making her look slightly less ominous than us.

"I need a basket," I say, turning back to him.

"I can't deny that you would look utterly adorable with a basket of flowers as you skip through town, but no," Kalstrop huffs. He lifts his drinking glass and peers inside. His eyes shift to glare at me from their corners as he frowns and places it back on the table without taking a sip.

Smiling, I bop his nose with my finger. "I do not skip," I say, making sure the P pops as he swats at my hand.

Moving my cup before me, I swirl my finger just below the surface. Currents and rapids in rivers clean their waters, so creating a swirl can't hurt. The whirlpool flows faster and faster until the bottom of the cup is visible and dry. Continuing the motion with my finger, I lift it from the water and grin at the debris floating in the cyclone that follows me.

Kalstrop snatches at the dirty water and quickly throws his catch under the table. "Stop it," he hisses.

"That was my pants," Beau growls through his teeth.

I watch my water settle back into my cup, filtered clean of all its debris. "Do you want me to do yours?" I ask the men.

"Please stop," Beau grumbles. "What has gotten into you?"

"I don't know," I answer, shrugging. "We're surrounded by something other than trees. There are people here, and they don't seem to want to kill me. Isn't that the least bit refreshing for you?"

Kalstrop places a hand on my arm as the marked man approaches us. He places four bowls on the table and stares at me. I smile, but his steely gaze remains unchanged. The man's eyes shift to each of my companions before he snorts and turns away.

"Well, that was weird," I whisper, fixing my eyes on the extra bowl. "Why are there four?"

"Kalstrop!" a man shouts, striding between tables from the direction of the vats. "Old buddy! I've missed you." He plops into the extra chair and slams his forearm onto the table. "See, everyone said you wouldn't come back. But I said, 'No. Kalstrop is a man of his word. He will pay me.' And here you are."

The man's eyes playfully flick around and settle on me. They soften as he grins.

"What do you want, Faus?" Kalstrop growls.

The man groans. "You are keeping delicious company these days," he says, resting his chin on his fingers. "I could take her as payment."

Beau slips his hand under the table and firmly grips my sword's handle. Kalstrop takes a deep breath and straightens his back while I stop Beau and raise an eyebrow at my guard.

"She's not for sale," Kalstrop answers as though these were everyday things to discuss.

The man shovels a spoonful of stew into his mouth. "Everything's for sale," he spouts, sloshing food around and spitting as he speaks. "Although your price is pretty steep most of the time. You remember that redhead? Oof, that was a ride."

Trying to hold back a grimace, I turn to Kalstrop. "So, this is a friend of yours?"

"Faus is not a friend," Kalstrop replies.

"Words hurt, Kalstrop," Faus huffs, glaring at him. He returns to admiring me. "But one night with you would heal any wound."

My look of disgust can't be contained. My eyes trail over our dining companion in a less-than-favorable way. His unkempt beard complements the greasy hair that falls into his eyes. Much like my guard, his muscles are barely contained by the fabric of his shirt. Faus has three swords hanging from his belt but has yet to reach for them, while Kalstrop and Beau are both braced to pull one out.

"It is nice to meet you, Faus," I say, extending my hand. "My name is Mary, and as my friend told you, I'm not for sale."

Faus stares at my hand for a moment before snorting. "Mary?" he scoffs. "That's the best you got?"

He pauses while I lean back, raising an eyebrow, confused.

"Princess Ember, we all know who you are. You didn't think you could hide here, did you?" Faus asks, raising an eyebrow. He shakes his head and breathes out a laugh as he returns his attention to his bowl. "Well, that was incredibly naive of you."

"Enough," Beau snaps. "You'd do best to move along, sir."

"And Beau, man, you haven't changed a bit," Faus says, turning to my friend. "There's a bounty on your head, too." He clicks his tongue and shovels more stew into his mouth. "Y'all haven't touched your food. Cook worked hard on that. Don't be rude."

Although Beau remains stiff to my left, Kalstrop lifts his spoon on my right and urges me to do the same. "You need your strength, Princess," he murmurs, nodding toward my bowl. "Faus was part of my unit. I taught him everything he knows."

Understanding that we're about to fight a formidable opponent, I taste the boar stew. Much like the beef stew that Alice had made, this meal contains softened vegetables but also includes an assortment of nuts. The boar's meat is sweeter than beef, giving the stew a light flavor. Chopped pineapple would be a perfect garnish.

"I don't want to fight you," Faus declares, chewing a large chunk of meat. "I just want her. You two can go, and we'll forgive the debt. Sweet deal, right?" The man nods, smiling, clearly thinking everyone should agree.

"Can you hear yourself?" Kalstrop scoffs. "Do you have any idea how crazy you sound?"

"Kal, my man, you didn't think you were just gonna walk out of here," Faus says, grinning. "You can think I'm crazy all you want, but you're the one stupid enough to walk into my town with the damn princess."

Faus tips his chin in my direction, and I'm hauled out of my seat. The arms that bind me are unyielding, but the sword pushing against my neck is what causes me to freeze. Men swoop in from all directions, standing between my guards and me.

"Now, unlike you, I'll keep my word," Faus states, stepping around the table. "I'll let you two go." He pats Kalstrop's chest and looks down at his belt. "Well, I'm gonna take these. Wouldn't want you to, you know, hurt yourself."

Kalstrop's eyes stay locked on mine while Faus removes his blades. I want to fight, jump, kick, and kill these men, but the blade on my neck has already cut into my skin. Each nervous bead of sweat rolling down my face seems to find the wound, causing it to sear. I wince, but my guard remains unchanged.

"Don't worry, man," Faus says, grinning at Kalstrop. "I'll take good care of her. King Faus sounds good, don't it?" He winks and turns to the men holding me. "Take her blades. And stop cutting her! I want my pony to be pretty when I take her for a ride."

The blade is removed from my throat, and I yank against the arms while the men laugh at me. My swords are pulled from their sheaths, and the leather arm guard is cut from my forearm.

"Remember what I told you, Ember," Kalstrop says, stopping my thrashing.

My brow furrows as I shake my head, trying to recall any words he might have referred to. The men haul me away from the canopy, between buildings, and shove me down a street shrouded in thick tree limbs. A stone hut stands beside a tall pine, using its shadow to hide from unsuspecting eyes.

I catch the door frame with my fingers and stop my captor from forcing me inside. My heels brace against the stoop, and I shove as hard as possible, trying to push the man backward. The men around me erupt with laughter as I'm thrown over my captor's shoulder and carried inside.

I kick my legs and release a volley of punches on the man's back, but this only seems to provide rousing entertainment for the men surrounding me. I try to lift away from the man carrying me, forcing him to put me down. My wrists are snatched, and shackles are locked on them before being yanked to prove their effectiveness.

Faus clicks his tongue disapprovingly as he walks into my view. "Princess," he whispers in my ear. "You shouldn't anger a troll. You wouldn't survive that." He jabs a thumb over his shoulder at the doorway behind him. "Lock her up in there while I make sure those other two leave quietly."

The man Faus called a troll drags me by my shackles into a bedroom that has never seen sunlight. There are no lanterns, torches, or candles in sight. The only illumination is from the open doorway. The man pulls me to a bed and wraps a chain around my shackles, locking it into place. He pulls it to test its security before shoving me onto the bed.

He stomps from the room, closing the door and leaving me in the dark. I can't hear anything over the pounding of my own heart. My stomach clenches so tightly that I roll over and hope that I throw up over the side of the bed. More than a few bites of stew come up before my stomach stops ejecting its contents.

"I need something to drink," I shout, wishing I drank the clean water because whatever they give me is going to be gross. "Please! I've been sick!"

The door opens, blinding me in even the low light. Someone with a smaller frame than the troll stomps toward me. They latch onto my hair and wrench my head back. I gasp in shock and choke on whatever they pour into my mouth.

I only wish it were the dirty water. This horrid, putrid gunk spills over the side of my face and never seems to stop. I have no choice but to swallow some of it. The room begins to spin, and I'm thrown back on the bed.

* * *

"Where have you been?" Ash barks, appearing before me.

He reaches his hand back as if to slap me, but I jump into him, latching onto his neck. Taken by surprise, Ash stumbles backward a few steps before slowly wrapping his arms around my waist. I hate myself for the heavy sobs I release as I shake and cling to him.

"Easy, sweetheart," he murmurs, holding me tightly. "What's wrong?"

I try, but words won't come out. Kalstrop told me to remember what he said. He told me that he would just let the dragons take me. He didn't even try to stop Faus. My captor learned all his fighting skills from my guard. But Kalstrop was my teacher too. Maybe he thought I'd know how to get myself out of this.

"Ember?" Ash says, leaning back and commanding my attention. He narrows his eyes at my tear-soaked face. "What happened?"

"I'm trapped in a room," I start, wiping my face. "My guards abandoned me. I'm handcuffed."

Ash releases a deep breath and rubs my back while he stares into the distance. "Okay, well, no one can just abandon you, Ember," he says reassuringly. "I'm so mad at you that I wanna rip your hair from your head, but I'm still here." He tugs the tips of my hair. "You're like a drug."

I sigh and press my forehead to his chest. "I need help, Ash."

"I know," he murmurs, petting my head. "Do you think you could take me to where you're being held?"

Confused, I pull away and furrow my brow.

"Like when you change our surroundings," Ash continues. "Can you show me where you are and how they have you tied?" He grabs my cheeks as I swallow hard and shake my head. "It's perfectly safe, Ember. I'll be right here with you."

He releases my cheeks to move around behind me. Ash's hands are gentle as they rub over my shoulders. His chest presses against my back in a familiar way that soothes me and slows my breathing.

"Don't leave me," I whisper, sniffling.

"I will be right here," Ash vows. One arm wraps around my waist while the other holds me against him by my chest. "I won't let anything happen to you."

I close my eyes and recall the dark room with the dirty bed. I feel the shackles on my wrists, and the chain clinks when I move my hands. Ash's arms tighten around me, giving me the courage to open my eyes and face the disgusting room in a new light.

Chapter 21

"It's time to go, Ember," Ash whispers. "Close your eyes." He moves behind me again and slides his hand between my stomach and the shackles. "We've practiced every scenario I could think of, and you are ready to take on whatever they throw at you. All you need to do is follow the plan."

I relax against his chest and sigh deeply. "I can do this, Ash," I say.

"I know you can," he murmurs in my ear. "I'll see you soon, my precious."

After spending the night with an uncharacteristically sweet Ash, I hate opening my eyes to the pitch-black room. It's cold and smells of mold and damp earth. I sit up and move my wrists to test the mobility of the chain. Ash spent hours teaching me where to hit Faus to cause the most pain while also rendering him speechless so he can't call for help.

Tiny claws tap against something wooden, a howl sounds in the distance, and a bird chirps loudly. Something shuffles on the floor outside my door before the handle rattles. I lift my chest, taking a deep breath and steeling myself for whatever happens next.

The light that floods in is dim, yet still blinds me. The figure in the doorway holds up a lantern before closing the door and moving slowly across the room. They walk to a small table in the corner out of my chain's reach.

"Glad to see you're awake," Faus says, removing his coat. "The boys are a little testy when it comes to women. Thought they might have killed you."

I remain quiet while my eyes readjust to the light. Faus has washed since he left, and he's trimmed his beard. In different circumstances, he might be a good-looking man. But since he has captured me, chained me to a bed, and presumably wants to do things to me against my will, I can only see the ugly that resides in his heart.

"I like your shirt," I say, as he hangs his coat on a peg. "Would you like me to remove it for you?"

Faus grins and slides his eyes over me from head to toe. Ash's directions were to compliment him about something. He advised that if it were something I truly liked, it would be more convincing. The white shirt is made of thick linen. I assume the leather laced across the chest is designed to hold it closed, but Faus solely uses it for decoration. Beau would look amazing in it.

"Only if I can take yours off," Faus purrs, lifting an eyebrow as he closes the gap between us. He stops before me and tucks some loose hair behind my ear. "I hear you've been kept chaste. I can fix that for you."

I stand up and let Faus step closer. I reach for his shirt, but he grabs my shackles and lifts my arms over his head. He is so tall that only my toes can touch the floor when he straightens his back. Faus's breath rivals that of a rotting carcass. I swallow hard and mask my horror as he tries to rub his lips over my face.

When Faus curls over me to lift my hair from my neck, he puts himself in a position I practiced with Ash. "Why is your hair blue?" he murmurs in my ear.

"Because I'm a water fairy, you dumbass," I spout.

Before he has a chance to react, I pull my right knee up, hard and fast, catching him right in the groin. Faus tries to exhale as he stumbles, but his breath is stuck in his throat. I grab the back of his shirt when he begins to double over and lift my left knee with even more force, slamming it into his face.

Faus rolls into a ball at my feet, clutching his privates and bleeding from his nose. I quickly wrap the chain around his neck and press against his back, holding it firmly until his life slips away. I release a deep breath and shake my exhausted arms, begging them not to give up on me.

I dig through the man's pockets, looking for a key. I narrow my eyes on the coat when his pants prove to be empty. The next step is to get the key. We hadn't planned for there not being one. I jump over Faus's body and run to the coat, but painfully hit the end of the chain before I can reach it.

I turn and try to kick it off the peg. I'm a few inches shy of the mark, accidentally kicking the table and sending the lantern crashing to the floor. The oil spills from the shattered glass. As the corner of the room erupts in flames, I can only stumble back to the bed and stare at it.

"That did not go according to plan," I mumble, rubbing my forehead.

I stare at the fire as it reaches the coat, engulfing it in flames. The faintest clink sounds as something drops from its folds. The key falls to the floor and reflects the brilliant reds and oranges of the fire.

"Great," I huff, staring at my only hope for freedom.

Although the air is heating due to the flames, it's still damp. I hold my hand out with my palms up and concentrate on the humidity. The dirt and wood around me must contain water to create this clammy sensation. I mash my lips between my teeth, stretch my fingers, and tense my muscles, attempting to be commanding, but nothing happens.

The flames leap high as if I were controlling them instead of the water that should be putting them out. A loud crash comes from outside the bedroom door, and something slams into it. I narrow my eyes and tense every muscle, trying to force the moisture into my grasp.

"Come on!" I growl through my teeth.

With a deafening explosion, the door disintegrates into tiny splinters, causing me to crouch and shield my face. Once the wood stops raining upon me, I look up to find Kalstrop standing in the doorway. He looks at the fire and then at the body on the ground.

"Uh, am I interrupting something?" he asks, tilting his head. "I can come back."

"Shut up and get the key," I hiss, pointing into the fire. "It dropped from his coat."

"Princess, I'm not fireproof," Kalstrop scoffs. He inspects my shackles before digging in his bag and producing the blue crystal. "It would be helpful if you could make it rain because I can't break those."

The crystal turns into a beautiful, liquefied ball in my hands. I pull a chunk off of it, but freeze when it turns to mud. "This isn't going to work," I hiss to Kalstrop, holding my hand out for him to see.

"Then make it rain mud," he growls, covering his mouth and nose with his sleeve. "I just need a path, Princess. I don't want to die here, so maybe we could move this along."

I watch Kalstrop try to progress through the fire and jump back when it reaches for him. He kicks at the floor to loosen the thin, hard-packed dirt. The soil does little to extinguish the fire. Instead, the flames quickly consume the freshly exposed wooden planks. When Kalstrop looks over his shoulder, the concern in his eyes points out how little time we have left.

Coughing, I look down at the crystal. "Come on, old friend," I heave. "I need you."

I press a few fingers beyond its surface and swirl them as I have in the pools and rivers. The water calmly winds over my hand and up my forearm. Closing my eyes to shut out the smoke, I exhale deeply and raise my hands.

My arms shake with tension as sizzling erupts around me. I gasp when something hits me and slowly oozes over my shoulder. I stumble backward, bumping into the bed.

"Easy, Ember," Kalstrop forcefully whispers. "Keep going. You're doing good."

I relax and continue urging the water to leap into the air, raining down on the fire and saving us from burning to death. Kalstrop scrapes along the floor and urges me quietly. I follow his voice and project the falling droplets in the direction I'm sure he's in.

"Shit," he hisses. "Hot, hot, hot."

I open my eyes to find him approaching me, flinging the key between his hands. Kalstrop is completely coated with mud. Streaks run down his face from his eyes' reaction to the smoke.

He looks up to find me staring at him. "I see I got the bulk of the mud," Kalstrop scoffs. "Come here."

Laughing, I release the mud wrapped around my arm and do my best to wipe Kalstrop's face clean, but I just end up smearing it around. My guard doesn't seem to notice as he unlocks my shackles and fusses over my wrists.

"You said you'd let them take me," I whisper once he slows. "I thought you left me."

Sighing, Kalstrop scoops the crystal from my hand and places it back in his pack. "That is not what I wanted you to remember," he whispers. Kalstrop steps up to me and cups my cheek, wiping mud across my face. "He didn't hurt you, did he?"

"No," I answer, smiling. "But I did miss your cinnamon sticks and mint leaves."

Kalstrop erases the space between us. He mashes his lips together and scans my face. His muddy hands pull my hair back and hold me just out of reach.

Something in my stomach tightens as images of my dream begin playing in my mind. I loved Kalstrop's soft hands as he gave all of my skin attention. Although I have nothing to compare it to and may never experience him like that in real life, I can't help but wonder if he would be that gentle with me.

"We should go," I whisper, lowering my eyes and turning away.

Kalstrop breathes deeply and steps back. "Yeah," he agrees. "It's nearly sunup. We gotta get going."

"I've been here that long?" I spout.

"Faus had a lot of men," Kalstrop answers, moving to the doorway. "It took me a while to kill them all. Come on. Beau's outside." He grabs my hand and drags me through the front room to the fresh air outside under the pine tree. Beau steps beside us and stretches his wing out of my way. "Your chariot awaits, Princess. Get on."

I quickly look around, finding bodies strewn about the yard. Not one is moving. I hate that I doubted this man who pushed through a throng of men, slicing and killing each one until he finally made it to me. I was proud that I had taken out Faus, but that small act could never compare to what Kalstrop has done to save me.

I turn to my guard before he can kneel to help me onto Beau's back. Smiling, I grab his cheeks and pull him to my lips. "You mean so much to me," I gush, pressing my forehead to his. "I'm sorry that I doubted you. I won't make that mistake again."

Kalstrop breathes a laugh. "I could never leave you behind," he whispers before kissing the tip of my nose. "The nag would never forgive me."

Beau reaches his back hoof, trying to kick Kalstrop and shoving me back into reality. I shake my head and step on Kalstrop's knee to launch myself onto Beau. Once my guard jumps up behind me, our winged friend darts into the forest. They've planned this escape so after only a few miles, Beau emerges into a field and spreads his wings.

* * *

After using the rest of the dark hours to move as far from the village as possible, Beau lands beside a cliff, and we disappear into the forest. Under the canopy of limbs and leaves, the shadows conceal us from anyone who might happen upon our area. Kalstrop and I gather wood while Beau changes back into his clothes. Watching him enjoy himself is a pleasure, but Kalstrop's right. He's our biggest target.

"We moved a little further from the castle," Kalstrop says, taking some of my wood. "We need to rest and stock up." He pulls my arm guard from his back pocket. "I thought you might like to have this back."

I smile broadly and accept the smooth leather cuff. Something had felt strange all night, but slipping my arm band back into place feels like finding my missing piece. I treasure each item Kalstrop has made for me during this journey.

When I glance up at my guard, I find him studying me with a lifted eyebrow. I twist my face and clear my throat. "We should avoid towns," I add, trying to fall back into our conversation. "They seemed so peaceful."

Kalstrop shakes his head. "So do you," he says, lifting an eyebrow. "Faus wasn't expecting any trouble from you. I'd love to know where that came from."

Softly laughing, I consider what answer I would give him. The man who says dreams aren't real would never understand how Ash had taken me back to that room and taught me how to take down my captor. Even the idea of sharing those details sounds crazy.

Besides, I like keeping these worlds separate. Kalstrop is my safety net when I need to feel protected and in control. Ash is the man who makes me want to throw it all away and be under his command. There is no in between. Their lines must never meet, and neither needs to know about the other.

"I took a self-defense class a few years ago," I lie, blushing. "A girl's gotta know how to protect herself."

"And you needed to know how to strangle a man with the chain he bound you with?" Kalstrop asks, frowning. "I'm beginning to think this ranch wasn't such a safe place for you after all."

"It was safer than here," I scoff. "I grew up listening to fairy tales and thinking how boring it would be to marry a man and settle in a castle like all of them." I walk beside Kalstrop as he guides me back to where we'd set up camp. "Now I think they were the lucky ones. I'm a fairy, and my tale is very different."

My guard drops his pile of logs and adds mine to the top. He pulls me into his arms and holds my head to his chest. "Do you know what I wanted to be when I was little?" Kalstrop asks, making me smile. "I wanted to be a bird."

"What?" I spout, giggling.

"Stop laughing," he grumbles. "I was young and dumb. I thought I could grow up to be a bird." He softly rubs my back as I attempt to stifle my giggles. "I wanted to fly. I miss my wings, but they were worthless. I wanted to soar through the clouds and reach the tallest mountains." Kalstrop takes a deep breath. "It's hard not to feel jealous of the nag, but I really liked flying with him."

I sniffle, unsure why tears are sliding over my cheeks. "I won't tell him," I whisper.

"I appreciate that," he murmurs, kissing the top of my head.

Chapter 22

I run through the hedges in my loose green pants and fitted leather vest. I appreciate that I've been allowed to wear my regular clothes as I race through the pathways. They seem to have changed since I was last here, and I can't find my small garden. I would love to visit with the mama duck, but I can't deny wanting to see Ash.

I turn a corner and realize I've seen these flowers before. It's like I'm going around in circles. The archways aren't here anymore, and there is no way out.

"Ash!" I call, hoping he'll just appear.

"Ember," he responds from deeper in the garden. "You should find me. I don't like it when you're so far away."

Moving in the direction I'm sure his voice came from, I smile at his playfulness. I don't doubt that I would not have survived our last encounter had I not been in danger. I only hope he's forgotten about me taking off on him when he clearly wanted to bed me.

"Marco?" I sing out.

"Who's that?" Ash asks, making me laugh. "No one else is here, Ember."

"It's a game, Ash," I reply. "You would say, 'Polo.'"

"But I am not playing a game, Princess," he purrs. "I want you to find me."

"Then you better keep talking," I urge, slowing to catch the direction of his response.

My breaths remain shallow as I listen carefully, trying to hear any hint of noise in his silence. Every tapping of a branch or shake of a leaf suddenly becomes the loudest noise in the garden. I stop and turn my head, trying to pick up any unnatural sounds.

"Ash?" I whisper.

Arms slide around me from behind. One hand presses over my vest along the buttons until it reaches my throat, pushing my head to the side by my jaw. The other slides around my waist and holds me against a warm body. Lips rub over my neck and pull at my earlobe, igniting things I didn't know could burn within me.

"I love it when you whisper my name," Ash breathes into my ear, causing a sigh to jump out of me without warning. "Do it again."

Through no direction of mine, my mouth opens, and Ash's name slips out so quietly that I can barely hear myself. He may not have heard it, but my attempt was enough to tell him he is in complete control. Ash groans deeply and rubs his teeth over my skin. I've been bitten by many animals—wild, feral, or tame—I never thought I'd whimper, asking to feel the pain.

Ash inhales deeply and rests his lips where my neck and shoulder meet. His kisses are sweet and tender before he lifts off me with a sigh. "No," he whispers. "I scared you. I don't want to do that again."

I rest my head back on his shoulder and slide my hand up his arm. When he lifts his fingers to thread them with mine, I know

I haven't done anything against his wishes. I smile and bring his hand to my lips.

"Thank you for your help," I murmur. "I don't want to think about what would've happened without your guidance."

"He would've felt my fire," Ash responds. "No one else is allowed to touch you."

I chew my lip and think of Kalstrop. I've never mentioned him to Ash. If he is threatening someone in the real world, I would guess he would try to harm someone I was with in my dreams.

"What's troubling you?" Ash asks, kissing my temple.

When I look up at him, Ash loosens his arms and allows me to turn around. I hold his shirt tightly in my fists and rest my forehead against his. Ash's fingers tangle into the belt loops along my back, and he sighs, closing his eyes to join my silence. The fear my impending future creates creeps in, and I want to cry, but showing Ash another weakness could cost me this moment.

"How am I going to make it to the castle?" I whisper after a while. "The moment I got close..." My voice trails off. I can't think about Faus without remembering his horrible breath. Ash would never let me live to see the next day if I threw up on him.

"I've been thinking about that too," Ash admits. "There are a great many men who think they deserve my treasures. I will guide you the rest of the way in. You must stay away from villages until you reach the outer bailey."

"What's that?" I ask, pulling back to look into his eyes.

"Where you will find safety, my dear," Ash murmurs, rubbing his fingers over my lower back. "It's the first line of defense. Until you reach the castle grounds, you are fair game, and these hunters are all very hungry."

Frowning, I tuck under his chin and rest my cheek on his chest. "I am not a meal," I grumble.

"If you were a man, you'd understand," Ash responds.

"If I were a man, we wouldn't be in this situation," I scoff.

"Very true," Ash agrees, sliding his hands up my back and reaching for my chin to push me out of hiding. "I also wouldn't find you so delicious."

Ash lifts his eyebrow and flashes a playful grin before pressing his lips to mine for a beautifully tender kiss. His fingers remain gentle on my chin as he holds me against him, and then lovingly brush over my cheek when he pulls away. Ash's kind eyes and the soft touch that sweeps my hair behind my ear make it difficult to remember why I ran from him.

"We will take a walk tonight, sweet Ember," he whispers. "Shall we go back to your field?"

"Um," I stammer, blinking a few times to pull myself back from the daze he created. "I can try."

Ash licks his lips, distracting me. "Add a picnic this time," he requests, turning me to press his chest to my back and covering my eyes.

Since I didn't create the last field we were in, I have trouble recalling the specifics. I turn my thoughts to a lake with a sandy beach. A red-and-white checkered blanket sprawls over the sand, boasting heaping plates of fruit and cakes, while covered bowls hold rolls and biscuits.

"Hmm," Ash hums quietly. "This is different."

I open my eyes to the world I created. Lakes wouldn't usually have waves, but I like the sound, so I added them for fun. "Would you like an umbrella?" I ask, smiling over my shoulder.

Ash only shakes his head and steps away. He reaches for my hand and winks when I give it to him. "Come feed me some of your imagination," he says, grinning.

We spend hours on the sandy beach talking about when we were children. Ash entertains himself by feeding me bites of everything on the blanket before eating what remains. I'm unsure why, but I'm incredibly jealous of every article of food that enters his mouth.

Once done, Ash lies back and holds his arm out to me. I smile and roll onto his shoulder, curling up to his chest and laying my leg over his. A squawk catches our attention, and we glance up the beach to find a magpie. I'm pretty sure it's the same one from earlier dreams.

"Magpies recognize themselves in a mirror," Ash murmurs, staring at the bird.

Lifting myself onto my elbow, I smile down at him curiously. "What?"

Ash's laugh is beautiful. I don't know why he keeps it so well under guard. "Most birds view their reflection as a friend because they don't know it's a mirror," Ash answers, still chuckling. "Magpies know it's a reflection of themselves. They can also mimic our words. Unlike a mockingbird that only repeats other birds' calls."

I try to hide my pinched smile with my hand, but I'm sure it displays across my whole face.

"I had a younger brother who studied birds," Ash tells me, rolling his eyes. "I couldn't care less and have never used any of the knowledge he forced into my head, but suffered through hours of pointless rambling while we went hunting together."

Moving my hand away, I show Ash my broad smile. "Ash, you have family," I gush. Throughout every childhood story Ash shared, he never mentioned any family members. "He sounds sweet."

"Had, Ember," Ash corrects. "I had family." He pulls my hair over my shoulder and slides his fingers through it a few times, twisting his face in thought. "Nepotism is only good for sacrifice," he continues. "Blood will only travel so far by your side. Once they are gone, the void becomes normal."

I don't know when my smile faded, but my frown hurts my face. "Do you miss them?"

Ash takes a deep breath and rubs his fingers over my face. "No," he answers. "I only miss you when you're gone."

I shouldn't. I know I'll pay dearly for it, but I lower myself onto Ash's lips. Many people in this realm and the last would say things to anger a person and get a rise out of them. Ash's words make me want to love him. No matter what he's done, his words hit my heart and make it want to beat for him.

I shriek in surprise and giggle into Ash's kisses when he rolls with me to trade places. He smiles and watches my eyes close as I lose myself to him.

* * *

Kalstrop spends three days cooking the meat we collect on hunts until it is as dry as leather. He calls it jerky, but it's nothing like what Alice made. If the bland flavor wasn't enough to kill my appetite, the texture threatening to rip out my teeth would do it. I glance down at my boots and wonder if they would taste better.

"You look like you slept well," Beau comments as we pack all the meat into our pockets. "You ready for this?"

True, I've been sleeping like a baby. I haven't seen Ash since our night at the lake. He usually stays away when he's angry with me, so I often find myself distracted, wondering what I could've done wrong.

"We need to reach the outer bailey without going near any other villages," I say, recalling Ash's directions. "We need to avoid people."

Beau lifts an eyebrow. "'The outer bailey?' Did your inner princess teach you that?"

I furrow my brow before realizing I used a term I shouldn't know, having not been raised in this realm. "I think I read about it in a book," I say, hoping I sound convincing. "It's the edge of the castle grounds, right?"

"Yeah," Beau says slowly, not looking convinced. "It's a wall, actually. Although only lightly guarded, it provides the first defense for the castle and surrounds the housing and shops for those most important to the royal family."

Nodding, I smile and accept his offered arm. "I read that also."

"Sure," Beau responds, studying me suspiciously.

"Come on, you two," Kalstrop snaps, distracting Beau. "We've got a lot of ground to cover."

"Mm-hmm," Beau hums in agreement. "So the princess has been telling me."

Kalstrop has been moody for the past few days and only provides sharp interactions when he bothers to acknowledge us at all. He's quick to storm off and lead the way while Beau and I trail behind at a comfortable distance. I watch my friend eat a few strips of the jerky before I have to speak up.

"How can you eat that?" I hiss. "It's horrible."

Beau raises an eyebrow. "Ember, this is pretty good," he says slowly, his concern written across his face. "Are you feeling okay?"

"I'm fine," I say quietly so as not to be heard by Kalstrop. "My shoes would taste better than that, and you're asking me if I'm okay? Come here." I pull his arm and reach up to feel his forehead.

Beau swats me away. "What's gotten into you?" he scoffs. "You used to eat mashed potatoes. Those things are horrible. They're grainy and lack anything that could be claimed as flavor."

"Beau, you literally ate grain," I spout, laughing heartily.

"Yes, but it had molasses," he states pointedly. "And that, dear Ember, is delicious."

My eyes water from how hard I'm laughing. Beau provided many humorous moments as my horse throughout the years, but I don't believe I've laughed this hard in a long time. It's almost funnier because it's true. Molasses syrup was a treat on pancakes whenever we had time to sit down for breakfast at the ranch. I even remember Beau stealing a cake or two when I'd roll them up and carry them out to the barn with me once we were done eating.

"At least we agree on something," I say when I finally catch my breath. I rest my head against his shoulder and watch Kalstrop slow ahead of us. "Beau, you're my best friend."

He smiles crookedly as I look up at him. "And you are mine, Princess." Beau kisses my forehead and rips another chunk off his jerky. "Even though your judgment of food is questionably flawed."

"Blah," I retch, grimacing. "Gross." I turn my attention to Kalstrop, who's now stopped, waiting for us. "What's up?"

"It's been nearly a century since I've been out this way," Kalstrop says, wincing. "I know there's a town. I'm just not completely sure where it is." He narrows his eyes on the split in the path before us. "Our odds are fifty-fifty. Should we flip for it?"

"Perhaps the safest thing is to leave the trails altogether," I suggest, making them both turn to me. "Roads typically lead to towns. Wouldn't trails do the same thing?"

"She has a good point," Beau chimes.

"I have a pretty good sense of direction, but even I can get turned around with the right spell," Kalstrop grumbles. "Trails are the best way to avoid that."

Sighing, I look through the trees surrounding us. They all look the same. Without these men, I would've ended up lost and died long ago. But flipping a coin is not a safe way to navigate these woods, especially with everyone wanting to eat me for dessert.

I laugh at the thought and recall Ash's words. Just then, a flash of light catches my eye. I focus on the area, trying to find what caused it. Stepping away from the men, I move along a few trees and catch it again.

The bright flicker of red and blue flames flashes against a tree's bark and is gone as fast as it came. I jog to the tree and rub my hand over where the light had been, finding it colder than the surrounding wood.

"This way," I call out to the guys. "Over here."

Neither looks as though they are interested in taking direction from me when they approach.

"Yeah," Kalstrop says slowly. "I just said I'm not leaving the trail."

"Ember, this does not look safe," Beau agrees.

I smile and place a hand on each chest. "This is the way we should go," I tell them, raising my eyebrows. "I feel it in my heart."

Kalstrop steps ahead to look where I'm trying to take them while Beau stays behind. "How do you know?" he asks, cupping my cheeks and studying my face.

"I just have a feeling," I lie.

Chapter 23

"You look beautiful tonight," Ash whispers, pulling me out of a deep sleep. "I have missed you."

Grinning, I turn and wrap my arms around his neck. "Where have you been?" I breathe over his smiling lips. "I was worried you were angry with me."

"No, my Ember, I've been busy," he answers, watching my hair blow across my face. "I have more work to do, so I can't stay, but I had to see you." Ash moves the hair from my eyes and tucks it behind my ear. "I couldn't stay away."

"Thank you for the help," I say, letting him guide me to the blanket on the sandy beach. "The marks are cold."

Ash lies down, propped up by his elbow, and waits for me to join him. "I'm glad you remembered," he murmurs.

"You were mad at me that day," I whisper, tracing my fingers over his jaw. "I was struggling and made you angry."

"I will work on my temper," Ash promises.

I smile and hold my hand out, beckoning to the lake's water. "And I have improved my skills," I announce as the small amount of water swirls into a sphere in my palm.

"Yes, you have," Ash responds. He slides his hand over mine and sits up, watching the water swirl over his skin. Ash lifts an eyebrow and curls his fingers. A ball of fire erupts within my sphere.

My eyes widen as I watch the flame dance within the confines of my ball of water. "Oh, wow," I whisper, unable to contain my excitement.

"You've greatly improved," Ash remarks, turning his hand over to thread our fingers and release the elements. "I have to go, Ember."

"So soon?"

Ash sighs deeply. "Yes," he whispers. "I have urgent matters that demand my attention. I have arranged for a visit, though." Ash cups my cheek and leans down for a kiss. "I thought you might like to spend time with an old friend."

"When will I see you again?" I ask before he can leave.

"Soon," he whispers, vanishing into thin air.

Behind where he had been, the mother duck waddles toward me with two new little ducklings in tow. Rolling to my side, I pat the blanket and smile. "Well, hello again," I gush. "Look at your new little ones. Aren't they adorable?"

The yellow ducklings settle with their mother at the edge of my blanket. I lay my head on my arm and reach toward the family. They let me rub their heads with my finger before the mother duck tucks her small ones under her wing and settles in for a snooze. I roll onto my back and let the waves from my lake lull me back to sleep.

* * *

I've lost track of how long we've been tromping through the forest. Without a trail to follow, progress is slower than usual, and the grime collecting on my skin has become more than I can bear.

We're all exhausted when we step onto the bank of a small creek just before sunset.

I walk into the water without worrying about my boots or pants. The creek is only knee-deep, but it's enough to quench this thirst and wash off the weeks of dirt covering my skin. We followed Ash's signs until we couldn't go another moment without water. I tried to pull it out of the ground a few times but failed, and used the absence of sound to find this creek.

Kalstrop kneels beside me in the water after taking off his boots. "You found it, so you can go first," he says, holding out a bar of soap and a rag.

"I think I can smell myself," I whisper, wrinkling my nose.

"Yes," Kalstrop whispers back. "We can smell you, too."

I scoff and shove him over in the water. "Shut up," I growl, snatching the soap. "Go stand guard."

As Kalstrop chuckles and retreats to the bank, I look up to find that Beau has already crossed the creek and is checking the thin bushes to ensure our privacy. Once he nods, I pull my clothes off and lie in the water, letting the ripples carry the evidence of our journey downstream.

Each swipe of the soap-filled rag is a beautiful sensation. My skin loses its stiff, sticky feeling and begins to glow again in the fading light. I used to think I was fit and athletic back on the ranch. We worked so hard that staying up until sundown could be challenging throughout the summer months.

Looking over my body now, I can see I was only a frail girl who had no hope of ever standing her ground anywhere. Although we haven't been on the move every day of the several months I've been here, we have trained each day. There are signs of wear and tear on my limbs, but the long, slender muscles tell a tale of someone who will not go down without a fight.

"I'll do your back," Beau says softly behind me. "We're all sticky everywhere, Ember."

I smile and hold the rag over my shoulder. "Are we close?" I whisper, eyeing Kalstrop's back on the other shore.

"Yes," Beau answers quietly. "We will reach the first gate tomorrow. I know this creek."

Although I'd asked the question, I'm not prepared for the answer. The castle and everyone within are the many things my parents didn't want for me. My grandfather should know that I am here, yet he has offered me no assistance in navigating his kingdom safely. Nothing about the end of our journey seems safe or inviting.

"In some ways, I want this to end," I admit. "The hiding, fighting, killing—I just want it to stop." I look over my shoulder when I realize my friend has paused with the rag on my back. "The next chapter isn't any better, though, is it?"

Beau's sigh speaks the words that no one is willing to say. The story wouldn't be pleasant, and the teller would not survive my guards' anger. My tale would wrap around a wedding to a stranger, constant battles between men who refuse to afford me any liberty other than to bear a child, and in the end, I would die, useless and unwelcome.

"You are not the royalty of the past, Ember," Beau finally responds. "I could never imagine you as a ghost that fades into the background. You are a warrior who will find a way to bring honor to the title 'Princess' and prove you are worth more than a head to mount on the wall."

"Well, that sounds unpleasant," I grumble.

I watch Kalstrop stand and hold up my pants, inspecting his work. My leather vest can't take the soap, but my pants needed a good scrubbing. My guard has never offered to clean my clothing.

"He washed my pants," I murmur. "He's never done that before."

"I think we're all a little unsure about what will happen once we cross the gates," Beau admits. "I believe it is simpler for us, having been in the castle before, but it doesn't make it any easier to stomach the unknown."

I glance over my shoulder to see that Beau has removed his shirt to wash it with my soap. His once flawless skin is now marked from each of our encounters since we arrived here. Even Percy accidentally cut him during one of our practice sessions. I noticed a scar on his back a few weeks ago. It turns out to be a wound his wing received during our first landing.

Beau looks up to catch me watching him. "You will be all right, Ember," he assures me.

I smile and turn to rub his arm. "I know," I whisper. "I'll have you."

"Come on, woman," Kalstrop grumbles, stomping through the water. "Now that I can't smell you, I'm upset about my own stench."

"A shower would be nice," Beau adds, lifting his eyebrows. "Here. I washed it so you could put it on while your clothes dry." He holds out the soaked but spotless, cream-colored shirt and narrows his eyes at its nearly see-through properties while wet. "We'll turn around."

Giggling, I accept the shirt. "You've both guarded me while I bathed," I say, pulling the shirt over my head. "I'm sure you've seen some of me after all these months."

"Accidents are very different from intentional," Beau states, lifting an eyebrow.

I stand and raise my hands out to my sides, palms up. The water lifts into the air in tiny droplets. I let them swirl above us and smile at the guys. "Are you ready, then?"

They begin to tear clothes from their bodies, and I release my hold on the droplets, letting them rain down. I close my eyes and turn my face to the falling water. Beau and Kalstrop shout things to each other, but I can't focus on them over my thoughts as I suddenly realize I've missed a bizarre fact.

"It hasn't rained," I spout, opening my eyes and glancing between the men. "Not once since we've been here has it rained. How is that possible? It's been months."

Kalstrop laughs quietly. "You just noticed that, huh?"

I was deep in thought until my eyes landed on my guard. Every detail of Kalstrop's body is a perfect reflection of my dream. I've seen his back many times, but can't recall ever seeing his butt or thighs, besides when he cut himself. I remember the little scar on the top of his right buttock in my dream, though.

Kalstrop scrubs soap over his arms before turning around to catch me staring at his backside. I swallow hard before returning my gaze to the sky and allowing the water to wash away my shame.

"In Calisbrya, the elements are controlled by the fairies, Ember," Beau says. "Although plenty of water is in the ground, only water fairies can make it rise. You would need to pull the water to make it rain and wash the dust away."

"Are there no others?" I ask.

"No," Kalstrop responds. "You are the last."

"But all fairies have a connection to an element," I spout, dropping the water and turning to the men. "How is that possible?"

Beau kneels in the creek to wash his pants. "Abilities are passed on to children," he starts. "There are many reasons why the gift is dying. The major factor would be that water requires purity. The element often rejects those who try to use it for nefarious purposes."

"Could that be why the crystal changed to mud? Because I was using it to cause harm?"

"Crystals are fickle, Princess," Kalstrop scoffs. "I've worked with them for centuries and still don't understand why they react differently to things. You'll be driven mad if you put too much thought into it. I've seen it happen."

Beau slips into his clean, wet pants and holds his arm out. "Come on, Ember," he urges. "Let's get you dried off."

I let him lead me from the water in a daze. I'll never pretend to understand the elements, what they are, and what they do. Ash told me to command water—tell it what to do as though I were a General in an army. But according to Beau, if I did, water would reject me, never to return.

"Are the other elements different?" I ask as Beau guides me to a tree on the bank.

"Yes, Princess," he responds, slightly irritated. "Each element is different."

"No. I mean, are they controlled differently?"

Sighing, Beau organizes a few branches into a pile. "I'm not a fairy," he answers, narrowing his eyes in thought. "I've never worked with elements. The only fairies I've known were your parents. Your mother was quite gentle with the gardens. She loved them dearly."

"What about my father?" I press.

"Prince Emory was also a water fairy, like you and your grandmother," Beau responds. "However, he did not practice his ability."

I furrow my brow. "We have a choice?"

Beau snickers. "Not normally," he scoffs. "Your father had many admirable strengths. I did ask him once why he didn't work with the element as his mother had. He answered, 'I will not give my father the satisfaction of controlling water again.' I have often wondered if that influenced his decision to send you away."

"How could my grandfather control the element?" This whole conversation started with me trying to find out if Ash was right about fire needing to be commanded, but every new bit of information Beau provides sparks several less relevant questions. "And what good would that do him?"

"Calisbrya is a vast land filled with many magical beings, Princess," Kalstrop states, dropping a pile of logs beside Beau. "When you rule over a grand territory, you must decide how. Will you love your people and allow them to love you back? Or will you threaten and punish them until they bow to your will?"

"No one was interested in your grandfather sitting on a throne. Everyone could see that it was the imps' desperate attempt for the crown. The shift in power came at a great cost. Lands dried up, food became scarce, and villages collapsed under the weight of his rule. In the end, they all bowed."

"When your grandmother died, he lost what little control he had," Beau continues quietly. "That sparked many battles. Although the memory of his tyranny lingered, no one was willing to allow him to remain in power. The only thing holding them back was the thread of hope your father presented. I have no idea how he's held the castle all this time."

"He had help," Kalstrop grumbles. "He has guards who are loyal, but he allowed sorcery back into the realm, and there was a dramatic shift in the air."

"Sorcery?" I fall back against the tree and rub my forehead. "Like cauldrons and potions? Wands and pointed hats?"

Kalstrop laughs heartily. "That would actually be hilarious," he spouts. "I don't think anyone would fear that."

"It's hard to explain, Ember," Beau murmurs, glaring at my guard.

Shaking his head, Kalstrop stands and extends a hand to me. "There's fish in the creek," he announces. "Why don't you help me, and I'll cook you something besides jerky?"

I let him pull me to my feet and step toward the water. The creek is generally calm, but low ripples throughout indicate stronger currents near the center. I look where Kalstrop points to see schools of fish circling in deeper pools by the edge.

"Think of it as cupping your hands along the bottom of a bowl and scooping them out," he says softly. "Keep your eyes open but change the view in your mind as you dig through the water."

Kalstrop steps behind me and slides his hands along my forearms and under my outstretched fingers. He turns my palms up and moves them slowly until my pinkies touch.

"Now relax and raise them," Kalstrop murmurs.

He gently lifts my hands, and I gasp when the pool of fish rises with them. The school doesn't seem to notice as they swim in their tight circle.

"Lovely," Kalstrop whispers in my ear. "Now hold them there while I grab a few."

I smile as I watch him pluck fish out of the pool. They would've scattered if he had walked over to them, and he would have no hope of catching one with his bare hands. However, trapped in the air as they are now, he can just reach in and grab the one he wants, and there is nothing they can do about it.

When he turns back to me, I see he's made a bowl with the front of his shirt and holds several fish for dinner. I release the rest of the pool and allow them to return to their natural habitat.

Kalstrop stops beside me and looks down. "If I'm cooking dinner, you're cleaning my shirt."

Chapter 24

The outer bailey appears as nothing more than a tall garden wall. It would keep deer away from the vegetables, but raccoons and squirrels could easily scamper up the jagged rocks and wreak havoc while hidden from sight by the thick barrier. Moss fills each crack, making the structure nearly blend into the lush forest as a backdrop until we step from the trees.

The road leading up to the gate is well-traveled but empty this afternoon. As we wait just inside the trees, Kalstrop counts the guards and times their rotation. He hushes me when I ask why, so I pass the time by watching Beau eat the remainder of the jerky with a disgusted look plastered across my face.

"You're giving me a complex," he mutters between bites. "You didn't eat much of the fish last night."

I take a deep breath and flick my eyes toward Kalstrop. "I wasn't hungry," I respond. My stomach has been upset for days. I tried the fish my guard had painstakingly cooked for us, but found it just as bland as the jerky and could only manage a few bites. "You two needed it more anyway."

Beau follows my gaze. "He's waiting for a specific guard," he tells me.

"What?" I furrow my brow, confused.

"I heard you question him earlier," Beau says. "I believe we'd all enjoy a quiet entrance and the ability to slip unnoticed through the streets."

"No one has let us just slip by yet," I scoff. "How would that even be possible this close to the castle?" I narrow my eyes at the gate. Ash's symbol has been pulsing over it throughout the day. I can nearly see his face twitching with impatience in my mind. "We should just go. It's not like they aren't expecting us."

"Knowing the past, what your parents wanted, and what we've been through lately, I prefer not to walk into a trap, Ember," Beau states, lifting his eyebrow. "We don't know what to expect, but we're pretty sure it won't be a welcome banquet."

My stomach turns slightly, and I wrinkle my nose. "If it is, we should avoid that too," I grumble, wondering how rude it would be to decline the King's food. "What's it like in there?"

Beau rolls his eyes. "Chaotic," he answers. "It was a relief to be stationed with your father's guard. The silence was beautiful."

I giggle thinking of our long days in the cattle fields. "That explains your irritation at the end of the roundups and branding day."

"Them damn cows," Beau grumbles. "All that mooing."

"Wrap it up, you two," Kalstrop snaps, making us jump. "Time to go." He glances over his shoulder at the gate while stuffing his things back into his pack. "Did you find anything interesting?" he scoffs at Beau. "Damn nag ate every piece of food we had."

Smiling broadly, I rub Beau's arm as he rolls his eyes. "Is that the guy you were waiting for?"

"One of them," Kalstrop says. He ties his pack closed and turns his attention to me. "Are you ready?"

"I want to be," I answer, sighing.

"Good enough," my guard responds. Kalstrop stands and reaches for my hand. "You remember that extra loop on your belt? Time to use it." He pulls his long sword from its sheath and delicately slides it through the leather loop behind my blades. "Careful, Princess. It's sharp."

"I know my way around a sword," I remind him. "You've all taught me well. I'll be fine."

Kalstrop cups my cheeks and leans down to look into my eyes. "Listen to me," he whispers so softly that I must strain to hear him. "Those are your blades. This one is mine. It will slice through that leather without a second thought. Your skin is no match for it, and I will not see you injured. Do you understand?"

Something about his expression and tone causes me to swallow hard. This is not the gruff soldier before me. He isn't even the guard who spoke softly to me across the fire at night. This is the caring man who spent hours within my dream, teaching me how to enjoy another's body and worshiping me in all the ways I don't deserve.

"Ember?" he whispers, raising his eyebrows.

Licking my lips, I nod as best as possible while still within his grip. "I understand," I mouth, unable to produce a sound.

"Okay," Kalstrop breathes. His jaw tightens, and his fingers dig into my neck before he sighs deeply and straightens his back. Kalstrop's eyes turn toward Beau. "Not a word, nag. Let me do the talking."

"You two would probably get along better if you'd stop calling him 'nag,'" I scoff. "Faus said there's a bounty on him. How is he going to get through the gate?"

Kalstrop steps forward and yanks Beau's sword from his belt. "As my prisoner."

"What?" I spout, stepping between Beau and the sword pointing at his chest. "No. You can't go switching sides!" Pressing the back of my hand to the broad side of the sword, I shove it aside. "We did not discuss this."

Beau places his hand on my shoulder reassuringly. "Ember, it's okay," he says softly. "There's no other way I'll get across the castle grounds." He waits until I turn my confused expression on him before continuing. "It's just for show, and we all have a part to play."

Kalstrop slings his pack over his shoulder and slips Beau's sword into the empty sheath on his belt. "Let's go," he murmurs. "It's now or never. I wanna hunker down for the night and hit the main gate in the morning with the crowd."

"You got some place in mind?" Beau asks, turning me by my shoulders to face the gate.

Kalstrop chuckles. "Yeah," he replies, holding his arm out to me. "Hopefully, she's still there. You'll recognize her."

I gingerly slip my arm through Kalstrop's and take a deep breath.

"It's okay, Princess," my guard whispers, watching my eyes nervously take in our surroundings. "Put your faith in me. Head high. Back straight. You're royalty, and I am very proud to have a woman so powerful on my arm."

Smiling broadly, I squeeze his arm. "Thank you."

"For what?" Kalstrop asks, stepping forward to escort me to the gate.

"Always knowing what to say," I respond thoughtfully.

Kalstrop hums, watching the gate guard. "It's easy with you, Princess," he says quietly. "I think you just like the sound of my voice."

I furrow my brow and lift my eyes in thought, letting them lose focus. I haven't paid much attention to what we discussed throughout our conversations, but he is right. Even during our nightly fireside chats, Kalstrop usually just said the first thing that came to mind and often made me laugh. It wasn't thoughtful, insightful, or even kind. He just said whatever he wanted, and I enjoyed it.

"Orin, I see you've moved up in the world," Kalstrop barks, snapping me out of my thoughts. "That robe looks good on you."

"Well, look what the cat dragged in," the gate guard says, extending his hand. "Kalstrop, there have been rumors."

"Hmm," my guard hums, lifting his eyebrows and taking the man's hand. "Are they at least interesting?"

The gate guard shakes Kalstrop's hand, but his gaze has remained on me since I looked in his direction. His eyes can't decide on the best place to stare, so they slide over my body until the moment becomes so awkward that I step back. Kalstrop holds me firmly, stopping my retreat, and yanks the man's arm.

"That's the princess you're offending," he growls.

The gate guard slowly licks his lips, humming as though savoring a good meal. "And yet I'd like to do more enjoyable things to her," he murmurs.

As he steps forward, I instinctively pull a short blade from my arm band and press it under his chin. Although his eyes widen, they remain just as intense, burning through my clothes to see what I keep hidden from sight.

"I trained you better than that, Orin," Kalstrop snaps.

The guard scans my face before stepping back. "It would appear you trained her, too," he grumbles.

"I did," Kalstrop responds, lightening his tone. "I'd watch out. She's spicy."

Orin smiles when I wink at him. "So I see," he says, nodding. "And who's that?" His attention turns to Beau, who's stood quietly behind me with his hand on my lower back.

"That's my prisoner, a deserter," Kalstrop answers.

"And he just willingly followed you to his death?" Orin scoffs.

Kalstrop chuckles. "Actually, yeah, he did," my guard answers, winking at me while Orin is distracted. "He's pretty attached to the princess—wouldn't leave her."

Orin narrows his eyes curiously at Beau. My companions are older than they appear, but this gate guard is clearly younger. Based on how he's studying Beau, he has no idea who he is.

I slip my knife back into my arm brace with a huff. "Is your interrogation over?" I bark. "We would like to pass."

Kalstrop groans quietly and squeezes my arm. "What the princess means is that we have had a long journey, and we would like time to clean up before presenting her to his majesty the King."

"You know I could help with that," Orin offers, eyeing me again. He scowls when he sees my look of dismay. "Fine, have it your way, but that one goes in irons." He points at Beau. "And you'll be giving me those blades."

I watch the men as Kalstrop removes his knives and, lastly, Beau's sword, willingly handing them to Orin. The gate guard has uniquely white hair and steel blue eyes. He is soft-spoken, and I imagine he easily finds his way into the bed of any woman he chooses with his beautiful skin and handsome features.

"Yours too, sweetheart," Orin says, arching an eyebrow. "Let me help you."

I snatch my arm away as he reaches for it. "Don't touch me," I snap, narrowing my eyes.

"Royalty doesn't surrender their weapons, Orin," Kalstrop says, scooping his arm around me to move between us. "She outranks you."

Orin winces and tips his head. "Things have changed around here, old man," he says. "But I do believe this one is a bit special. I'll let her slide." The gate guard carries the swords and knives he'd collected to a tunnel cut into the gate's archway and returns with shackles. "Here, since it would seem you lack the appropriate equipment for prisoners."

As Orin locks them onto Beau's wrists, I pull Kalstrop away to hiss in his ear, "I can tell you trained him."

He scoffs and rolls his eyes, making me smile. "The guard that trained him would've let him have you," he whispers.

I wrinkle my nose.

"Yeah," he grumbles. "I've changed."

"Where you headed?" Orin asks, reminding us he's there.

Kalstrop twists his face. "The castle," he answers, annoyed. "If you're done here, we'll be on our way."

Orin watches Kalstrop collect his bag and hold his arm out for mine. "Listen," he says, sighing. "Things have changed since you were here. Be careful, Kalstrop. I don't think this will end how you want it to."

"Yeah, we'll see," my guard grumbles, turning me away from Orin and moving into the busy side street.

* * *

From the moment we enter the bailey, the streets come alive. There was no hint of the activity hidden within these walls from our hiding spot in the woods. Bakers are placing bread on their window sills while women shake out laundry, children run and kick a ball between buildings, and someone sings the most beautiful song somewhere deep within the dwellings.

"Wow," I whisper, looking around.

"I'll show you the town tomorrow, Princess," Kalstrop murmurs, ushering me along. "We need to get you inside before anyone figures out you're here."

I let my guard direct me through the streets and between buildings while I look around. Beau remains so close that his shackles bump my elbow. Kalstrop glares over his shoulder at him a few times, making me giggle. I'm nearly out of breath when he stops beside a quaint lodging with a hay shack beside it.

"Wait here," he breathes in my ear, pressing my back to the door frame. He looks over his shoulder at Beau. "Stay with her. I'm gonna go around back."

Beau lifts his arms over my head and covers me with his body. As we relax, his shackles lie over my shoulder, and his chin rests on my head. "You nervous?" he asks.

"I feel a lot of things, Beau," I answer honestly. "None of them is very comfortable."

"I get that," he whispers. "It's almost over, though. We'll have all the answers tomorrow, and you'll be safe inside the castle walls."

The noise of the street is silenced by the wall Beau's broad shoulders create. I could never describe how secure it feels to know he's scanning the area for threats. After spending nearly 18 years as my horse, thundering over the mountains and fields with me, Beau's build rivals Kalstrop's. His muscles constantly twitch and flex even while he remains still.

A crash inside the dwelling makes me jump, and the door flings open. "Beau!" a woman gushes, grabbing her chest.

Beau shoves me through the door before lifting his arms off me. "Hailey," he whispers, taking her hands. "You made it out."

The woman turns to me and gasps. "And you saved her," she breathes.

Smiling, Beau steps back. "Princess Ember, allow me to introduce Hailey," he says, guiding the woman toward me. "She was your nurse and your mother's loyal aide."

Hailey cups my cheeks with a broad smile. "You look just like your mother," she blubbers, tears streaming down her face. "Although she was very royal." The woman pulls a rag from her pocket and brushes it over my forehead and nose. She releases a deep breath, shaking her head. "I will draw you a bath, Princess."

She spins on her heels in a flourish, squealing and crying as she runs deeper into the house. My brow furrows, but I still smile at her excitement.

"What was that?" I ask, turning to Beau.

"That was Hailey," Kalstrop answers, storming through the house. "She's the only surviving member of your mother's staff." He pulls a small blade from my arm guard and works on Beau's shackles. "You'll be safe here tonight, and apparently you'll be taking a bath."

I only get a short hug from Beau before Hailey returns to usher me into the back of her cottage. I'm unsure how to feel about her methodically removing my clothes, but the therapeutic sensation of the steaming water erases all other thoughts. Sighing, I relax and rest the back of my head on the edge of the tub.

"The men tell me you aren't interested in palace life," Hailey murmurs, placing a rag in my hand. "Princess Timber didn't want to be queen either."

I narrow my eyes thoughtfully. "She didn't?" I ask, confused. "She married into the family, though."

Hailey smiles gently. "She loved your father very much," she responds. "But I think she had other reasons for entering the royal family. She always spoke of righting wrongs—fixing things that had gone awry."

"Do you know why she promised me to a dragon?"

Smiling, Hailey pulls a stool beside the tub and offers me a few differently scented bars of soap. "I traveled with her, but wasn't allowed in the meetings," she finally answers. "I was there. I remember shaking in my boots as I stood outside the room under the watchful eye of several guards. They didn't even blink. It felt like they were questioning my soul and drawing out all my secrets."

She swallows hard, frowning.

"Your mother never told anyone why she did it," Hailey says. "Although Prince Emory wasn't happy with her, he never left her side. You were in their arms when she died."

Hailey would have answers for the many questions I've always had about my parents, but I can't bring myself to ask them. Tears slowly drop from her eyes as she helps me wash the day's dirt from my skin and hair. Her sorrowful smile when she helps me from the tub is enough to squash any attempt at an inquisition.

Once I'm dry, Hailey helps me slip into a soft satin robe and crosses it over my chest. She ties it closed with a ribbon around my waist before gently rubbing a towel over my hair.

"Your parents would've been very proud of the woman you've become," Hailey whispers, cupping my cheek. "I'm sorry you didn't get to meet them, but you were everything in their eyes." She holds my hand and leads me to a small bed. "You can stay in my room tonight. It would be my honor."

Unable to find words, I drop onto the mattress and watch her speedy departure. I've always had questions about my parents, but never considered how they felt about me. I'm ashamed that I'd always assumed they had abandoned me. In my soul, the fact that they had died was sad, but hearing how they felt about me and each other hit me in ways I didn't know were possible.

My hand rubs over the pillow at the head of the bed. My mind races with a different set of questions that will never be answered. I can't help wondering what they thought of me and if this is the path they would want me to take. How would they want me to proceed now that I'm so close to the life they both despised?

I flop onto the bed and mash my face into the pillow. Every emotion I've had over the past few months bursts through me, demanding to be felt. Tears stream from my eyes as I scream into the fabric and pound the mattress with my fists.

It's been days since I've slept, so my emotional breakdown is short-lived, and I limply collapse on the bed, defeated. My heavy breaths are disrupted by a hand sliding over my back.

"Hey," Kalstrop whispers as his weight presses on the bed. "You all right?"

Without a care as to how inappropriate it would be, I grab my guard and pull him down with me. Understanding my need, Kalstrop silently rolls onto his back and kisses my forehead as I curl against him. He rubs my back while I stare at the wall, trying to make sense of my feelings.

"Why don't we forget about the past for tonight, Princess?" Kalstrop offers. "Close your eyes and go somewhere happy and safe."

Chapter 25

Waking with Kalstrop in my bed seems almost natural after spending the night wrapped securely in his arms. He told me to go somewhere safe, and I only have one place that has always been my haven—his cavern. He didn't even seem surprised to see me when I entered the big bedroom and climbed over the blankets into his awaiting arms.

A few birds chirp in the low morning light while I slide my fingers over my guard's collarbone. The memory of his hands on my body and lips on my skin causes a tightness in my stomach. I can't help wondering if the real-life experience would be the same. Would my enjoyment cause me to call out to him as it had in my dream?

"That tickles," Kalstrop mumbles, scaring me. He turns his head as I look up and kisses my forehead. "I trust you slept well."

The heat spreading over my face could only be from an embarrassingly deep red that I wish would have stayed at bay. "I was in a safe place," I respond, trying to nuzzle my way back under his chin where he won't see my shameful hue. "My parents lost their lives trying to protect me from this life. I shouldn't have come here."

Kalstrop sighs deeply and rests his chin on my head. "This is the only safe place left in the world, Princess," he murmurs. "When given this mission, I was assured of your safety. Still, I've taken precautions to assist if necessary." Kalstrop's protective nature is a comforting shield that has carried me this far through our journey.

"What about Beau?" I whisper, afraid of the answer. "What will happen to him?"

"I don't know," he answers honestly. "He wasn't part of the deal."

"But you'll stay with me, right?" I ask, looking up from my hiding spot.

Kalstrop squeezes my shoulders. "For as long as I can, Princess," he responds.

We lie in silence, letting today's impending journey fill the air like oppressive smoke. My chest tightens at the thought of losing my two guards. They have been my constant companions, friends, and sometimes something more.

I lift my chin to rub my lips over Kalstrop's neck before pulling them between my teeth to taste him. The familiar flavor causes a shaky breath to escape my lungs. "I don't regret you," I breathe quieter than a whisper.

"What?"

"Sometimes I wonder what it would've been like if I'd taken another path," I answer thoughtfully. "But if we had done anything differently, I may not have met you. I would feel your absence."

"I've always been here, Princess," Kalstrop answers. "You just didn't know what to look for." He takes a deep breath and groans, rubbing my back briskly. "Hailey's making biscuits. It's been a while since we've had them."

I smile as his stomach growls. "Are you admitting your cooking is flawed?"

"I stand firmly by the belief that you are broken," Kalstrop grumbles. He slides out from under me and sits on the edge of the bed. "Hailey said she would make you presentable," he says, smiling down at me. He winks before adding, "I made sure she didn't make it a dress."

Rolling over, I reach for his face and smile when he leans forward to give it to me. "Once more," I whisper. "In case I dare to forget."

Kalstrop licks his lips as I guide him to mine. His kiss is tender and warm. "I would never let that happen," he professes. Kalstrop's next kiss is more than our first. I could only compare it to my dreams. His flavor, our motions, and my body's reaction to him are all vivid memories of my safe place.

* * *

"Are those really necessary?" I ask, eyeing Beau's shackles.

Beau slips his hand out of the cuff and cups my cheek. "It's just for show, Ember," he assures me. "You look very royal, though."

"I'll admit, I'm a little afraid of you," Kalstrop agrees, stepping from Hailey's hut. He holds his arm out and grins at the additions to my wardrobe.

Adhering to Kalstrop's orders, Hailey had not placed me in a dress. I had appreciated the pants Kalstrop found in the armory cave, but they now fit my body like a glove, moving with me instead of flapping or rubbing against my skin. My leather vest has been altered several times, but Hailey's skill is unmistakable, as it now fits like a second skin.

The unexpected addition that makes Kalstrop watch me from the corner of his eye is the sleeveless trench coat-style vest. On top, it's comfortably snug around my chest and stomach. The cut opens and falls away at my waist to allow free movement of my legs, but closer to the hips, the fabric cascades to my ankles, hiding all of my blades.

"That's only because you know what's under here," I say, winking.

"No one needs to see what's under there, Princess," Kalstrop replies, patting my hand. "But I would fear you more because I know who trained you."

Our journey through the bailey is somehow quiet and exciting at the same time. I occupy my mind with thoughts of the woman who helped me dress. Hailey was too emotional for words. Her tears freely streamed all morning as she carefully slipped my clothes into place. I asked a few questions, but she only shook her head and rubbed her nose with a handkerchief in response.

The shops and storefronts begin to catch my attention as we walk deeper into the bailey, replacing my memory of Hailey. Women in aprons, men carrying large trays and pans, and children with nothing to do but play fill the streets and alleyways. Although many glance in my direction, none seem aware of who I am. I smile at everyone who meets my eye, but no one returns it.

"They don't seem very happy," I whisper to Kalstrop.

"Castle life isn't as glamorous as it's made out to be," he answers, looking around. "Many of these people work for very little money and are taxed out of every bit they should be making. They are forced to remain due to the balance they owe."

"So they're slaves?" I ask quietly.

"Most, yeah," Kalstrop answers. "Those who aren't will be soon." He takes a deep breath and adjusts the robe Hailey had made for him. "Those young and able will eventually join the royal guard out of financial obligation. The remainder will die in the tombs after being taken into custody for the crime of making too little money."

My eyes scan the townsfolk in a different light. "Why would anyone come here?"

"When no one ever gets out, it's impossible to hear about how hellish it is in here," Kalstrop responds, narrowing his eyes in thought. "Outside of these walls, they see someone brought within as an important addition to the royal yard. The prestige behind it is enough to make any man's chest swell. They are unaware of how the story ends as they never see that person again."

"This was my grandfather?"

"This has been the way for a few centuries," he says, turning us down an alley. "With each newly crowned royal, there was the opportunity for change, but no one seemed to see a problem with the way things were."

"Well, I do," I grumble.

Kalstrop laughs. "I'm sure you do," he says, stopping as the alley meets another street. He turns us around to face Beau, who's biting into a strip of smoked meat. Kalstrop raises his eyebrow. "Could you at least try to look like a prisoner?"

"Shut up," Beau snaps, rolling the meat around in his mouth. "I'm hungry."

Kalstrop adjusts his sack and steps before me. "We're nearly there," he says, leaning down to catch my eye. "Remember what I said. Leave the blades alone. Just keep your head held high and follow my lead."

He waits for my reluctant nod before setting himself up on my right side. Kalstrop gestures to Beau, who steps to my left and holds his arm out. I hook my arms with theirs and gain the confidence I need to take the first step from the alleyway into the street.

We were clearly walking through an outlying area based on the difference between this street and the last. The vibrant colors, bustling shops, and forgeries are loud and exciting. Still, no one is smiling, but there is a distinct hustle in their steps and a hint of hope in their tone.

I nearly question their activities when I see why they are so motivated. The towering gate of the inner bailey is so grand in scale that it could be claimed as a landmark on its own. Two guards stand on each side, looking straight ahead. Their robes match Kalstrop's, but they have thick belts and long swords hanging from each hip.

"State your business," a fifth guard demands, marching toward us from directly under the arch. He doesn't even look my age, but stands at least a foot taller. The young guard eyes Beau's shackles before turning his attention to me. "Declare your business or be on your way."

"We're here to see the king," Kalstrop snaps, moving forward just enough to place his body in position to protect me. "Official business."

The guard snorts, smiling. "Oh yeah? And who the hell are you?" His eyes haven't left me, so it's unclear who he's talking to. "I asked you a question," the guard growls, stepping forward.

Kalstrop slides between us and leans his back against my chest. "That's the princess you are addressing, son," my guard snaps. His right hand slides along my belt until he finds his blade's handle.

"Is that so?" the young guard says, a hint of humor in his voice. "And she wants to see the king, huh?" He peeks around Kalstrop. "This oughta be good."

To my surprise, he steps aside and bows with a flourish, allowing us to pass. Kalstrop keeps himself between us while Beau remains steadily by my side. I can feel the young gate guard's eyes on my back until we step into a crowd and disappear among the yards of fabric.

"This doesn't feel right," Beau hisses.

Kalstrop eases back to my side and hooks our arms. "Agreed," he murmurs. "But we're too far in to turn back now."

The inner bailey is nothing more than a garden of flowering bushes and tall fountains. Women in extravagant dresses and men in strangely feminine suits stroll along gravel paths, pointing and talking. News of my arrival seems to travel in a wave, as one by one, each stops to gawk at me.

The castle looms over us in all of its splendor, threatening to squash our hopes and dreams as it had for all the people in the outer bailey. There are no guards posted at the smaller archways leading into the hallways, which seem more like tunnels. The lit torches along the wall are no match for the cold, damp air within.

Curiosity might be the only thing driving me forward as I allow my guards to continue guiding me through the halls. I had watched movies with castles and royalty with Alice. There were always grand paintings and enormous tapestries along the walls. This castle's only decorations are the sconces holding the torches.

After a few turns, we emerge into a hallway massive enough to allow trucks. Taking a deep breath, I look up to find the ceiling painted with a never-ending mural. The swirl of colors sings a ballad of epic battles and dramatic victories. Flags fly high on hills while men and other beings lie beaten and bloody below.

Small clusters of fire and ice burst through trees while arrows and explosions rain down upon them. Hidden within the images are crests and seals, barely visible if you weren't looking for the extra details. While focusing on them, I notice something monstrous in the forest depicted at the edge of one side. I pick out a few spikes and one large eye.

Kalstrop clears his throat and steps into the room at the end of the hall. I blink a few times to adjust to the room's brightness. It's enormous, with a raised seating area containing a single chair. The blue velvet covering the cushions looks unused. The black carpet leading up the stairs nearly shimmers like satin.

"We request an audience with the king," Kalstrop announces.

Although there aren't many people in the room, the hushed silence they create thickens the air and makes me want to shrink to the tiny size I thought fairies were. Kalstrop stands tall while Beau's grip on my arm threatens to break my bones. The few people before me step aside, and a voice I didn't think I'd ever hear outside of my dreams breaks through the silence.

"Ember," Ash whispers.

My jaw slackens to help me move the extra air I need in my stunned state. "Ash?" I breathe, shaking my head. I slide my arms from my guards' grips and step toward the man I thought only existed in my dreams.

Ash's smile is one of pride. "I knew you would find me," he says, grabbing my arm and pulling me to his chest. His arms slide tenderly across my back, but his body tenses, and his breathing deepens. Ash's fingers dig into my skin as he snarls, "Although some things are not as they should be."

Surprised by his change in tone, I pull away and look into his angry eyes. "I'm sorry," I whisper, unsure of what I'm apologizing for.

"I know you are, sweet Ember," Ash murmurs. He glances over my head before taking my chin and guiding my lips to his. "And forever you shall be. I told you that you are mine. You should've listened." He pulls away and stares into my eyes. "Hold them."

Boots move quickly across the floor behind me.

"I'm sure you recall your vow to me, Durcarash," Kalstrop growls.

"And I distinctly remember telling you to stay off her," Ash snaps.

I jerk against Ash, but he holds me firmly before him. My heart pounds with such force that it may burst from my chest. Nothing makes sense, but if Ash is real and knows me outside of my dreams, it is quite possible that what I did with Kalstrop while sleeping could have actually happened, too.

"Ash, I didn't..." I start, unable to complete my lie. "I wouldn't..." Panic takes hold as I swallow every inch of respect I ever had for myself. "It was my fault. Punish me, not him."

"Hmm, Ember," Ash groans. "Have no fear. You will both get exactly what you deserve."

Ash's face turns nearly unrecognizable as he places his right hand on my stomach. Pain shoots through me, burning from within. I scream as my insides melt in a pool of lava and my legs buckle, unable to hold my weight any longer. Ash braces me upright, reveling in my torment.

"You gave me your word," Kalstrop barks.

"And you said you wouldn't touch her," Ash snaps, narrowing his eyes over my head.

"She asked for me," Kalstrop replies. "I would never deny her."

"You should have," Ash shouts, releasing me.

I roll to the floor, curled into a ball. My stomach is undamaged as I clutch it, but the burning within has barely subsided. I open my eyes to see Kalstrop fighting against the two guards holding his arms. I whimper from the pain, causing him to jerk away and fling himself on the floor before me.

Just behind him, I catch Beau being dragged from the room. He's fighting and thrashing around with his mouth moving, but I can't hear him. Everything hurts, and my only wish is to return to my safe place with my guard in his cavern.

"I will not leave you," Kalstrop whispers, digging at my hip. He yanks his blade from my belt and drops his pack as he stands.

"You assured me of her safety," Kalstrop growls, sharply enunciating each word.

"Oh, she'll be safe, brother," Ash purrs. "I haven't hurt her yet. I only took care of a little problem you created."

I push myself up with my arms, and a flash of light illuminates a pool of blood under my hips. I gasp and look around. Kalstrop's blade is on fire, and the red crystal drops on the floor beside him. Blood coats my pants as I slip in it, trying to climb to my feet.

Kalstrop swings his fiery sword, lunging at Ash as he screams, "You will pay for all of your lies!"

Ash catches the blade and steps into Kalstrop. "Did you really think you could hurt me with fire?" he growls. "You can't kill me, little brother. I made sure of that." He yanks the sword from Kalstrop and flips it to hold the handle. "You, however, will wish for death."

Kalstrop doubles over as his blade is plunged into his gut. Ash's laugh hits my soul more painfully than that blade ever could have. I crawl toward my guard as he crumbles to the floor with blood pouring from his wound.

"Why?" I beg, bawling and shaking my head at my guard, confused.

"His words mean nothing," Kalstrop whispers hoarsely. "Never stop trying to get away. You can't believe anything he says."

"Get her out of here," Ash barks.

Hands latch onto my arms and drag me away from Kalstrop. I scream for him and try to reach for his outstretched hand, but Ash's laugh breaks through my pain. I'm hurled through a flourish of fabric and dresses, reminding me that we are not alone in the room. I try to grab one of the spectators, but they all move aside to give the soldiers room to maneuver.

"Put her in a dress," Ash orders. "I want my crown."

Pronunciations

Arica - AH-ri-ka
Calisbrya - KAL-uhss-brei-ah
Durcarash - DUR-kar-ash
Faus - fows
Kalstrop - KAL-strahp
Leif - Layf
Tragae - T<r>AH-gei

L M Lissette is known for her ability to connect readers to her characters. After living all over the US, she has settled into a quiet country life with her daughter and writes about the sweet love she hopes still exists. Her sense of humor, sarcasm, and wild imagination emerge in her writing, creating worlds where destiny and heart-pounding adventure collide.

Prepare to immerse yourself in her world of fantasy, love, and unbreakable family bonds while she cures your "bully blues."

www.ingramcontent.com/pod-product-compliance
Lightning Source LLC
LaVergne TN
LVHW030343070526
838199LV00067B/6420